Our Forever STARTS TONIGHT

REBEL HART

OUR FOREVER STARTS TONIGHT

REBEL HART

ARIA

When my alarm began to fill the room with my 'favorite songs' playlist, I groaned. I thought I was more prepared to make the transition from my summer schedule to my school one, but the fact that I would rather step on Lego bricks than get out of bed proved otherwise. To make matters worse, my chocolate lab, Hazelnut, was curled up with her head over my legs and sleeping right through the music. Surely my mom would understand me skipping my first day of school. A sweet pup was snoozing in my lap.

"Aria! Wake up, sweetie. You don't wanna be late for your first day!"

Guess not.

"Yeah. I'm up!" I called back. Hazelnut let out a huff on my bed and I eyed her. "Easy for you to say. You get to stay here."

I gave her head a few scratches, then started moving my legs so that she knew she had to move. She did move her head away from my legs, but stayed curled in bed as I climbed out and stared with disdain at the moving boxes still littering my bedroom. I probably should have forced myself to pull out everything I needed the night before so I wouldn't have to do it while drowsy and dreading the day.

I was still in denial.

It wasn't like I missed my old home. This one was much nicer, and I obviously wasn't going to miss my old high school, but starting over just for my senior year felt a little like overkill. Did I love it there? No. Did I have a ton of friends I was leaving behind? Just the one. But I would have much rather finished things out in the realm of torture I was used to rather than a whole new one.

Putting the thoughts out of my mind, I dug through the boxes I'd yet to unpack two months into living in the new house. I found my shower set with all the advanced hair products I used to put myself together for school, my makeup bag, and a few other things, then headed towards the door. Almost as if she was trying to alert me, I heard Hazelnut's collar shake. I turned to look at her and saw the door to my attached bathroom.

"Right," I said out loud, turning around and heading for it instead.

After two months, I was still very unused to having my own bathroom. In our old house, my mom and I shared a bathroom. Now we each had our own, plus a spare for, I don't know. What did people do in third bathrooms? Eat caviar?

Hazelnut hopped down off the bed and I heard her scratching at my front door. I set my stuff down, rolling my eyes. I walked back to my front door and opened it so Hazelnut could lazily tromp her way out to get to her breakfast. Normally, my door would be opened for her when I left to go to the bathroom. Having a nice, new house was still taking some getting used to.

After letting Hazelnut out, I returned to my bathroom and commenced showering and getting ready for the day. As I stood in the shower, I could admit I was happy I wasn't going to be walking into my garden variety bullies today. Granted, they'd be feeling the high of satisfaction for running me out in a couple of hours when they discovered that I was gone, but I would take at least one day where I was the freak because I was new, and not because I was slightly overweight. Nothing was wrong with a girl with curves. Marilyn Monroe built her empire on it, but give me a size 14 pant size, and I'm public enemy number one.

"Aria!" My mom's voice carried through the closed bathroom door. "Sweetheart, hurry up! Do you want me to make you breakfast?"

"No!" I screeched. "No, I'm coming. I'll do it."

I loved my mom, but god bless the woman, she was not a cook. My dad had done all of the cooking when I was a little girl, but once they split, my mom took up cooking to do her best job as a mom. But generally, if you make it all the way to your forties without cooking much more than a PB&J, it's difficult to become a passable chef. I begged my dad to teach me how to cook so that I could do it at home, which he did until just before his passing when I was twelve. I did a majority of the cooking at our household, and we were firm believers in takeout.

Couldn't imagine why I carried a little extra weight.

"My cooking wouldn't kill you," my mom grumbled back. "I'll give you ten minutes, then I'm starting. You need to eat before your first day."

My mom meant business whenever she used food to

threaten me, so once I heard her retreat, I turned off the shower and climbed out. While my curling iron was heating up, I wiped a portion of the mirror off so that I could apply a thin coat of makeup. I didn't require much. My skin was naturally bronze thanks to my father's Native American roots, and my mom's dark brown eyes tended to pop off my face on their own, but I did like to cover up a few of my blemishes with concealer and give my eyes a nice winged eyeliner. Nothing too extravagant.

Once my curling iron was heated all the way, I got to work giving my hair some loose waves. It was dark brown, though already cresting towards the near-black color it turned during the winter. It looked best, in my opinion, when it was able to hang down and thin my cheeks a little bit, but curl away from my dimpled smile—the feature I liked most about myself. With that behind me, I quickly slipped back into my bedroom, donned the simple designer-ripped jeans and baby-doll plaid blouse that I'd picked out, and made my way downstairs.

Hazelnut was chomping at her breakfast kibble and my mom was in the process of making good on her threat to cook. She had a pan over the stove heating up, and had dragged eggs, bacon, and potatoes out of the fridge. Fortunately, she hadn't actually gotten started on anything yet, so I quickly took over, shooing her away to sit and enjoy her coffee in the kitchen nook.

"I love this little nook so much," my mom squeaked. "Doesn't it feel weird? Like we still aren't used to this house after two months."

"I was just thinking that earlier. I damn-near walked out of my room to get ready for school this morning."

She snickered at that. "You forgot that you have your

own bathroom? I've been walking into mine periodically just to stand there and stare at it."

I could envision my mom just randomly walking into her bathroom and standing there. "I believe that."

"So. Are you excited for your first day at the new school? This is what it's all been building towards," my mom said.

I stirred around the eggs I was cooking in a pan, unable to decide how best to answer that question. "Um…I mean. Change is always good, right?"

"What's with that answer?" my mom replied. "You aren't looking forward to it?"

"I don't look forward to school in general, Mom. You know that."

She shook her head and scoffed a little. "Don't you think it's that attitude that makes it so bad?"

"Yeah, Mom. I think all the popular kids attack and ridicule me because I don't have a good attitude about school," I snipped back.

Her coffee cup hit the table with a thud and I glanced over at her, seeing her annoyed expression. "That was your old school. This is going to be different."

"I think you have too much faith in people."

"Aria. I transferred jobs and bought a house probably a little more expensive than I can afford just to give you an opportunity to go to a school that will be better for you. The least you could do is be grateful."

That wasn't really a fair position to put me in. I didn't ask for any of that. "Mom, if you'd told me that you were going to put yourself in a bind just to send me to a different school, I'd have told you not to bother. Just like my old school had bullies, this school is going to have them too. For as long as I'm alive and fat, I'll be bullied. I've made my peace with it."

"You're not *fat*," she hissed back. "And I have a very hard time believing there are going to be more kids just as vile as the ones at your last school. You're incredibly beautiful and charismatic, and if you aren't so pessimistic and actually give people a chance to see that, it *will* make a difference."

"It's so easy for you to say when you've never been larger than a size two, even when you were pregnant," I snapped as I dragged a couple of plates down to plate up the food I'd cooked. "You don't know what it's like."

"I know what bullies are like, Aria."

"*Your* bullies are very different from *my* bullies. *My* bullies have access to social media and cell phones to really get all their best insults out in record time. If someone wants to upload a picture of me to the internet with a trough of pig slop in front of me and a snout photoshopped on, they can do it with ease. I just don't give them the time of day. They have stuff they wanna say, I let them say it. They want to laugh at me, I let them laugh. I appreciate what you did for me, but I regret to inform you, it probably isn't going to make much of a difference." I slid her plate down onto the table in front of her, "but if it makes you feel better, I'll exclaim once I'm in the door that I'm in a really good mood and positive that this is the United States' *one* school where the cheerleaders and football players love palling around with the overweight debate dork."

Instead of a response, my mom let out a drawn out, frustrated sigh. "I don't understand you. Your outlook on life can change things."

I looked down at her, right into her eyes so she knew I

was serious. "Mom. I don't hate myself. I like what I see when I look into a mirror, which is why people who actually *do* get to know me call me confident. I'm not projecting some sort of self-hatred onto people around me, these kids are just disgusting human beings. You can't throw a rock without hitting one these days, and as much as I wish my perspective changed that, it doesn't. It's much better to be cynical and prepared for what's to come than overly-optimistic only to be shot down when people behave exactly as I expect them to."

I walked back to the pan in the kitchen, and instead of keeping my ingredients separate, I stacked them to make a sandwich. I wrapped it in foil, grabbed a bottle of water from the fridge, and started for the door.

"You're not going to sit and eat?" my mom called after me.

Slipping my feet into a pair of my white sandals I called back, "I've lost my appetite." Then I grabbed my backpack and keys and left.

My car was a twenty-year-old beater Toyota that I'd bought off of Craigslist after saving my earnings from work for close to a year. It wasn't the most luxurious vehicle on the road—and definitely not in our new, ritzy neighborhood—but it was made of tough stuff, so it did better to contain my screams as I slammed into the driver's seat and let out as loud a howl as I could muster. My mom had always been beautiful and stick-skinny. I'd gotten her looks in the face, but always held onto extra weight. It didn't make me unattractive, at least I didn't think so, but society had long since decided that the more you weighed, the less beautiful you were, and her 'just see the good in the world' attitude wasn't going to change that core tenet. If my outlook on the world was going to change the way people treated me, I wouldn't have been so bullied by the kids at my old school that my mom was hearing about it at her office job ten miles away. Maybe it made her feel better to think the world wasn't so bad, but I knew better.

My phone rang, and I let out a sigh of relief. "Amazing timing," I said out loud. I quickly plugged my phone in, setting it up in the rigged-up hands-free mode I'd created and then started my car. "Hello?"

"Hey!" my best friend Lucky's voice came across the car's speaker. "Good morning." I imagined his freckled face and blond hair, smiling at me and waving like a dope.

It actually did make me feel a little better.

"Morning," I grumbled.

"Uh oh," Lucky responded. "What's wrong?"

"Oh nothing. Just my mom thinking that *I'm* the reason I'm bullied. Because I'm pessimistic."

"I'm sure that's what it is," Lucky replied in a deeply sarcastic tone, making me laugh.

"I said the exact same thing."

"Great minds," Lucky replied. "So I take that to mean you aren't looking forward to your first day?"

When I got to my first stoplight, I unwrapped my sandwich, ripped a piece off, and popped it into my mouth. "I'm never looking forward to school. It's just not my place."

"You would look forward to it when I was there," he replied, and there was genuine sadness in his voice.

"Correction," I said. "I looked forward to seeing *you,* but I can also see you at work, or anytime we decide to hang out. I don't have to be at school for that."

"I know what you mean," he responded. "I already wasn't a huge fan of this school, but now knowing I won't get to see you makes everything worse. That being said, I already know you're gonna knock 'em dead. I'm worried you're gonna make a bunch of new friends and forget all about me."

"I could never," I said. "Besides, we still work together."

"And we're going to meet up for coffee after school?" Lucky said, hope hanging in his voice.

"I can't right after school, because I'm going to check out the debate club, but we could grab dinner after that? I don't really want to discuss it with my mom anyway."

"Yeah, let's do that. My treat."

I smiled. "Ooh. Deal."

After about twenty minutes of absently chatting with Lucky and finishing my sandwich in bites, I finally got to my new school. Unlike the single-level, cracked-brick building I used to attend, Northwest End High School was where all of the state's tax dollars went. It was a three-level, four-leaf-clover-shaped school, with a wing dedicated to each grade, a pool, its own professional-grade sports arena, and an actual parking garage. It looked like a glistening, luxury resort sitting on the horizon in the distance, and there were almost exclusively brand new cars lined up to get into the parking garage.

Nothing like the bucket I was driving up in, was clattering like rocks in a tin can and almost more brown than blue from the rust.

As I pulled into the parking garage and headed up to the senior level marked by a glistening gold '12' wrapped in a boa constrictor, the school's mascot, the other students piling out of their cars stopped to look.

"Great," I grunted to Lucky, "everyone's already looking at me."

"To be fair, you're driving a literal explosion waiting to happen, so I don't think you can blame that on anything else."

"I suppose." I knew all too well the way they whispered to one another and pointed as I pulled into the parking spot assigned to me. "This is going to be awful."

"Probably. Just internalize it and we'll get it all out tonight," Lucky said. "Good luck."

"Thanks. You too. Love ya, kid."

"Love you too, Aria," Lucky said, and then the line hung up.

I took a deep breath, then grabbed my backpack from the front seat. "Well. I guess here we go."

2

ARIA

Though I was trying my absolute hardest to keep Lucky's words focused in my mind, I couldn't help but feel uncomfortable as everyone's eyes stayed trained on me. Unlike a normal school, the walk to the front doors of Northwest End involved walking all the way across the senior level of the parking garage, waiting in the elevator room to go down to the main floor, then walking through the school's massive, expensive courtyard towards the front doors.

Long after I was around people who hadn't heard my car go rattling into the parking garage, they were still staring at me, and my skin tingled with embarrassment. Sure, they were probably staring at me mostly because I was new to the school, but I couldn't be the only one, right?

Instead of making eye contact, which I knew would add fuel to any fires, I kept my eyes straight and made my way for the huge front doors of the school. The building itself was modern in design, made of white stone and capped with a flat, steel gray roof. Outdoor pods dubbed 'Study Buddy' by the painted-on signs had five or six seats surrounding a cement table with a pop up podium with charging ports in it. Several pods were scattered near the doors, and students in these pods watched me walk in. I picked a group to smile at as I passed, but they quickly averted their gazes, so I went back to staring forward.

Outlook, my ass, mom.

Passing through the big glass doors, the 'stem' of the school's cloverleaf shape was where a majority of the lockers were situated. Unlike being ceiling-to-floor and lined along the walls like my old school, past a round reception desk just past the front doors, groups of lockers that stopped at around the seven-foot mark were bunched together in groups of eight, and there were several groups polka-dotted about five feet from the next group over. I could stare straight to the top of the building from the first floor and could see banisters surrounding the second and third floors. My locker was up on top, so I passed the groups on the first floor and made my way up the stairs to the top floor.

"I don't know," I heard one of the freshman hiss as I walked past. "Maybe from South?"

I rolled my eyes. What right did a freshman have to treat *me* like I was walking new territory. I was, but so were they. And yes, I *had* transferred from South End High School, the lesser-funded school in the poorer part of town, but it wasn't like I was wearing that on me.

At least I didn't think so.

Students got older the further up I traveled, and eventually I was on the top floor where lockers were lined in similar groupings on the left and right side of the banister. I hesitated here, because I couldn't entirely remember if my locker was to the left or to the right. The principal had been kind enough to invite me and my mom to see the school a couple of weeks ago when the doors opened officially for pre-season sports practices. It was totally empty then, and allowed me to find my locker and classes with ease, but now that the place was full of students, I may as well have not seen it at all.

"Um, you okay?" I turned to the right and to see a girl standing with a group of about six others. "Do you need help?"

She looked nice enough, so I decided to take a risk and nod. "Yeah. Is it obvious I'm new? I'm looking for my locker."

"What's your locker number?" she asked.

"Great question," I said, one I did not have the answer to.

She giggled at me and stepped a little closer. "Here. Did you download the app?"

"Oh, yeah." I pulled out my phone and navigated to the school's official app. That was a far cry from the 'we'd rather not know cell phones were invented' rules at my old school. I opened it and it loaded up all my information, including my schedule and an electronic version of my student ID.

The girl clicked a few buttons and brought up locker information along with a giant 'unlock' button. There was a '381' number on top. "381, so you'll be on the right. It's easy to remember because 300 to 350 is on the left, 350 to 400 on the right."

"That is easy," I said with a smile.

"Just press the unlock button when you're in front of your locker," she said, then started off with her friends. "Bye."

"Thanks! Bye!"

Okay, so not *all* bad at least.

Despite feeling like there was a good possibility that the girl was hazing me, I made my way to the right and followed the locker numbers until I got to 381. There was no lock on the front of the locker, no place for a lock even to hang, so following my aid's instructions, I set my phone a little closer to the locker and hit the unlock button. I heard a mechanical unlatching noise and then the locker popped open.

"Holy shit!" I screeched. Several kids near me stopped and turned and I just waved with an awkward laugh. "Sorry. Technology. What a marvel, huh?"

I got a few laughs, but otherwise they ignored me in interest of returning to their conversations, so I opened my locker door and started stuffing all of my things inside. There was a little shelf inside with a raised circular pad. I set my phone there mostly out of impulse and it started charging. My jaw dropped. Being in a technologically-advanced school was insane.

My first few classes only required one big text book, then a small journal-sized book, and I'd invested in a multi-subject notebook to cut down on my carrying. I grabbed the three items, my pencil case, cell phone, and headphones, then closed my locker. To be sure that I'd be able to get my backpack again—and partially for the hell of it—I clicked the unlock button on the app again and my locker popped right open.

I snickered and a few kids next to me watched me with amused smiles. I looked at them. "Long way from combination locks, eh?"

One of the guys raised an eyebrow. "You must be from one of the southern schools, huh?"

"Am I not hiding it well?" I asked. "Don't worry. I won't be this irritating all year, just maybe the first week or two."

The guy shook his head. "Nah, it's cool. It's kind of adorable."

One of the girls standing with him squealed. "Jeez, just go for it, why don't you Yunmir?"

I could feel the heat rising to my face, so I waved goodbye and turned my back to them. Everything in me was inclined to think that guy *wasn't* hitting on me, but that was kind of what it seemed like. I'd have to run it by Lucky later for his expert male opinion.

My first class was down on the second floor, so I started back towards the stairs when I felt the intense looming of a gaze on me. People had been watching me all along, but no one had been full-fledged staring, but now I felt like someone was about to cut me open. I looked slowly to my right and there was a guy peeking around the lockers at me. My heart sank when I focused on him. He was the typical jock type—tall, with short, swooping brown hair, alluring hazel eyes, and even in his shocked expression he had one deep dimple on his left cheek. He was fit and wearing official NWE gear; there was no doubt in my mind he was a football player or something.

The exact type of guy that loved to torment me.

I locked eyes with him briefly so he knew I was looking, but that didn't seem to make a difference, so I just kept walking. I passed the next block of lockers at the exact same time that he did, almost anticipatory as he came around the block, staring right at me. I swallowed hard, certain he was just biding his time until he came up with the perfect insult to hurl at me. I took a deep breath and kept walking. If I didn't acknowledge him, he'd leave me alone.

But I passed the next set, and he was there again, staring over at me.

For the nice girl that helped me find my locker and the flirtatious guy, I was hoping I'd get a little further in before bumping into one of *these* guys, but luck was something that rarely roosted near me. Instead of continuing on, I turned around entirely, planning to hopefully lose him in the crowd and take the long way around to get back to the stairs. Moving a little faster, I passed the block of lockers back towards mine, but one block shy of my own, the guy stepped through the gap and right into my path. I froze, staring up at him, knowing he was about to make his move.

"Can I help you?" I snapped. "Yeah, I get it. I'm the ne—"

"Aria?" he said.

I recoiled a little. How did he know my name? "Uh… yeah? How did you know that?"

A smile rose to his face that set my heart to racing. It was stunning. He held out his arms as his eyes widened with joy. "It's me. Tristan."

My speeding heart stopped and went clattering up into my throat. Flashes of a little boy—tall, lanky, awkward looking—went across my brain and didn't mesh with the man I was looking at now. I'd been friends with a kid who fell victim to bullying himself back in elementary school, until his family moved away and I never saw him again.

"Tristan?" I said. "Like…"

"From the news?" he responded with a raised eyebrow. "I'd show you the scar on my pec from that stick, but that'd be a little inappropriate."

"Oh my god!" I screeched. "Tris!"

I was jumping up into a hug before I could stop myself, but thankfully he was lowering himself into one already. I wrapped my arms around his shoulders, feeling how broad they'd gotten. He was just a knee-high stick bug last time I'd seen him. How was he this super-hunky jock man?

"Man," I said, pulling back. "It's been…"

"Like eight years," Tristan responded. "Since my dad got remarried."

Tristan lived up the block from me in our old neighbor-hood. On top of the fact that he just *looked* like a kid that would be easy to push around, he got the wrong kind of attention when his mom made local news for going on a drug bender and attempting to kidnap him and his older brother. A lot of kids in our neighborhood and school punked him for it, until I finally got sick of it and stood up for him. We were really good friends from then until he moved away when we were around 10.

"Eight years." I shook my head. "I can't believe it. I had no idea you went to this school. Honestly, when my mom told me you guys were moving away, I think I just assumed it was out of state."

"It felt like that. Being dragged away from you when you were like my *only* friend was terrible. I…" His eyes widened like he was staring at an angel. "Can I hug you again?"

"Yeah," I said. Damn it. I was going to have to tell my

mom that this move worked out. "So… wow. Time has been good to you."

"I was just about to say the same," he responded, his eyes painting me up and down and bringing goosebumps to my skin. "You look incredible."

For anyone who'd ever told me that before in an attempt to boost my confidence, it actually sounded true coming out of Tristan. "Thanks. You must have discovered a gym somewhere along the way."

"Yeah, turns out if you don't build muscle to match the height, strong winds blow you over," Tristan responded and then cracked out into laughter and I couldn't help but join. "Uh, where's your first class? Can I walk you?"

"Yes," I responded, hating how breathless I sounded. I'd had a few crushes in my day, and in an attempt to prove that my weight had nothing to do with my ability to get guys, I'd lost my virginity back during my junior year and was maybe a little too vocal about it. The guy didn't like that. Tristan on the other hand… Why was my heart beating so fast? Why couldn't I stop smiling? "I have World History with Mrs. Hammerskill."

His jaw dropped. "Me too!"

This was it. This was the way god was repaying me for years of pain. "Amazing."

"Let's go," he said, and started off for the stairs and I was all too happy to follow him. "How are your parents doing? Ever get that little sister you wanted?"

"Only a four-legged one," I replied, pulling my phone up to show Tristan my lock screen. "Hazelnut."

"Oh she's so cute," he said. "And your parents?"

"Um…" My heart hurt a little bit. "My mom's good.

She took a promotion at a different office so we could move here, so she's a little busy and stressed, but good otherwise. My dad, um… he died. They were split up most of our friendship actually, and then called it quits officially right after you left, so not a great year for me. I guess my dad got a little too into liquor after that and ended up homeless. He was sleeping out in a tent in the dead of winter, got hypothermia and… yeah."

"I'm so sorry, Aria," Tristan said, and he seemed legitimately saddened by the information. "You guys were so close. I'm really sorry."

"It's okay. I work at this homeless shelter now, so I actually *feel* like I'm doing something to combat that. It's good," I replied.

"Wow. That shouldn't surprise me. Something so ambitious for you."

"Do you have a job?" I asked.

He seemed a little embarrassed. "No. Between sports and school I just don't really have time."

"Sports?" I said with a perk to my voice. "You could barely throw a ball when we knew each other."

"Yeah, well… I kind of threw myself into bulking up after I moved. I didn't have you to stick up for me anymore, so I figured I had better work on myself. Kind of got into sports as a way to work out, and now I play football in the fall and baseball in the spring. I'm captain of both teams."

"Sports *captain*?" I shook my head. "You've come a long way."

"Yeah." Tristan was looking at me with a warm, romantic expression that gave me butterflies in my stomach. "So have you."

We walked into the classroom, and my marvel over the school's modern environment continued. All the desks had clear, plastic covers, protecting the built-in screens that were mounted in the tops. The seats were a little more plush than the seats I was used to, and each station had an attached side-basket for any materials and even a charger for an electronic device. Not only were kids on their phones, but even the teacher had her phone out and seemed to be exchanging some sort of information with every student that walked in.

"Oh!" the teacher said as we entered. "Tristan, don't tell me I have to deal with you here too?"

"Hey, Mrs. H," Tristan responded. "Finally, I get to take one of your classes. You can yell at me here *and* on the field." He looked at me. "Mrs. Hammerskill is the football coach here."

My eyes widened. "That's amazing. The *head* coach?"

Mrs. Hammerskill flexed an arm and winked at me. "The *head* coach." She had dark red hair pulled back into a ponytail and a full face of makeup, plus she was wearing a bright yellow sundress. In terms of images I'd been indoctrinated with since birth, she did *not* look like a football coach, which made it that much more awesome. "And who might you be?" She stuck out a hand to shake.

"This is Aria!" Tristan answered for me.

Mrs. Hammerskill's jaw dropped. "Wow. Aria. I never thought I'd get to meet you. Did you know she was coming, Tristan?"

He shook his head. "Nope. Big surprise for me today."

"Well congrats." She held out her phone. "Open your apps. Check in for attendance and enter the ID on the board for the class info." Tristan did this with ease, but I fumbled my way a little bit. It was hard to think there were schools out there like this one while I was dragging myself through a rundown building with one textbook for every two kids. Once we'd checked in, Mrs. Hammerskill waved her hand. "Pick whatever seat you'd like and we'll get started after the second bell."

Tristan held out a hand for me, so I looked across the room and picked a seat in the center row near the back. Tristan sat in the desk in front of me, but quickly turned around to face me. "Tech in the desks. Crazy, huh?"

"It's unbelievable." I tapped the desktop and the smartscreen beneath it reacted to my touch. "It's gonna take some getting used to for sure. At least my mom can be comforted that she made the right choice to give me the, as she quotes it, 'Best high school experience,' for my senior year." I looked up at him and tilted my head to the side. "So… um… have you talked about me before?"

A light pink hue came to Tristan's face. "Oh… yeah. Uh. Not like creepily or anything, but ya know. You were kind of my inspiration to become tougher and stuff. You've come up a time or two." He flashed a blinding smile at me then. "What can I say? You're kind of my childhood hero."

The concept almost brought tears to my eyes. I just thought I was doing the right thing by protecting someone innocent. I had no idea I'd been such an inspiration. "Thanks."

"So, listen, what are you doing after school? We don't have practice since it's the first day of school. Do you wanna grab coffee or something? Continue to catch up?" He did a little half-shrug. "My treat or whatever?"

My eyes widened. Was he asking me out on a date? "Um…"

"Tris?"

Tristan and I looked up, and a disgustingly beautiful woman had entered our space. She appeared to be of Asian descent, with shimmering green eyes, a high-fashion bob cut to her black hair, and full, plump lips. She was clearly wearing makeup, but it was clear she didn't need it, and had donned a white, frilly crop top along with skin-tight black pants and platform boots. She had her nose and ears pierced and her fingers were tipped with matte black nails that came to a perfect point.

"Hey Ceradi," Tristan responded.

Ceradi gave me that look I was expecting from Tristan when he first turned up. That disdain, like I didn't even belong on the earth with someone like her. "Who are we talking to?"

"This is Aria," Tristan said. "We were friends as kids and I didn't know she was coming here."

"How lovely," Ceradi replied, though she clearly didn't mean it. "Come on, we're all sitting over here."

I frowned a little as I was looking forward to Tristan sitting in front of me, but I knew what to expect when I saw him. Whether or not it felt like it, he was one of *those* kids.

"Okay," he said, then looked back at me, still smiling. "Think it over and I'll catch up with you after class."

"I will."

Tristan gave me one last cheery smile, then stood up and followed Ceradi away from my desk. He walked over to a small group gathered at the desks nearest the door and they looked much more like the students I was used to avoiding. Along with Ceradi, there was a very pretty, wafer-thin blonde girl, somehow with curvaceous hips and bust, and a few dictionary definition jocks, one of whom was even wearing a letterman jacket. Tristan remained blissfully unaware, but the second Ceradi landed there, she turned and threw me an icy glare, and the blonde and a couple of the other jocks turned and did the same.

Great. Maybe bumping into Tristan was both the beginning and the end of my good fortune.

3

TRISTAN

"**W**ell, it's time for another exciting year here at Northwest End High, and for all of you, it's your last year. I know it's as exciting as it is sad, but just be sure you study as much as I'm sure you all will live it up!" Mrs. Hammerskill began. "For those of you who don't know, the deal here is that your first class of your first day is not only your first academic class, but also your homeroom. So take a good look around. Me and these students are going to be the raft that helps sail you through your final year here."

I used the excuse of looking around to look back at Aria. It was still so unbelievable to me that she was actually sitting right there. It was also unbelievable to me how beautiful she had gotten in the last eight years. Not only was her face still as much of a knockout as it always had been, more so even, but she wasn't an overly skinny girl like the ones I normally hung out with. There was no problem with either, but if I had a choice, I'd definitely pick someone with curves and substance like Aria.

Hell, I'd just pick Aria.

"I typically take this time to ask if anyone is willing to volunteer to be our class liaison. Don't worry, it's not a difficult job. You'll occasionally run messages for me to other classes or the office, and there are a few times a year that we'll work as a class and will need to send a representative to a few meetings. Low effort, but looks great on your resume and college applications," Mrs. Hammerskill asked. Everyone looked around a bit, waiting for someone to volunteer, and then when a few seconds had passed, Aria's hand went up. Mrs. Hammerskill smiled. "Aria?"

"Yeah. I don't know the school super well, so what better way to learn?" she replied.

Mrs. Hammerskill nodded. "A girl after my own heart. Okay. Aria it is. Keep an eye on your school app. I'll send you any responsibilities through there."

Aria nodded and gave a quick, dorky thumbs up. "Great."

"How do you think Hammerskill's ass smells?" Ceradi murmured behind me and a few students snickered.

Whatever. It wasn't like any of them did it.

Mrs. Hammerskill clapped her hands before picking up a stack of packets off of her desk. "Okay. With that sorted out, let's get onto the boring class stuff. Yes, I do know it's boring, but it's important for you to learn it. This is a packet to let me know where you are in your history studies. This is our chance to round out what you know and prepare for your SATs. Feel free to work with others around you or independently. It's totally up to you."

Mrs. Hammerskill walked up the rows of desks, handing packets to each student, and I noticed as soon as Aria got hers, she made a joke about it to the guy to her left and he and the girl in front of him started to chuckle. They continued to chat and eventually decided to work together. Throughout class, Mrs. Hammerskill made a few comments to the students in general, and Aria boldly and wittily bantered back and forth with her. Everyone laughed and enjoyed talking to Aria, and I quickly found myself jealous. She was still just as confident as I remembered.

I imagined speaking out loud during class in front of everyone and my stomach gave out just thinking about it in my own mind. Yeah, I'd managed to create an ideal body, and I was the captain of the football and baseball teams, but when it came to public speaking, being charismatic, or just generally anything that required being out of my comfort zone at all, I was horrible at it. It was something she'd always had down pat. No wonder she was able to just come to a new school and start over fresh senior year. I could never do something like that.

"Tris." I looked over to my right and my best friend Hannah was holding the packet like it was covered in toxic sludge. "Please help me with this. I'm horrible at history."

Ceradi flicked up some of Hannah's blonde hair. "It's not like Tristan is so smart. You'd be better off just guessing. You'll probably get more correct. It's not like it's graded."

Hannah and I locked eyes. History was actually my best subject, which Hannah knew, but the rest of my friends thought I was as dense as they were. "Yeah," I said, "but at least if we guess on all the same ones, we'll know that we're the same amount of stupid."

Ceradi accepted that, letting out a shrill laughter. She turned her attention away from us and started working on her packet on her own, mostly using her phone. Hannah slid her desk close to mine and we started working on our packets together. Occasionally, I would hear an explosion of laughter and look over to see Aria in the middle of some pleasurable conversation. Part of me wanted to walk over and join in so bad, but I knew how it would look to walk away from my dedicated group of friends.

"Are you looking forward to your party this weekend?" Hannah asked. "The big 1-8."

"Yeah," I responded. "Super stoked."

"Were you able to get your brother's place?"

I sighed. "Kinda. He's going to be there and his girl-friend, but at least I was able to ditch my old man. I'm sure Taylor will be much more chill."

"I assume you *didn't* tell him you already invited over a hundred people to his house before even asking him to use his house."

I snickered, imagining Taylor flipping his shit if he knew that. "No. I creatively chose to leave that out. He let me use it anyway, so no harm, no foul."

Hannah shook her head as she laughed at me. "I guess. Do you have a date?"

"No. Why? You jealous?" I asked.

"Yeah totally," Hannah said flatly.

Hannah and I *had* dated right after she joined our friend group sophomore year. She was gorgeous and seemed to accept more of my authentic self. It went okay until we started to get intimate and realized that the romantic aspect simply wasn't there. Dates went fine because we legitimately enjoyed spending time together, but when it came to doing anything beyond that, it was just awkward. We called it quits and had been close as best friends ever since.

"Anyway. People are going to talk if you bring someone,

so just being open and available is probably better anyway," Hannah explained.

"Yeah. Probably." Once again, my eyes drifted over to Aria. I wondered if she would go with me if I asked?

"What are you doing?" Hannah asked. "Why do you keep looking at that girl?"

"Oh," I said. "She's an old friend from when I was a kid."

"So?" Hannah said. "Stop looking at her. You're going to cause a scene."

I furrowed my brow at her. "Now you really *do* sound jealous."

"No. I'm just worried about you," she replied.

"Worried? About what?"

Before she could respond, the bell went off, signifying the end of class. "Okay guys," Mrs. Hammerskill said. "That's it for today. Continue to work on anything you haven't finished tonight, and we'll have a little more work time and then review tomorrow. Enjoy the rest of your day."

Everyone packed up their things and started to leave the classroom. I hung around outside the door, and it didn't surprise me to see Aria lingering behind, caught up in conversations with the new friends she'd made. Ceradi, and some of our other friends, Josh, Milton, and Capito, blew right past me on their way to their next class, but Hannah noticed me hanging back and came to stand at my side.

"You okay?" she asked.

I nodded. "Yep." As Aria was walking out, I called out, "Aria!"

Hannah side-glanced me. "What are you doing?"

Aria quickly waved goodbye to the people she was

walking with and turned around to come over to me. "Hey."

"Hey!" I said, my heart already fluttering a little harder with her closer to me. "This is my best friend, Hannah. Hannah, this is Aria."

Aria offered her a bright smile; one of her best features. It could light up even the darkest of rooms. "Hi."

Hannah put on a significantly less bright, more courteous smile. "Nice to meet you."

"Did you have a chance to decide about that coffee?" I asked.

Aria turned her sweet smile to me. "I'd really love to, but I'm checking out the debate club after school and then I promised a friend I'd meet up after that. What about this weekend?"

"I can't this weekend, I'm having a birthday party. Although, you could totally come if you wanted." Hannah shifted weirdly next to me, but I just ignored it.

"Oh, sure! I'll have to see if someone can swap shifts at work, but it shouldn't be a problem."

I dragged my phone out of my pocket, excited that I was already going to get to see Aria outside of class. "Okay. What's your number? I'll send you the details." Aria and I dropped our contact info to one another, and I quickly sent her the time of my party and my brother's address. "You could also, you know. Text or call, if you need anything or whatever."

She got a little bashful, but nodded. "Yeah. Same with you."

"I could walk you to your next class if you want?" I asked.

"Actually," Hannah cut in. "I was hoping you could

walk me to my locker. I don't want that creep Dre bugging me again."

I exchanged looks between Hannah and Aria. A guy in our grade named Dre had an unrequited crush on her, but she'd never had trouble dealing with him before. "Uh…"

"It's okay. You go," Aria said. "I'll see you later."

Disappointment filled my gut, but I smiled nonetheless. "Yeah. Okay. See ya."

Though I wanted to ask Hannah what her sudden interruption was all about, I didn't want her to be upset with me, so I didn't. We didn't even see the guy on our way to her locker, and all she did when we got there was swap a blue pen for a black one. It seemed she specifically didn't want me going with Aria, but I knew that Hannah didn't have feelings for me, so I wasn't quite sure what that would be about. If it happened much more, I'd have to muster up the courage to ask her about it. For the time being, I let it go.

Unlike most normal kids, lunch was typically my least favorite part of the day. Not for any reason other than the fact that all of the popular kids piled up at the same table and spent the entire lunch period talking trash about other people. It wasn't something I particularly enjoyed, Hannah either, but we weren't the targets at least, so we just sat and took it in stride. Teenagers could be ruthless, especially those like Ceradi and Josh, a fact they proved in earnest almost every single day. I was glad to be a friend, not a foe. They weren't the kind of people you wanted against you.

Ceradi pierced the drone of voices all talking in the lunchroom at once with one of her shrill laughs. It was one of my least favorite sounds. I'd heard Ceradi laugh in earnest. It was much deeper and could turn into a snort if she was amused to that degree, but she wore her witch's cackle instead when she was in the spotlight.

"So, what do we all think of the *new girl?*" she asked.

I eyed her nervously. "Aria?"

"Oh that's right," Ceradi said with a pitying tone in her voice. "Wasn't she an old friend of yours? Is she trying to hang around you like she did when you were kids?"

I hesitated to answer, opening and closing my mouth a few times, then Hannah kicked me under the table before rolling her eyes. "That's what it seems like to me. I had to make up a lame excuse to take him with me to my locker just to get her to leave him alone earlier."

Ceradi perched a few of her manicured nails on the end of her chin. "Really? That's so sad. Who in their right mind thinks that you can just pick up with someone from elementary school? Tragic."

"Wait," Josh said. "Is she that whale that I've seen swimming around?"

One of the other guys in our group, Milton, nodded vigorously. "Yeah. I had to keep a wide fucking berth from her earlier. I thought she was gonna knock me over the bannister." The table erupted in laughter.

Not only were they over-exaggerating, but they were being downright cruel to someone they didn't even know. I opened my mouth to say something, but Hannah stabbed her fork into my mouth with a bit of macaroni and cheese at the end. "Can you try this for me and tell me if it's any good."

My nose burned with frustration as I chewed the bland, barely cooked noodles. I swallowed hard, punctuated with a glare at Hannah before I said, "Yeah, it's delicious."

She gave me a fake smile. "Thanks."

"Well, poor you, Tris," Ceradi continued. "That thing following around after you like a little puppy dog. Hopefully she'll just lose interest eventually."

"Maybe she'll shag one of the nerds. There are plenty of lingering virgins for her to choose from," Josh said.

"Aw, how sweet. A fat kid love story," one of the other girls in our friend group, Neerah, said. "They need love too."

Milton let out a snort. "Do you think they do anything other than eat on dates?"

"Rude," Hannah said. "They're people too." All eyes shifted to her, and I was just beginning to think she was going to stand up for Aria when she tacked on. "They have to get in their exercise too. Huffing and puffing their way from the restaurant to the car."

Ceradi and the others broke out into laughter again, and Hannah turned an amused look to me.

She did *not* get one in return.

"What?" Hannah said. "You act as if you care about them at all. When did you get all high and mighty?"

"You like her?" Neerah said with disgust in her voice.

Ceradi gasped and slapped her hands to her mouth. "Is that why you were talking to her?"

The intense gazes of everyone at the table settled on me, along with Hannah's 'I told you so' expression. I never liked being backed into a corner. Though regular people had been born with fight or flight, it was like I only had panic. My gut instinct was to survive, as was most people's, but whether fighting or fleeing was best going to get me to that goal, I never knew.

Everyone was watching me, and there was a sly smirk

on Ceradi's face, almost like she was waiting for me to confirm so that she could dial in.

And I panicked.

"N-no," I said. "I was just being nice."

"Ugh, you are painfully sweet," Ceradi replied. "I guess that's acceptable."

"He's the best one of us if he can sit and talk to a dorky behemoth like that," Capito said.

I forced a laugh and the attention left me in the interest of continuing their ribbing, so I ignored everything from then on. I just blamed their attitude on the fact that they didn't know Aria at all. If they did, they wouldn't be so harsh.

Maybe my birthday party would be a good chance for me to introduce her and let them see how wonderful she really was.

When lunch was finally over and I was able to get on with the rest of my day, things were much better. On top of the first class that we had together in the morning, Aria and I had an additional two classes together in the afternoon. Fortunately, one of them had very few of my friends in it because it was an advanced course. Only Hannah was in it, and we chose to keep it a secret that we'd placed higher up the ladder.

Anyone with above average intelligence was considered a nerd and harshly criticized.

It was the last class of the day, so as slyly as I could, I said my goodbyes to Hannah after the last bell rang and caught up with Aria on her way back to her locker. "Hey."

"Hi," she replied, knocking me out again with that killer smile. "AP Math huh? Nerd." When she said it, it was much less painful to hear. It felt almost more like a compliment.

"I guess you could say that," I replied. We got to her locker and she used her phone to let herself in, letting out a little squeak of excitement when it popped open. She looked at me, with pure amusement. "I don't think I'm ever gonna get over how cool that is."

It had only been a day, but she already gave me butter-flies. How could anyone be so mean to her? She was perfect.

"So, debate club, huh?" I said.

She nodded as she pulled all of her stuff out of her locker. "Yup. I was on the team at my old school too, but we didn't have a ton of money. In fact, we didn't have any. We had to fundraise anything we needed on the front end, and let me tell you, people with no money aren't keen to give some of that no money to a debate club. We had to skip out on most tournaments and mostly just competed against ourselves and other South schools."

"Jeez, I'm sorry. Well, you won't run into that issue here. The academic clubs get more funding than the athletic and creative ones. It's because our principal believes in educa-tion above anything else, so he pours everything into stuff like that."

She flung her backpack over her shoulder and shut her locker. "I got that sense. He was very excited when I mentioned the debate team. He was excited for me to join." She looked in a few different directions, then back at me. "Would you mind pointing me in the right direction?"

"I'll do you one better." I held out my arm in a loop and Aria giggled a little and then looped hers through mine with a smile. "I'll accompany you."

A blush came to her cheeks. "You're such a gentleman."

We started off from her locker arm-in-arm, but it didn't

take me long to notice people watching us. Students whispered to one another and pointed, and I knew it was probably just a matter of time before one of my friends showed up. I remembered their ridicule from lunch and Hannah's attempts to keep me from embarrassing myself and knew I had to get my arm released from Aria's somehow. I waited until we'd taken a few more steps, then unlooped my arm from hers to fish my hand into my pocket for my phone. Her smile faded a little, but not totally, and I was just hoping she couldn't see that I was trying to distance myself a little.

"Do you normally have football everyday after school?" she asked finally.

"Mondays through Thursdays," I responded. "Fridays are typically game days, and if they aren't, we get the day off. Coach is strict about making sure we have time to take care of ourselves and our studies too, so she makes sure we have a good balance."

"Are you planning on trying to get a scholarship?"

I smiled a bit wider then, even puffing out my chest a little bit. "Yeah. I've already had a couple of recruiters talk to me and Coach says this year will be instrumental in getting me out there. I was featured on ESPN's high school and college channel last year. She really thinks I won't have a problem getting noticed."

"That's awesome," Aria said.

"What about you?" I asked. "Any post-high school plans?"

She wrinkled up her nose. "Honestly, I think I'm going to end up taking a few years off. Don't get me wrong, academics are my thing. I really wanna get my degree in social work so I can keep moving up at the homeless shelter, but

I'm looking forward to getting away from all the politics of being in a public education institution."

I tilted my head. "What do you mean?"

She gave something between a scoff and a snort. "Well, I know you're super popular and hot and all that, so your experience is probably not so bad, but here at the bottom of the food chain, things are a little different. I've been bullied, called every name in the book. Hell, my mom thought we had to completely move out of our city for me to be free of the torment. Maybe I'll do online school or something. I just don't think I can jump right into more of the same, especially not mixing in people who can legally drink."

So Aria's experience had been the same at her old school as Ceradi and the rest of my friends were already trying to make it here. That killed me. If she knew that I even tacitly agreed with anything they said, she'd probably never talk to me again. It was honestly something I just didn't understand. From being a victim to now being friends with the people who do it, bullying didn't benefit anyone. Why was it so necessary to break others down just to feel powerful? What was the point?

"Honestly," Aria continued. "I'm a little surprised you're friends with those kids. Don't get me wrong, I'm not judging, and I don't even really know them, maybe they're great. It just seems like they're not all that far from the kids who gave you that scar ten years ago."

My pec throbbed a little as if to remind me. I had a permanent scar from my shoulder to my ribcage where a kid had broken the skin pretty badly when he and some others were whipping me with sticks. Simply because my mom had lost it and been in the news, they felt that gave them the right to both verbally and physically abuse me, and while they were turning me into a human pinata, one particularly sharp stick caused permanent damage.

"They're not so bad," I said, and the words felt problematic coming out.

We turned down the wing of all the club rooms and came to a stop in front of the door to the debate club. I relaxed a little bit, knowing none of my friends would be anywhere around. "So… uh. Could I call you tonight maybe?"

Aria looked up into my eyes and my stomach did a backflip. "Yeah. I'd like that. I'm having dinner with a friend after this, but I should be home by 7 or so."

"Okay. Then I will call you around 7 or so." I opened my arms and Aria walked into my embrace. I wrapped my arms around her and it felt amazing just to be holding her close. "Have a good meeting."

"Thank you." When she pulled back, our eyes met, and sparks of electricity flew between us. Finally, she turned, saying "I gotta go, or I won't go." Then walked into the debate room.

It was like I was a guy in a romance movie. My heart was fluttering and my whole body was riding a high I never knew was possible. Eight years we hadn't seen each other, but it didn't seem to matter.

"Why are you doing this?" I turned and came face-to-face with Hannah, looking concerned. "Tristan. This is a mistake."

4

ARIA

I'd be lying if I said I didn't stumble into the debate room after my playful flirting with Tristan. It was crazy to me still that after all of this time, we'd reunited, and it was even more incredible that apparently we were hitting it off. If someone had told me a year ago that I'd have my arm looped through the arm of an unbelievably gorgeous guy, whose personality gelled with my own like we belonged together, and seemed just as interested in me as I was in him, I'd have told them to fuck off. Tristan was the exact kind of guy I'd avoid in the past, now I was looking forward to our planned phone call.

Way to go, Aria.

I shook my head, pushing the thoughts of Tristan away for the time being. I'd been looking forward to getting my hands on the rich school's debate club since I first found out my mom was transferring me. It was the one thing that I felt was going to salvage an otherwise horrible situation, and even though the school swap itself was turning out okay, I was still anxious to see what the debate club had to offer.

Boy were my expectations *way* too low.

Here I thought the thing I'd be most astounded by was the fact that it had a dedicated room as opposed to being shoved in an unused English classroom. Not only was that the case, but it was a true, actual debate hall. At the front of the room were two tall wooden podiums raised slightly off the floor on a platform with stairs leading up both sides. Slots on each side of the podium would hold either paper notes or a tablet for electronic notes, and small microphones jutted up from the center of the podium for the debaters.

Facing these podiums, towards the center of the room, was a legitimate judge's table along with clocks for keeping time and scoring stations. Behind those were rows of college-style seats with the side desks that could be pulled up for writing on, or tucked away if they weren't needed. The wall opposite the podiums had what appeared to be a smart board for any kind of use both for the club itself or the specific debaters.

From the number of kids gathered around, I could tell the club supported both solo debaters and teams. I'd never had a team opportunity in the past before, mainly because so few kids participated in the debate club to begin with. Maybe there'd be a chance to do some duo tournaments now that I was there.

It was incredible.

"Oh my god," I heard someone say behind me as I marveled at the space. "*Please* tell me you're gay."

I turned around and saw a beautiful girl looking back at me. She was a handful of inches taller than me, and had blazing pink hair, with the sides shaved, and the top swooped over to the side and flowing down to just above her shoulder. Her eyes were a cool, almost lilac color, and popped due to the piercing in her left eyebrow. Her ears held gauge earrings and she had a labret piercing as well. Her style could best be described as punk chic, and for a very brief moment, I wished that I was.

"No," I said with a smile. "Unfortunately, I am totally straight."

"Dammit," she hissed. "Straight men get all the goddesses."

My cheeks burned in the wake of the compliment. "Uh, that's not a word I would use to describe myself."

She rolled her eyes. "Ah. You're one of those beautiful people who doesn't realize you're beautiful, huh? Damn. The rest of us fight for it all day long, and then here you come just walking around." She waved that thought off. "Consider me backing off. Hi. I'm Arden." She stuck out her hand.

I grabbed it and shook it. "Aria."

"We've had a few classes together, but I never got the chance to say hi. We're actually in homeroom together," Arden said.

It wasn't a shock to me that I hadn't noticed the electric pink hair over still being gobsmacked that I'd run into Tristan. "Oh cool. Yeah, I didn't notice much of anything. Still getting the lay of the land."

"Don't sweat it. If you need any help with anything, just let me know. I'd be happy to help out," Arden said.

"Cool. Thanks."

She turned and started walking off, waving a hand and she moved. "Come on. Get comfy, meet the gang."

I followed after her, excited that I was skipping past awkward introductions and seemed to have made a friend already. Her stuff was piled in one of the "audience" seats towards the back of the room, so I stacked my stuff in the one next to hers and then let her lead me to a group of students sitting in a group not far from there.

"Guys, this is Aria. Aria, this is the crew, well some of 'em," Arden said.

One guy stood up and held out a hand. "We're the seniors, so the most important ones." He had short, curly brown hair, caramel skin, and warm, brown eyes, and as I shook his hand, his smile grew.

Arden put a hand on his shoulder. "That's Devario." She moved to a girl with thick glasses and the longest, straightest red hair I'd ever seen. "This is Colleen." She pointed at a pair of twin boys with short brown hair, pale skin, and freckles. "One on the left is Luke. On the right is Micah." Then she moved to a girl with rainbow dyed hair pulled up into a ponytail. "Rainbow Dash here is Bea. Also not gay, I have tried."

I laughed. "Hi. Nice to meet you all."

They all offered their own greetings, before Devario sat back down, but kept his gaze trained on me. "You actually have perfect timing. Settle a debate for us."

That sentence lit me on fire from the inside out. "I'd love to."

"Catwoman or Poison Ivy?" he asked.

"Easy, Poison Ivy," I replied instantly. "She's a strong, independent woman who don't need no man. She's got *actual* powers and stands up for herself. Besides, I live for her natural aesthetic."

"Four strong points and delivered in less than thirty

seconds," Luke said. "Not to mention she chose the *obvious* right answer. Kids, I think we've got a real winner here."

Arden looped her arm around my shoulders. "That we do." The seniors immediately started to debate amongst themselves about other notable Batman villains while Arden pulled me back to our seats. "You can thank me later. They'll go on for hours that way."

"I'll thank you now. Don't get me wrong, I love a good, nerdy conversation, but that could have gotten over-whelming fast," I said. "So, give me the talking points of Arden. What do I need to know?"

Arden fell down into one of the seats and kicked her legs over the armrest, flashing her white combat boots with pink flowers painted on. "Let's see… Well, you already know I'm the tragic lesbian character, but if I were to high-light a few other things about me, I'd say you wouldn't like me when I'm hangry, and I have two adorable shih tzus named Joel and Benji."

I smiled. "Madden, I assume?"

She flicked her finger at me, shaking her head. "Aria, you and I are going to get along just fine."

I nodded. "I think so, too."

"And, I'm an aspiring inventor. Not one of those 'next big thing' types. I want to invent something that's going to change the world. That people are still using in twenty or thirty years, ya know?"

I sat down in one of the seats a row in front of Arden and looked back over the seat at her. "Any big ideas?"

She let out a barking laugh. "Come on, Aria. I like you and you're super hot, but I can't just go giving away my secrets like that."

I held up my hands in surrender, laughing as I did so. "You're right. Sorry about that."

"One last thing," she pointed across the room to where a massive, golden trophy was situated in the middle of a trophy case, towering over the others around it. "I'm the reigning champ. If you want to take me down, you're gonna have to bring your A-game."

As a highly competitive person, I burned with a desire to do just that. "You're on."

A loud bang and scatter of papers preceded a man stumbling into the room. He had hair that had been dyed black, but the blond roots were showing through at the crest of his head. Arden sat up, wincing. "Ugh. I'll have to get your notes later. This is our fearless leader."

"Are you sure?" I asked.

She walked over to the door and started helping him pick up the papers. Out of impulse, both for wanting to help, and not liking the mess, I started picking papers up as well. Arden collected the papers I stacked up and handed them to the man. "Forgot how to walk?"

"Ha ha," the man grumbled back. "Lay off me. I got a whole new class of freshmen today. It's not easy." His eyes scanned over and landed on me. "Oh. Hello."

"Hi," I said, holding out my hand. "I'm Aria. I'm a senior that just transferred here this year."

"Ah." He took my hand and gave me such a vigorous shake that I nearly fell over. "I'm Beck Hanson." I opened my mouth and he cut me off. "Ahhh, yes. Stop it. Don't ask. I am not *that* Beck. He spells his last name with an e, I spell mine with an o. Why do you think I dye my hair black?"

"Was your mom a fan?" I asked.

He shook his head. "I have never asked that question because I don't want to know. Anyway, just call me Beck."

"You got it."

"Nice to meet you, Aria," Beck said. "You're here to join the debate team, I imagine."

"Yeah. I participated at my last school, but it wasn't a lucrative operation so we didn't have a ton of opportunities there," I explained.

Beck set his papers down on a small desk behind the podiums as he spoke. "I've been there before. Don't worry. If you've got the drive to participate, we've always got an opening for the ambitious."

That made me more excited than I could imagine. "Yes."

"Okay!" he clapped his hands. "Come on up to the front rows, guys. We're gonna hit the ground running this season." Arden and I took a couple of seats near the front as everyone else in the room flooded into the front few rows of the audience section of the room. "Listen, I'm just as excited for a new season as all of you are, but we're gonna have to catch up fast. I just got an email literally five minutes before I came in here that East End is hosting a tournament next weekend. New Year, New Meet." Snickers and sputters erupted all around the room and Beck held up a hand. "I know. I know, but a tournament is a tournament. It's going to be a lot of hard work, but if you guys are up for it, I'll submit us for it." There was no hesitation. The entire room responded with immediate affirmations and positive responses. "I knew you'd go for it. Let's do it."

My heart started beating faster immediately. I was so used to being the one working overtime and being the most ambitious. Everyone in the room was raising the bar, and it was unbelievably exciting.

Finally, I'd found my people.

For the first time in my entire life, I was actually a little disappointed to be leaving school. My classes all went so well, I reconnected with Tristan and it seemed like there could be a flame, and I was already making new friends in a new, electrifying debate club. It was unbelievable.

That said, I was glad to meet with Lucky and talk about how his first day without me there had gone. We met at a diner close to where I used to live that we used to frequent together. We exchanged hugs and cheery greetings while we were seated and ordered and then got into the nitty gritty.

"So. Did South fall apart without me?" I asked sarcastically.

"The whole school? No," Lucky said. "Me. Definitely."

"Aw. What happened?"

He just shook his head, his unkempt blond hair flopping around his head. "It was just a trainwreck. Even though we were both the target of the big bullies, it's like, with you gone, everyone feels like they can do it. I was beating people off with a stick today."

That broke my heart. It was similar to how things were with Tristan when we were kids. I could handle the pressure more, so I would defend him and keep kids away from him, and those who still couldn't resist the urge to bully, would bully me instead, and I would take it and shield him from it. I didn't even realize I was doing the same for Lucky.

"I'm sorry," I said. "If I'd known…"

"No, hey, come on. Gives me a chance to figure out how to stand up for myself, huh? I'll be fine. Don't worry about me."

Lucky wasn't an unattractive guy. In fact, if it weren't for his association with me, he may have been able to sift himself more into the run-of-the-mill students, or maybe even aim for the top. He was a little under six feet tall, but had some bulk to him, and a nice face, the kind that you'd see in a magazine. His freckles were adorable and if he put some effort into styling his feathery hair, it'd be similar to the kind of hair that people paid thousands of dollars to get. Maybe it was hard at the outset, but without me around, maybe he could do a little better.

"Tell me about you. How was your first day?" Lucky said. "Not too awful, I hope."

That stabbed me straight through the heart. I couldn't rightfully tell him that I'd had an amazing first day when he'd had such a terrible one. "You know… school is school."

Lucky looked up from his food and locked eyes with me. "Why are you lying?" I tilted my head and he gave me a hooded gaze. "Aria. I know you better than anyone on this planet. I can see that you're lying to me. Was it terrible?"

"N-no…" I said. "It was good."

He recoiled a bit. "Good?"

"Yeah… I know, it's shocking."

"Well then tell me," Lucky said. "Tell me about your first day."

"Okay," I said. "Well, frankly, it was incredible. The school, first of all, is super technologically advanced. Like… my locker opens via an app on my phone, and all the classes, they don't demand that you don't even use your phone, they have chargers and special holders for them. All the desks have screens."

Lucky's eyes widened. "Wow. How the other half lives."

"No kidding. Their debate club, it's an actual club room. With podiums and a judge's table and all this fancy stuff, and I made a new friend there, Arden. She's awesome. We have a few classes together, so I don't feel so alone," I said. "And… I met someone… Well, I re-met someone."

There was a clatter as the fork Lucky was holding hit the plate. "You met someone? Like a guy?"

"Yeah. I had this friend back in elementary school before I met you: Tristan. He was lanky and awkward and kids picked on him for… reasons. Anyway, I kind of stood up for him like I do, and we were close, but then his dad got remarried and they moved and I thought I'd never see him again. He goes to this school, and honestly, we kind of hit it off. Exchanged numbers, he asked me out… I turned him down because I already made plans with you, but I'm… excited."

"Wow," Lucky said. "Uh, that's great, I guess?"

I crossed my arms. "What's with that reception? You were the one who wanted me to tell you."

"Who knew that while I was doing so shittily, you were doing so great," Lucky spat, popping a fry into his mouth. He'd never acted like that before.

"What's your deal all of a sudden? Misery loves company? You would have preferred me to have a shitty day just like you?"

He must have been able to sense something in my tone, because he looked up and his demeanor changed instantly. "What? No! Obviously I'm happy you had such a good first day. That's awesome. I just… I missed you so much. I guess it would have been nice to know you missed me too."

I reached across the table and gave the top of his head a little smack. "What are you talking about? Of course I missed you. I wish you could have been there with me. I couldn't wait to get to dinner and catch up with you."

That seemed to calm Lucky, who smiled at me. "Yeah?"

"Yeah, you dope. Who do you think is my best friend? No school, or debate club, or Arden, or Tristan could replace you."

Lucky's smile turned blinding. "Oh. Good."

I shook my head at him. "Honestly. Don't get so jealous."

He rubbed the back of his head, a coy expression on his face. "Heh, yeah. I'll work on that."

5

———————

TRISTAN

As I drove home, I couldn't get the last thing Hannah had said to me out of my head.

"You're only going to create problems for both of you," she said. *"It's not just you that you have to think about, but it's her too. If it weren't for you, she could probably just ease into life here and Ceradi would get bored and go back to her regular victims, but if she thinks she could get a two for one deal, she'll do it without a second thought."*

I hadn't considered the fact that I might be making things difficult for Aria. Yeah, Ceradi and some of our other friends liked to look for people to gossip about, but was my simple involvement with Aria going to put an unintentional target on her back? The very last thing I wanted to do was cause Aria any stress or pain, but if I liked her and she liked me, what business was that of anyone else's?

What if there was a possibility of showing my friends

how awesome Aria was by involving myself with her further? That had certainly happened in our friend group before when one of us started dating someone and they worked their way further in. Hell, that was halfway what happened with Hannah, and now she was closer with all of us than anyone any of us had dated in the past. When I started dating Hannah, it gave her that in to work her way further into our group and eventually Ceradi and the others accepted her too. Long after we stopped dating, they were all still friends with her.

Now, the fact that she blossomed over the summer helped. She finally got her braces removed and grew into her lithe but curvaceous form, so she was more the norm for our group, but Aria was just as beautiful.

No, she was *more* beautiful.

Hannah was good looking, but as far as I was concerned, Aria was my dream girl. It wasn't just the history that we had or the fact that our personalities gelled like we were born to be together.

She was fucking hot.

How anyone couldn't see that simply because she wasn't a twig, was beyond me.

Turning the corner onto my block, I noticed a familiar maroon Impala parked in the driveway next to my step-mom's car and smiled. It belonged to my older brother, Taylor, whom I never turned down a chance to spend some time with. Despite him being about eight years older than me, we'd always been incredibly close. I pulled up and parked along the sidewalk, given that Taylor had taken my driveway spot, then grabbed my backpack and hopped out.

I wasn't even to the sidewalk leading up to the door when the front door opened.

"Hey!" Taylor threw his hands in the air. "There he is! The big senior!"

I waved. "What's going on?"

Taylor looked like a taller, bulkier version of me. He had my same short brown hair and resting face dimples, though he had my mom's green eyes instead of the hazel one's I had inherited from my dad. Though he'd never been big into sports, and was more of a band and music guy, he'd always run muscular, and developed a love for the gym when I started dragging him there daily to help me beef up myself. He was also unbearably tall, standing well over 6'6".

Making my way up the sidewalk, I walked right into his open embrace. He squeezed his arms around me, dwarfing me with how much larger he was than me in every way.

"You know I had to come see how your first day of senior year went," Taylor asked.

"Are you staying for dinner?" I asked as I pulled back.

"You know it," Taylor replied. "Andrea's making tater tot hotdish, so I'm obviously not missing out on that."

I grumbled. "It's pretty good I suppose."

Taylor looped an arm around my neck and dragged me through the front door. "Don't be like that. I know it's one of your favorites, and you always flip when Molly makes it. I love the woman, but hers is *not* as good as Andrea's. Don't be such a Cinderella."

"You *do* realize that Cinderella had every right to hate her step-mom, right?" I asked.

Taylor stopped and looked up towards the ceiling as he processed the statement. "You're right. That was a bad example. Andrea's a good woman, and she loves Dad. Don't be so rude."

I didn't respond. We'd gotten into the argument about my step-mom more than once. It always felt to me like my dad got remarried really fast, and while I was still trying to get over everything that had happened with my mom, I was suddenly being shoved before this random person, telling me that she was going to be my new mom and take care of me the way my mom couldn't. My dad never understood why that upset me so much, and instead of cooling his jets, he charged forward, full-steam ahead, including moving away from Aria and my old life and throwing me into an entirely different type of lifestyle that I wasn't prepared for.

It was terrifying.

"Anyway, my first day was… interesting." I looked at Taylor to see how he was taking my sudden shift in subject, but he was just nodding and smiling. "I got Coach Hammerskill as my homeroom teacher."

"No kidding? That's pretty cool. Gotta be nice to have a teacher you're already really comfortable with," Taylor said. "Is that it, though? No offense, baby bro, but that's not all that interesting."

"No, that's not it. I, um… well, I think I might be going down in history for the fastest crush ever developed."

Taylor looked at me with wide eyes as we sat down on the couch in the living room. "Yes! Tell me all about her. What's her name?"

"Aria," I replied.

In response to the name, Taylor furrowed his brow. "Wow. How strange is that? You found *another* Aria. That's not all that common of a name."

I side-eyed him. "No… it's not."

He read my expression for a few seconds, then he leapt up from the couch, turning around to look down at me.

"Wait! It's *that* Aria? From the old neighborhood?" I nodded and he started to clap his hands. "Oh my god, I am *so* excited. She goes to your school? Has she always?"

"No. She just started this year. Her mom relocated and she had to transfer. I probably came off as a creep at first. I was walking up to my locker and saw her and recognized her right away. She looks mostly the same." A heat started to rise through my chest and into my face. "Although, she's *way* more beautiful. The years have been amazing to her."

Taylor was damn near buzzing with excitement. "I can't contain myself. This is *incredible.* I always loved Aria. She brings out something in you. Well, I mean, this," he motioned to me. "You're sitting there grinning like you have a banana stuck in your mouth."

"Yeah. I'm excited too."

"I feel like I need to tell someone."

"Tell someone what?" In our excitement, we hadn't heard the door open, but my dad came striding around the corner in his suit with a loosened tie. "Tell me."

"Hey Dad," I said.

My dad wrapped an arm around Taylor's shoulders. "I love it when I have both my boys. No football, no law practice, just like back in the day."

"Dad, you'll never guess who Tristan has a crush on?" Taylor sang the last few words like a middle-schooler mocking his friend. "You remember Aria from before we moved?"

"Wow," my dad replied. "You were crushed when we moved away from her. I didn't realize she went to your school."

"She just transferred," I replied, then glared at Taylor. "Good to know you can keep secrets."

Taylor waved his hand at me. "Whatever. It's Dad."

"So today's the first day you've seen her in, what, eight years?" my dad asked. "You developed those feelings pretty quick."

"Well, adolescent attraction to beauty, father," Taylor replied.

"It's not just that," I snapped. "When we realized who we were, we clicked instantly. It was like no time had passed at all. She's still just as smart and outgoing, *and* she's super ambitious. She's joining the debate team, volunteered to be our homeroom rep, and she works at a homeless shelter. She wants to get her degree in social work."

Taylor and my dad looked at each other with matching looks of amusement, then Taylor quietly muttered, "Uh oh."

"Uh oh what?" I said.

A whistle came out of Taylor's lips as he puckered them. "Nothing. I legit thought this was just a physical attraction, but you learned all that about her in one day? You got it bad."

"Did you ask her out?" my dad asked. "I mean, is it a mutual thing? We're too cool for you to come off desperate."

"Ha ha," I said flatly to the man who had gotten both his current and ex-wife by wearing them down over time. "I did ask her out, but she was busy after school. She asked if we could do it sometime this weekend instead, but I have my party, so I invited her there instead."

Taylor clapped his hands and then pumped his fist in victory. "Hell yeah. Activate embarrassing brother mode."

"No, you can't. I'm trying to be impressive right now. At least wait a few weeks or something," I begged. "Dad."

My dad laughed. "Don't drag me into this. This is between you and your brother, just like this party." Then he looked at Taylor. "Which I surely hope is going to be a responsible, but fun time."

Puffing out his chest, Taylor smiled. "Of course. Me, Mol, and her younger sister Sherelle are chaperoning, so we'll keep things on the up and up. I capped his invitees and I'll be frisking kids at the door. Don't worry, pop. It's gonna be fine."

"Better be." He loosened his tie and twisted his head to the right. "Alright, let me go kiss my wife. I missed her today."

"Gross," Taylor and I said in unison, but my dad just wandered off without responding.

Taylor walked back over and dropped himself down onto the couch. "Hey, look," I started. "You aren't going to be lame this weekend, right? That's why I asked to have it at your place instead of here."

He tapped my leg. "Come on. I'm just putting on a show for our old man. I remember what it was like to be your age. I'm not gonna let you be stupid, but I'm gonna let you have your fun, don't worry. You're 18 now, an adult, and you had better act like one." He poked a finger into my cheek. "I'm letting you use my house that I worked my ass off to buy, so you had better not trash it. Molly stressed me out enough with renovations as it is, let alone cleaning up behind a bunch of children."

Molly was Taylor's live-in girlfriend, and in my opinion, way out of his league. She could be a bit neurotic though. Knowing she'd be at the party made me a touch nervous. "Nothing like that is going to happen. It's just kids from my grade, and not even half of them at that. We're just gonna hang out and have a good time. That's it. I promise I'll treat your home with respect."

"Sounding like a boring old man already," Taylor replied, shaking his head, and I punched him in the arm for it.

Dinner was a comfortably quiet affair. When Taylor wasn't over to visit, we rarely even ate together. Andrea and my dad normally sat at the table while I typically collected my plate and retreated to my bedroom. Not being Andrea's number one fan, I tried to spend as little time with her as possible, but Taylor always felt like a glue for us. A forceful adhesive, sure, but an adhesive nonetheless. He started a few conversations about how things were going for Andrea at the boutique she owned and designed expensive wedding dresses for, and how my dad's job was going now that he was a general manager at his office job, but after a few back and forth comments, all the conversations died. Still, it got us through a meal as a 'family' which is probably all Andrea and my dad wanted to begin with.

After we were done eating, I said goodbye to Taylor. I got flack for running him off until I told him I made plans to call Aria, then he was all too happy to send me off. I cleaned up my place at the table and then made my way up into my bedroom. I pulled out the little bit of homework I'd gathered from the day and went and sat down at my desk. It was a little before seven, so I kept myself busy with work until seven on the nose.

Then waited until seven-oh-two to make the call, to not seem too hasty.

"Hello?" Aria greeted.

"Hey," I said, my heart thumping a little harder at the sound of her voice. "How are you?"

I could hear her smiling on the other end as she said, "I'm good. You?"

"Good. Taylor came over tonight to have dinner and see how my first day went, so he just left," I replied.

"Oh man, Taylor. I nearly forgot all about him. Is he still as dorky as he was before?" there was a complimentary tone to the way she said it.

"You know it," I replied. "He's doing awesome though. He's got his own law practice and lives with his girlfriend Molly. She's a knockout too. A model. Like… way too good for him."

Aria giggled. "I always kind of suspected that he would end up like that. He's so charismatic."

"Yeah, yeah, yeah," I grumbled. It wasn't the first time people had lauded over Taylor to me. "Anyway, how was dinner with your friend?"

"Really good. He's having a tough time without me there, but he was glad to hear things are going well for me," she said. "The debate club was incredible. I've never seen anything like it."

While we were talking, I found myself shoving my homework away and pulling out one of my sketchbooks. I hadn't set out to draw anything specific, but in no time at all, I realized I was working on a pencil drawing of Aria. It was nice to have her smile in front of me as I spoke to her and then, my stomach twisted as I got an idea.

"Hey… uh. Can I send you something?" I asked.

"Like in the mail?" she sounded confused and border-line concerned.

"No," I said with a chuckle. "A text."

"Oh. Sure."

"Okay. Hang on." I pulled the phone away from my ear

and took a quick picture of the drawing and texted it to Aria. "Just sent it."

There was silence for a minute and then a bright gasp. "Oh my gosh! Tristan this is beautiful! You're still drawing. That's amazing."

"Thanks," I said. "Yeah, not many people know I do it, but I still love it. Whenever I can, I try and sketch something out." It felt refreshing to have someone around who knew me a little more authentically.

"Well, I know what I'm getting you for your birthday now."

"Oh yeah?" I said with a snicker. "Honestly, just having you there would have been enough."

Aria replied with a warmed hum. "Well, consider it a bonus then."

My own smile grew. Hitting the ground running with her was going to be enough of a bonus on its own. I couldn't wait to see what the future held for us.

6

ARIA

I couldn't believe it. An entire week at the new school in the books and it had actually gone pretty well. The debate team was firing on all cylinders, classes weren't awful—I was actually making friends—and then there was Tristan. His birthday party was coming up the next day and I couldn't wait to spend some time outside of school with him. The only things that stood between that and me were my final debate team practice for the week, which was just ending, and my shift at work.

"What do you say, gorg? Wanna grab a bite?" Arden said as we packed up after the practice. "We can go over our notes for the tournament next week."

"Sorry," I said. "I have work tonight. What about Sunday?"

"Sundays are terrible for me because my family insists on dragging their obviously gay daughter to their very Catholic church to smile and pretend like everything is fine. It's a whole ordeal and by noon I'm exhausted," Arden explained. "Saturday?"

I laughed. "I can't do it Saturday."

"Jeez!" Arden yelped. "I'm beginning to think you just don't wanna hang out with me."

"Hey, I'm not turning any religions upside down on Sundays, that's you," I snipped back, "and normally Fridays work for me, but I had to swap shifts so that I have tomorrow off. I have Tristan's birthday party."

We were headed towards the front of the school and Arden grabbed my arm and pulled me to a complete stop. I looked at her, expecting her typical, jester-like demeanor, but she was wearing the most serious expression I'd seen thus far. "What?"

"What?" I said.

"Tristan Castrone?" Arden said. "Captain of the football team, reigning overlord of the pops? That Tristan?"

"The pops?" I said with a tilt of my head.

"Yeah, come on, Aria, keep up." Arden shifted her weight and turned me to face her fully as if she was about to give me the most important information of my life. "In terms of hierarchy, Tristan, Ceradi, Milton, Josh, Capito…" She hesitated for a beat. "…Hannah, they're the popular kids at this school. They're the top tier and they do not socialize below their station. I call them the 'Pops,' short for popular—duh. Anyway, most of the school's students are in the middle, but anyone who attends anything in *that* wing," she pointed towards the academic club wing of the school, "are the losers." She flipped her thumb between the two of us. "We're losers, they're Pops, and Pops don't like us losers. Did you buy an invitation or something?"

The dynamic that Arden was explaining sounded so much like my old school, it was terrifying. The thing was, at least from the first week of school, it didn't seem like things were all that bad, and for all the horrible things the popular kids at my old school had done to me, I just couldn't see Tristan being that guy. Even his friend Hannah, although a little icy, didn't seem that cruel. Was there really a whole layer I was missing?

"No, I didn't buy an invite, he invited me. We're actually childhood friends," I said.

Arden's eyes widened. "Wait… really?" She seemed surprised, but not in the way I was expecting, more of like a planar shift had taken place. "You and Tristan?"

"Y-yeah?" I said apprehensively. "We lived in the same neighborhood growing up. I kind of looked out for him, because believe you me, he was *not* that bulky as a kid. We were really close. Then his dad got remarried and they moved away. I assumed they moved far, like out of state, but I show up here for my senior year, and here he is. We're getting along really well, and he invited me to his birthday party tomorrow."

Arden slowly started walking again and I kept pace with her. "Well, okay, but be careful. You'll find that deep ties don't matter much to these guys."

It sounded like she was speaking from experience so I asked, "Something that happened to you?"

"That girl Hannah. I have pictures of the two of us in diapers. We are, quite literally, generational. Our mothers were best friends, their mothers were best friends. I still see her mom often. Always asking whatever happened between Hannah and me. It's not like I can say, 'Oh, well, your late-blooming daughter grew some boobs and had her braces removed, which were two of the criteria for becoming a cosmic *bitch*,' so I just say we grew up and grew apart." She sighed. "I picked lice outta that girl's hair and now she won't even look at me. It was kind of Tristan that started the whole thing actually."

My heart skipped a beat then. "What do you mean?"

"Oh, you know, she got all hot so he asked her out. I kept trying to hang with her, but they were dating, so she always ran off with him. The most irritating part was that they only dated for like two weeks. Our entire, 15 years of friendship got flushed down the drain for him to get interested and bored with her in two weeks. Terrible."

"Wow," I grumbled. "I'm sorry that happened to you."

Hearing Arden telling it like that *did* make me a little nervous. I wanted to believe in Tristan, that he would never do that kind of thing to me, but if it happened with Hannah, one of the most beautiful girls in the entire school, why *wouldn't* he do it to me?

But then I shook my head.

No. Tristan was a good guy, and he'd been just as excited to reconnect with me as I was with him. If he was as vapid as Arden was making it seem, he never would have invited me to his party. In fact, he'd already remained friendly with me even with his friends around. We had a ton of history. Everything would be fine. I believed that Tristan would treat me much better than that, and if he really was starting to fall in line with the asshole popular kids, I could help him work through that too.

"No offense, but I don't think it'll be the same with Tristan and me, though. I mean for as much as kids our age don't really think about love or anything like that, when Tristan and I were together back then, I remember thinking that I hoped we could stay that way forever. He approached me when he saw me, not the other way around. I didn't even recognize him at first. I think it'll be okay."

Arden shrugged. "For your sake, I hope so. But hey," she nudged me playfully, "if it goes horribly wrong and you need to just get drunk and make out with a friend, I'm here for you."

"Gee thanks," I said, rolling my eyes.

Arden held out her hands on either side of herself. "Hey. Don't blame a girl for trying. It's your fault for being so stunning, but I'll get used to it eventually. Maybe."

"I really don't think I'm all that special," I said. "I mean that Hannah girl is way prettier than me."

"Yeah, okay," Arden said with a scoff. "I bet she's better at debating and also works for a homeless shelter." She shook her head. "God I hate it when beautiful people don't know they're beautiful." Just as we were entering the parking garage, one of the other debate club members, Devario, was walking by. Arden snagged his arm and said, "D. Please tell this woman she's a knockout. She doesn't believe me."

"Oh, I get it," Devario replied. "It's like that thing where supermodels tell normal people that with a little effort, they can be just as beautiful."

Arden fell out laughing. "Exactly."

"I really don't see what you guys see," I said.

"Attractive people never do," Devario said. "In fact," he yanked his arm away from Arden, "let me go before I embarrass myself. I never do well with beautiful women."

Arden held up her hands as he walked away. "You do fine with me!"

"I said what I said," he called back.

I cupped my hands over my mouth to stifle a laugh as Arden flipped him off. It was all in good fun anyway. Though her look was a little eclectic, Arden was really gorgeous too, but she didn't seem like the kind of woman who liked people lauding about it, so I couldn't return her gracious favors.

"I have to go," I sputtered out between snickers. "I'm gonna be late as it is."

"Fine," Arden said, roping me into a hug. "Call me later."

"I will."

We waved goodbye and I set off for my job with Devario and Arden's words ringing in my mind. Tristan had said I looked good when we first saw each other, but I wasn't sure if it was just courtesy or if he actually meant it. Hopefully he shared their same sentiments. I certainly felt that way about him.

"Evenin' kid!" The homeless shelter I worked for was a refurbished three-star hotel just outside of the city. A man named Billy—a kind, older guy with ruddy cheeks, salt and pepper hair, and a wide grin—greeted people at the front reception desk. "I ain't realize you was workin' today."

"I have a party tomorrow, so I swapped with Shaina to come in tonight instead," I explained.

"Party?" he said, furrowing his brow. "You don't like people though."

I giggled. "Yeah, you're right about that. This is a special case though. An old friend invited me. I'm hoping to reconnect with him, so I'm going to go and deal with the widespread disease that is *people*."

He chuckled. "Alright, well Zami is back there already, and I believe Lucky's coming in too today. It's been slow so far. Soup's in about two hours though."

"From uptown or downtown?" I asked.

"Downtown," Billy replied.

"Yeah, it's gonna hop up then. Thanks Billy."

Billy waved a hand. "No problem, kid."

Beyond the front desk where Billy was sitting, I could head back into what had formerly been the hotel's kitchen, but was now our functioning kitchen for feeding any guests that came through our door. To the left were all the ovens, sinks and prep stations, and to the right were a few tables set up for us to take breaks, along with a long line of lockers for staff to put their stuff in. One of these lockers was my regular one, so I made my way towards it and started to pile my stuff into it.

"I thought I heard someone dinking around back here." A familiar voice echoed off the tiles. "Hey Aria."

I smiled. "Hey Zameera. How's it going?"

"Even better, now that my favorite employee is here."

A scoff came out as I shook my head. "I bet you say that to all your employees."

"Trust me, I don't," she replied, giggling.

I got the rest of my stuff put away and pulled out my work apron. I pulled it over my head and stood up, shutting the locker as I did. I turned to see Zameera sitting at one of the staff tables with a wide smile on her face. She had thick, frizzy black hair and caramelized skin a few shades darker than my own. Perfectly round rimmed glasses shielded her dark brown eyes, and sparse freckles covered her nose and cheeks. She was my boss, and as far as bosses go, I got pretty lucky. She was awesome.

"Sit," she said, motioning to the chair across from her at the table. "You're technically not on until 6, and we're pretty light anyway. Tell me about your new school."

I grabbed a bottle of water from the cooler reserved for staff and then slid down into one of the chairs. "This is going to sound a little shocking, but… I actually really like it."

"Yeah? That's great! Much better than the old place?" she said.

"So far," I responded.

"See?" she reached across the table and thumped me on my head. "All that flak you gave your poor mother and it's working out."

"I know, I know. I already apologized to her," I said.

Zameera was only a handful of years younger than my mom and lauded over me like a surrogate. My mom and I were almost identical in personality, apart from her optimism for my pessimism, so we butted heads fairly frequently. When I was having issues with my mom but still needed that motherly advice, I came to Zameera.

"What's so good about this new school?" she asked.

"Well, the debate club is incredible. It has its own dedicated room with real podiums and timers and stuff, and I'm making new friends there too. So far, the one I'm closest with is this punk chick named Arden. She's awesome, if not a bit jaded from being at the bottom of the totem pole."

Zameera raised an eyebrow at me. "*That* sounds familiar."

"Yeah," I said snickering.

"And you've already been invited to a party, and you're going, so that's *two* unexpected things," Zameera said.

At that moment, the door from the lobby swung open and Lucky came waltzing back. He had a muted, bored expression on his face, but then he looked over and saw me and lit up. "Aria! What are you doing here? I thought you had work tomorrow?"

"Figured I'd surprise you. I had to swap shifts," I said. With much more exuberance, Lucky walked over to his locker, made short work of pushing his stuff inside and grabbing his apron, then he sat down at the table perpendicular to both Zameera and myself. "I have a party to go to tomorrow."

"One I'm still waiting to hear about," Zameera said.

"You're going to a party?" Lucky asked, shocked.

"Yeah, you remember that guy Tristan I was telling you about?" I said, then turned to look at Zameera. "There's this guy—"

"Wait," Zameera cut me off, leaning half across the table. "Like… a *guy*? More than friends guy?"

"I hope so," I said. "I knew him as a little girl until his family moved away, but he goes to this school and we totally hit it off. He invited me to his birthday party this weekend. Arden thinks it's a bad idea to go, but I'm going to go anyway. It'll be fine."

"Why does Arden think it's a bad idea?" Zameera and Lucky said in unison.

"Because Tristan—that's the guy—is one of the popular kids at the very top of the school and we're the dorks at the bottom. They don't intermingle, and Arden thinks I'm going to end up getting hurt. I don't though. I trust Tristan, and it's clear he likes me, so he'll probably just leave his friends out of it," I replied.

"Hm," Zameera said. "I've just decided I really like this Arden girl. I appreciate when people look out for you where I can't. Jury's still out on this Tristan guy, but we'll know for sure about him after this party, right? Do you think something is gonna happen?"

"I mean…" Heat rose to my face as I thought about it.

"I'm not *aiming* for it or anything, but if he starts something I'm certainly not going to stop it."

Zameera was all giggles, but Lucky frowned fiercely next to me. I wanted to ask, but I had a feeling I was just going to get another speech like the one Arden had given me, and I didn't need it. I'd already resolved myself to going to the party, and I was just going to have to expect the unexpected.

7

TRISTAN

I parked my car in the third spot of my brother's garage, and then used my key to let myself in. The whole house smelled delicious, and the entire place was already decorated with the simple, understated options I had requested. Streamers were strung across the ceiling of most of the rooms, in forest green and gold, my school colors, and there were only a couple of bundles of balloons, sitting just inside the front door. Most of Taylor's living and dining room furniture had been pushed against the walls or removed altogether, creating lots of extra room for party guests. My excitement grew and grew with each passing second.

Trusting Taylor with my party had been the best course of action, and I was happy it worked out.

"Tris?" a voice called out and I recognized it as Taylor's girlfriend Molly.

"Yeah!"

I walked through the living room and sizable den, into

the kitchen. Molly was in there, along with her younger sister Sherelle, and they were working over the oven, preparing a bunch of finger foods en masse. Molly and Sherelle looked almost identical, with chest length, wavy, dirty blond hair, and bright blue eyes. They owned a catering company together and had agreed to do the food for my party. They were putting together about ten different appetizer options, in large quantities, on different plates for serving in different rooms throughout the house.

"Hey there, birthday boy," Molly greeted, taking a quick break from her work to wrap an arm around me. "Food's almost done, the house is decorated, as you can see. Taylor just went to gather…" she gave me a half-lidded gaze, "…refreshments." I smiled then. At least he followed through on letting us have *some* booze, which Molly didn't seem thrilled with. "You *do* realize you're not legal right? Your brother is a lawyer. If he gets caught letting you guys drink, he could be disbarred."

Sherelle walked over and clattered her spatula on the countertop. "Mol, stop. You promised Taylor you wouldn't do this."

"I know," I said to Molly. "I know that Taylor's taking a big risk. Not only am I aware of that, but I've made sure all my friends are too. We're going to do the solo cup thing, keep empties in the trash, not drink outside, and make sure not to make too much of a ruckus so that there's no reason to even call the cops or anything. I know I'm kind of a shit-head, but I'm not trying to ruin my brother's whole life. I just want one good party. That's it."

Molly took a deep breath in and then out. Sherelle was standing between us like a ref between two boxers and finally Molly shook her head. "I'm not some loser who doesn't get it, you know? I was eighteen once too, but it's not just you, it's your brother, too. You both have really bright futures. I don't want it to be ruined."

"I know." I put a hand on Molly's shoulder. "I know. I'll be good. I promise."

As if summoned by the mention of him, the back door to the kitchen opened, and Taylor walked in with a couple of brown paper bags balanced in each hand. He set them down and then walked out again, returning a few seconds later with a couple more bags. After a few trips, he'd gotten all the bags inside, along with a couple of big coolers and several bags of ice, then he walked over and gave me a hug.

"What's going on, bro?" he said. "Nearly there for your party!" He snagged a pig in a blanket off one of the trays Molly was preparing and popped it in his mouth. "Got the drinks."

"What'd you get?" I asked, walking excitedly to the counter where he'd stacked the bags. "You said you compromised."

"I did. I'm not about to serve a bunch of single-minded teenagers vodka and whisky, so…" He reached into one of the bags and pulled out a six-pack of wine coolers. "You get 6% or less."

I snickered, anticipating something of the sort, but not knowing which way he was going to go. "Hey, this works for me."

"We've got coolers, hard cider, and just regular beer, plus a few selections of hard sparkling water. I'm gonna split 'em between up here and downstairs in these big ass tubs I got, and once they're gone, they're gone." He turned and stabbed a finger at me. "And I swear to god, Tristan, if

I see anyone at this party with hard liquor, I'm ending it, and calling the cops. I'm not joking."

"Narc," I grumbled, but then when Taylor threw me a stern glare, I waved my hands through the air. "Don't worry. I was just telling Molly, we're going to follow all the rules. Keep it low key. I'm grateful that you let me use your place, so I'm not gonna take advantage."

"Better not," he muttered back. "I've also got water, soda, and stuff for punch for non-drinkers. Much more of that even in the back, so go crazy with that."

"Thank you so much." I looked at Molly and Sherelle. "You guys too. This is really awesome. I'm going to have the best party ever." I turned back to Taylor, bouncing with excitement. "You said downstairs, so does that mean we get to use the man cave?"

Taylor rolled his eyes. "Yes. I'm letting you use my man cave, but—hey!"

Taylor wasn't even done with his sentence before I bolted from the kitchen and through the door that led to a staircase leading down. What had started out as an unfinished basement when Taylor first bought his house, had been revamped into an entertainment paradise. Against the wall furthest from the door, there was a projector screen that would take feeds from the projector mounted to the ceiling a handful of feet away. A couple of movie theater style loveseats were situated in front of it for relaxed movie watching, and a functioning popcorn machine sat against the wall to the left of the chairs.

Behind that, was a pool table, with electric pink felt instead of green. The casing for the table was see-through, so that when the balls went into the pockets, you could watch the ball roll in, and the pocket would light up.

Against the wall nearest to the door was a bar that was normally well-stocked, but I could see it had been emptied of all of its options. Chilled bottles of water and cans of soda were stacked on the shelves instead, which I was perfectly okay with, because the neon underside of the shelves shimmered through the water and looked awesome. The entire thing was topped off with an original Galaga and Pacman arcade machine, sandwiched together on the wall between the basement door and the door to the downstairs bathroom. My decorations theme continued down there, with streamers along the ceiling, and twinkle lights in the same color scheme draped along the bar and molded sills.

"Yes!" I said. "This is totally going to be the hot spot of the party!"

Taylor whacked me across the back of my head. "Listen. There is fifty-grand worth of shit down here. If you break anything, it's coming out of your pocket."

"Nothing will be broken or damaged, I promise," I said, then walked over and slumped down into one of the comfy, movie chairs. "I need it to start already. I'm anxious now."

"Just a couple more hours," Taylor replied, sinking in next to me. "Is Aria coming?"

"Yeah," I said. "She says she is anyway."

"I can't wait to see her again. God, I hope she sticks around," Taylor said. "I know I haven't seen her in years, but I just know she'd be good for you."

"I'm a little nervous actually. My friends are being a little weird about her," I said.

"It wouldn't have anything to do with the fact that they're shallow and mean, would it?" Taylor asked.

"Hey," I snapped. "Can you not be like that? They're my friends."

"Sorry, Tris. They're terrible people. Hannah isn't completely awful, but I think you should just drop all of them. You turn into this snob when they're around, and if they're being mean to Aria, I don't know why you'd keep them around anyway. Let them go and see what the future holds for you without them holding you back."

"You don't know them like I do. They have the capacity for kindness. We're all good to each other," I said.

"Are you?" Taylor asked

I opened my mouth to offer a rebuttal, but didn't have anything solid and closed it. Taylor stared at me knowingly until I finally dismissed the subject by saying, "They're my friends and they're not going anywhere, so let's just drop it."

Taylor crossed his arms as he sighed. "Fine, but I sincerely hope you wouldn't pass on an opportunity to be with Aria for them. I've always been my true blue, geeky self, and I ended up with a real babe."

"You got that right." Taylor and I looked back in the direction of the bar, and Molly was dropping a couple of food supplies on top of it. She threw an eyebrow up at us, before heading back upstairs.

"Don't you walk away from me!" Taylor huffed, hopping up from his chair and rushing over. I heard Molly giggle as they clamored up the stairs.

A longing twisted my stomach into a knot. It wasn't just because Molly was stunning that I was jealous of my brother's relationship with her. They'd been thick as thieves ever since they met, and what started out as a tight friendship blossomed into true love as they both came to realize they were made for each other. They could do all that sappy, romance-movie stuff like finish each other's sentences and be around each other for weeks on end without getting sick of one another, but they were also just so obviously in love. From the little things they did for one another to the minor details of their relationship that proved they were both all-in.

It was what I wanted more than anything.

I pushed the thoughts from my mind, because I didn't want to be a sappy, lovelorn mess at my party. Standing up from the chair I took another look around Taylor's man cave, certain that it was going to be the hit of the party, and made my way back upstairs to see if there was anything I could do to help setting up.

Though the party started at 7:00pm, at about five minutes 'til, people still hadn't arrived. I wasn't concerned, knowing that it was the *cool* thing to show up fashionably late, but it made waiting that much harder. I figured it'd be until 7:30pm or maybe even 8:00pm before people started arriving, but at about 7:07pm, there was a knock at the front door. Taylor smiled as we walked over to the door, and when we opened the door, his excitement doubled.

As did mine.

Aria was standing on the other side of the door, with an orange bag in hand—my favorite color that she must have managed to remember from *years* ago. She also looked incredible in a navy blue, silk shirt dress with a multi-colored collar, and a matching tie around the waist. The ensemble showed a tantalizing amount of her legs and cleavage without being too revealing, and her hair was pulled back into a high ponytail so that her beautiful eyes could be the highlight of her face.

"Aria!" Taylor screeched before I could get any words out. "Hey!"

"Hi!" she said with a smile. "How are you?"

Taylor opened his arms and Aria walked into his embrace. He gave her a tight squeeze. "I'm much better now. When Tristan told me that you two had reconnected, I was elated."

"You and me both," Aria said as she pulled back from Taylor, then she looked at me. "Hi. Happy Birthday, well, a day early."

I shook my head and smiled. There were two, *maybe* three people who I'd invited to the party who knew that my actual birthday wasn't until tomorrow. Aria's memory was incredible, and it made me happy to have someone around me who actually knew me. "Thank you."

I slowly turned my head to look at Taylor and he laughed and held up his hands. "Right. Sorry. I'll leave you guys to it." He waved at Aria. "I'm glad you're here. If you need anything, just let me know."

"Thanks," Aria said.

Then Taylor took one last look at her, complete with a dorky smile, then looked at me and walked off. I stood aside so that Aria could walk in, and once she was inside, I wrapped my arms around her and gave her a huge hug. "I'm glad you're here."

Aria's arms gripped around me. "I'm glad I'm here too." She pulled back and held out the gift to me. "For you."

"Oh, thank you!" I smiled. "Uh, wanna find a comfortable spot? Taylor's entertainment room downstairs is awesome."

She nodded at me with a warm smile. "Yeah. Let's do

it." I led the way downstairs with Aria chuckling behind me. "I feel like such a loser showing up so early. I tried to be late, but I'm still first."

"You think ten after seven is late?" I asked.

"I mean… by definition it is," she replied. "Yeah, you're right, it's not. I'm lame."

We got to the bottom of the stairs and I turned to face her. "It's not lame. I was chomping at the bit for you to arrive."

A light blush came to her cheeks. "Maybe we're both lame."

"Maybe," I replied.

Aria wandered around the basement room, glancing at all the cool gadgets. "Wow. This really is an awesome space."

"Yeah. I spend a majority of my time here, down here." I looked down at the gift in my hands and my stomach turned over a little bit. I'd get maybe one more gift from anyone I invited if I was lucky. A small handful of people *might* send me $20 in a cash app, but that was it. Most of them didn't even know me well enough to get me a gift at all; they were just in it for the party. "Can I open my present?"

It brought Aria's attention flying back to me. "Of course! It's yours." She walked over and leaned against the pool table and I came to stand in front of her with the gift in hand. "It's not much, but…"

"Are you kidding? I wasn't even expecting a gift. This is really nice." I lifted the light orange tissue paper out of the bag and set it on the pool table and then reached into the bag. There were a couple of things inside, so I pulled the larger out. It was a really nice flip-top spiral sketchbook.

"Oh wow!" I reached back into the bag and there was a box of drawing pencils in different gradients. Aria said it wasn't much, but I'd bought the same set before, and knew they weren't cheap. "Aria, this is incredible."

"Like I said, it's not much, but after I saw that you were still drawing, I knew I had to get it. I know you're really into the football thing, but you're *so* talented. I just wanted to support *that* hobby, since I'm sure you get no shortage of people telling you you're good at sports."

It was such a considerate gift, but the fact that she honestly believed it wasn't much made it even better. "Thanks, Aria."

I stepped forward to give her a hug, and she wrapped her arms around my back. "Of course."

Everything changed at that moment. Maybe it was the thoughtful gift, maybe it was the dress she was wearing that was revealing and hung onto her shape so nicely, but wrapping my arms around Aria set my heart to racing wildly. My entire body heated up and I suddenly wanted more. I pulled back from Aria, but kept my arms wrapped around her. I was testing the waters, seeing what she felt about the sudden closeness, but as soon as she realized I wasn't going to pull my arms back, she leaned against me a little more.

"So I guess you like the gift then?" she joked.

I stared down into her intoxicating eyes and smiled. "Yeah. I like the gift."

Before I could stop myself, I was leaning in, and to my satisfaction, Aria's eyes drifted closed and she leaned in as well. My lips pressed to hers and sent a jolt of electricity flying down my spine. I'd kissed other girls before, but it was nothing like the way it felt with Aria. Her full lips felt like silk against mine, and with her hands clasped behind my back, I took a step forward and pinned her against the pool table.

Whatever had come over me must have come over her as well, because she repositioned herself so that she could pull her arms up around my neck. Her fingers flicked across my neck, leaving chills in their wake. With her warm reception I decided to push the envelope a little more and slipped my tongue out. Aria's lips parted, allowing me to push forward. She let out a breathy moan that threatened to have me showing my rapidly developing arousal. I suddenly regretted that I was at my brother's house with a hundred people on the way.

All I wanted to do was be alone with Aria and see how far we could go.

"Tris!" Molly yelled down the stairs. "More of your friends are here."

I let out an audible growl and Aria laughed. As frustrating as it was, I stepped back from Aria, glancing down to make sure I was okay, which made her laugh more.

"Why did I invite a bunch of people to our first date?" I asked.

Aria's face was totally flushed and her eyes fluttered with happiness. "I don't know. It's probably a good thing though. I'm not a first date, first time kind of girl but... I wouldn't have stopped you."

I shook my head. "Don't tell me that. I'll shut this whole shit down."

She giggled. "Fine by me."

I looked at her and wanted so desperately to lean back in, but there was nothing I could do. "Maybe, when the party is like... up and going, we could slip away again?"

My heart jumped when she nodded. "Yeah."

"Okay. I'll come track you down later." I started off, but looked back at her and didn't want to go. She flicked her hands at me to shoo me off, so I groaned again and made my way upstairs.

As I got to the landing at the top of the stairs, I could already hear Ceradi's shrill laugh. I rounded the corner into the kitchen and saw Ceradi, Hannah, Milton, Josh, and Capito standing there, already with drinks in their hands.

"There you are," Ceradi said. "I was beginning to think you were going to leave us here on our own."

Hannah smiled at me. "Happy birthday."

"Thanks."

"Ooh, what'd you get?" Milton said, snatching the orange bag with Aria's gifts out of my hands. When my arms wrapped around her, I stopped thinking about the fact that I was holding it.

"Uh," I said, but then decided to let them journey further and test the temperature.

Milton shoved his meaty hand into the bag and pulled back out the sketchpad and pencils. His face screwed in confusion as Hannah's eyes widened and flicked to me.

Ceradi grabbed the tag on the bag and opened it up. "Aria? That new girl? She's here?"

I waited for a minute, with no one doing anything to indicate which way they were going. Milton looked at Ceradi, then Hannah, then me, and then after a few seconds of silence, they burst out into laughter.

Ceradi looked at me with tears in her eyes. "What did you think when she handed it to you?"

I quickly glanced at Hannah, and she gave me a subtle shake of her head, then I cracked a smile. I didn't want to be embarrassed or ridiculed in front of all of my friends.

The party was just getting started. "What do you think?" I said. "I was like, is this girl serious? A coloring book? What am I, five?"

Though she didn't laugh, Hannah let out a sign of relief, while Ceradi, Milton, Josh, and Capito roared.

8

ARIA

My heart was still pounding out of control. No matter how long I sat there, the feeling of Tristan's lips on mine and his hands caressing down my back lingered. I wasn't sure if I was happy or sad for the interruption of his other party guests beginning to arrive. We were a speeding train, and I could say with certainty that if he tried to push for more, I would have let him. I didn't expect that he would actually make a move that quickly, but something about that last hug we had snapped a strand of resistance that had already been pulled completely taut.

If he hadn't made that move, I probably would have.

Hopefully we'd have a little more time later to continue to explore. I wasn't sure if I wanted to go *all* the way with him just yet—we should probably go on a date first—but again, I wasn't in any position to slow us down. If he wanted to keep going, so did I.

Over the course of the next ten or fifteen minutes, party guests arrived in droves. I could hear the rumble of dozens of sets of feet on the floor above, and eventually, people started to spill their way downstairs. The music started to rock a little harder, and people started indulging in the food and drinks.

It was a party. A totally new experience for me.

I did see that there was a giant tub with ice in it, and the drinks people were pulling out appeared to be alcoholic. I'd never drunk before, and if I had any control over it, I never would. My father died because he was homeless and got so drunk in the middle of the winter that he didn't realize how much heat his body had lost. The warmth of the booze convinced him he was fine, and he sat out in the cold until he froze to death. At work, at least half of the clients I helped at any given time came in completely wasted. A majority of our financial counseling was convincing people that liquor was a black hole of finances and that the beginning of not being without was not spending money on things like that.

In short, I hated alcohol. Nothing good came from it.

That said, I wasn't *that* much of a loser that I didn't understand that it was all the rage, especially among people who weren't legally supposed to be doing it. It was considered "cool" to get drunk as a teenager who could barely decide when they needed to use the bathroom or not, even if I didn't understand the allure. It did seem, at the very least, that they had restricted the booze to low percentage malt liquors and coolers. Probably Taylor's doing.

"Aria?" I looked to my right and the guy who had a locker next to mine, Yunmir, was standing there. "I didn't expect to see you here."

I snickered. "Yeah. I'm full of surprises. I also just happen to be old friends with the birthday boy, so…"

"Ah." Yunmir nodded his head. "Well, how's it going?"

"Pretty good. How are you?" I asked.

"Not bad. Can I get you a drink?" Yunmir asked. "I've seen soda, booze, water?"

"Oh, um…"

Behind Yunmir, I could see his friends standing and whispering to one another. I remembered on my first day, Yunmir had seemed to make a pass at me. He'd been kind to me the remainder of the week, but had never made any additional moves. He was smiling brightly at me, and his behavior seemed to suggest he maybe *was* a little interested. I was flattered, but he didn't do for me even half of what Tristan did.

"Thanks, but I actually need to go and find Tristan now. He asked me to save him from mingling." It wasn't entirely false. He did say we'd meet up later on.

Yunmir seemed unbothered, nodding while tipping his beer towards me. "No problem. Maybe we can chat later on?"

How did people normally turn people down that they just had no interest in? "Yeah. For sure."

He waved. "Okay, see ya then." Then he walked off with his friends in tow.

In order to ensure that I could get as far away as possible from what could only get more awkward, I headed towards the stairs and started up. I had to slide along the wall, excusing my way past people as the expected popularity of the basement entertainment room grew. A few people stared at me as I passed, no doubt sharing Yunmir's surprise to see the newest school loser at a popular, senior kid's party, but I just ignored it. I was there for Tristan, and he'd beyond proven that he was happy I was there, so that was all that mattered to me.

On the upper level, the music was so loud that people had to shout to speak to one another, a problem most people were solving by not talking at all, but rather dancing and drinking instead. I scanned the sea of students, looking for Tristan, but he was nowhere to be seen. Taylor was making his way around the room, making sure everyone saw him and knew that he was there, and when his eyes met mine, he gave me an excited wave. I waved back, giggling, before continuing my search for his brother.

Finally, I turned to walk into the kitchen, where I saw Tristan standing along with his friends. He had the bag that I'd given him his gift in, and one of his friends was holding the sketchpad and pencils. I found it unbelievably adorable that he was showing his friends the gifts I'd gotten him, so I stopped in the doorway of the kitchen to see if I could hear what they were saying.

Unfortunately, I could.

"I mean," Ceradi said, laughing so hard she was dabbing at tears in the corners of her eye. "How sad is it? She got it *this* wrong."

"These pencils are all shades of grey," one of the guys who I'd learned throughout the week was named Josh, said. "The least she could have done is get you some colors."

It hurt, but I expected it from the popular kids. They didn't understand Tristan's true self, nor seemed smart enough to recognize a true artist's tools when they saw them. Tristan's back was to me so I couldn't see his face, but then he reached out and grabbed the sketchpad and pencils and shoved them back into the bag. I wasn't sure if he was going to defend me or just walk away, but I was hoping for the former.

"What does she expect me to do?" Tristan said. "Draw a gray football?"

My stomach twisted and I felt like I was going to throw up. His friends erupted into laughter, and he doubled over like it was the funniest thing he'd ever experienced in his life. "I mean, is this what losers give each other as gifts? I've never been there, so I wouldn't know."

"Maybe?" another one, Neerah, said. "They show up uber early to parties and give lame gifts. That could be their thing."

"I thought we were bad showing up at 7:30," Hannah said. "When did she even get here?"

"No lie," Tristan replied immediately. "Like ten after seven. Maybe even sooner, and she thought she was late." He started roaring alongside his friends. "Who does that?"

"Why did you even invite her?" Ceradi asked.

Tristan shrugged. "She's an old friend and I kind of felt obligated to."

Ceradi shook her head. "Ugh. The sooner you ditch that nice guy attitude, the better off you'll be."

That was considered a nice guy's attitude?

One of the guys, Milton, held out a hand. "Hey. At least you can say you had two people show up that early." His friends gave him looks of confusion, so he explained. "Oh, sorry. I'm counting her as two people, you know, because…" Then he warped his arms out on either side of himself and puffed his cheeks out like he was a balloon.

"Oh, I was just confused because I was counting her as three," Tristan replied.

It snapped my heart in half. Tears rose to my eyes and I

was certain I was going to puke. A hand settled on my back and I looked up to see Taylor standing next to me, looking furious. He looked down at me, then used his hand on my back to pull me away from the kitchen doorway. He shoved me past the dense collection of students and over to the front door so we could step out into the fresh air. I let out a loud gasp as if I'd been holding my breath that whole time and I could no longer stop the tears from running down my face.

"Aria," Taylor said. "I'm so… He's not… I just…" He shook his head. "I'm sorry. Can I get you something to drink or something? If you want, you can go take a breather in my and Molly's room. No one is allowed upstairs."

I shook my head, biting the inside of my cheek. "No. I just want to go home."

"I understand," Taylor said, then he pulled me into a hug. "I'm sorry. These kids make Tristan an entirely different person."

Tristan's hurtful words rang through my brain and radiated out until every ounce of me just felt weak. After being so excited to be reunited with him and thinking that things were going somewhere between us. How could he say stuff like that about me? I was actually beginning to think that maybe I was going to be that lucky person that got to be with their school sweetheart. After everything.

How could it end like this?

"Thanks, Taylor. It was nice to see you."

"You too," Taylor replied, sounding almost as heartbroken as I felt.

I walked back to my car, passing the people who were still just arriving, and climbed into the driver's seat. I was barely there before I broke down sobbing, and only just barely managed to get my car a block away before my eyes were too blurry to drive safely. Talking was only going to be a trainwreck, so I opened up my phone and sent a text to Arden that just said, "You were right." She called me right away, but I couldn't bring myself to answer and tacked on, "Can't talk now, I'll call you tomorrow."

"Definitely," she replied. "Lunch on me."

The thought that I would be able to see Arden and talk things out was enough to calm me to the point that I could limp home. I drove so slowly I was certain a cop was going to pull me over, but after a long thirty minutes, I was finally pulling into my driveway at home. The living room light was on, which meant my mom was still awake, a fact I was less than happy with, but I walked in nonetheless, preparing myself for the conversation that was sure to take place.

"Aria?" she yelped as soon as she saw my face, standing to rush over to me. "What happened?" She wrapped her arms around me and pulled me over to the couch to sit down. Something about a mother's love always made emotions feel stronger, and I started bawling in earnest. She pulled my head down against her shoulder and petted my head gently. "Baby. What happened?"

"Tristan," I whimpered. "He called me fat and a loser. He said he liked my gift but then he trashed me in front of all his friends."

I'd told her about Tristan, and even apologized to her because of him, because I thought he was going to make this whole experience worth it. I couldn't have been more wrong.

"Honey," my mom said sadly. "I am so sorry."

After all of my worrying, all of my fears, and all of my

anxiety, trying to give people the benefit of the doubt had turned out to be an egregious mistake. I wasn't even upset that the popular kids were bullying me—that was a reality I'd come to accept—but hearing those words come from Tristan's mouth, less than an hour after making out with him, was something that was going to haunt my nightmares for many days to come.

I was hoping for a new adventure, but it was beginning to look like it was going to be more of the same. Maybe even worse.

9

TRISTAN

I t took a while, but eventually I got my friends to move on from the topic of Aria and the gift she'd given me. Pretending to hate it and dislike her as much as I did made me feel gross. If I'd known that it was going to be so problematic, I actually might have opted to invite Aria to my birthday lunch with my family rather than the party with all my friends. I didn't expect them to be that cruel, and I was really hoping I wouldn't have to jump in. With the party just beginning, I didn't want to cause any problems that would ruin things for everyone, so I did what I had to do to get through the conversation, but it wasn't fun.

As long as they all had drinks in their hands and were off talking about someone else, I took my gift from Aria and slipped away from the pack. Honestly, I didn't want Aria to cross paths at all with Ceradi or the others, so I figured it would be good if we could just slip to a quieter place and continue spending time alone. Maybe I could even use my new sketchpad and pencils to draw another portrait of her, more accurately with her right in front of me.

I did the cursory scan for her, but didn't see her right away and could see people looking at my gift. Whether out of curiosity or guilt from not having brought anything of their own, people kept staring at the bag, so I decided to take it upstairs to keep it out of the view of others.

When Taylor bought his house, he thoughtfully kept me in mind, and I had my own dedicated bedroom. I walked in and set the gift down and then took a few minutes to pack up my bag and backpack that I'd brought with me for staying overnight, and even lit a candle to make the room smell a bit better. At the very last second, I made sure the bed was made and that there was a nice, calming and romantic playlist going. In my backpack was a box of condoms that I kept on me just in case, and I moved them from my bag to the drawer next to my bed. I wasn't expecting anything from Aria, obviously, but if things went in a certain direction, I wanted to be prepared.

Once I was confident that my room was prepared for eventually bringing Aria up to get away and spend more time together, I walked back out of the room and returned to the first floor, where everyone seemed hellbent on distracting me as I looked around for where Aria was. It wasn't the worst thing, because I did need to show my face, especially considering the fact that once I got Aria alone, I may just stay there until the end of the party. I took pictures, enjoyed a drink for a few minutes with a handful of different people, expecting that, at some point, I'd see Aria wandering around too.

But I couldn't find her.

After an hour of not seeing her anywhere, I started to just full-fledge look for her. She had to be somewhere—we agreed to meet up again—but I checked the living room, the kitchen, the backyard, and the man cave, and couldn't find Aria at all. Did she get uncomfortable and leave?

The only person as excited as I was that Aria was there was Taylor, and if I knew him at all, he'd probably been keeping an eye on her. He, Molly, and Sherelle had been making sure to keep a presence all around the party so that people knew not to misbehave. It was much easier to find Taylor, who was in the kitchen with Molly, refilling food trays and restocking the drink supply.

"Taylor," I called out.

Taylor turned and looked at me, and I thought his gaze was going to freeze me over. I side-eyed Molly, who was shifting her gaze between what she was doing and Taylor, eventually throwing me a nervous glance. "Uh… What's going on? I was wondering if you guys have seen Aria?"

The mention of Aria's name had Taylor's fist tightening around the bucket he was holding. He looked at Molly, then back at me, and Molly reached out and took the bucket. "I'll deal with this, you deal with that."

"What?" I asked.

Taylor walked past me, heat emanating off of him. "Follow me."

I looked at Molly, nervous. "Am I in trouble?"

Molly nodded quickly. "Yeah. A lot of it."

My heart started to beat a little faster, nervous that maybe one of the guests had broken or damaged something. I had just finished a complete loop of the house, and everything appeared to be in order. I'd been upstairs and no one else appeared to be up there. As far as I could see, everyone was behaving themselves and treating the house as if it was their own.

So why was Taylor so angry?

He led me through the side door that attached the house into the garage. He leaned against his car and crossed his arms and watched me with anger. I shifted from side to side before finally breaking the tense silence. "Um, did someone make a mess or something? I didn't see anything that looked damaged, but I promise if someone spilled or something, I'll spend time cleaning up."

"No. Nothing is damaged," Taylor growled at me. "You were looking for Aria, right?"

"Oh, yeah," I said, confused at the shift. "Have you seen her? I expected that you would have seen her hanging around."

"I did see her." He gave me an irritated eye roll. "I saw her standing in the doorway of the kitchen when you were talking to your friends earlier."

I furrowed my brow. "She was…" Then my heart came to a stop. My mind raced back to the conversation; showing all of my friends the gift she'd gotten me and mocking it and her in the wake. "How… long was she standing there?"

Taylor's leer was answer enough, but he still hissed, "A while."

I dropped my head as disappointment fell over me. "She heard everything?"

"Most of it," Taylor responded. "She certainly heard you ask if only losers give the gift she got you, and compare her one body to that of three people. Aria's stunning. What the hell is the matter with you?"

"She *is* stunning," I yelped. "I just said that because I didn't want to make waves with them?"

"So you let them dog Aria out and you even join in?" Taylor said. "What have you gained? These people, who don't even know you well enough to know that what Aria got you was actually really considerate, are still your friends, and you lost someone who actually knows and cares about you. Well done. I've never been more proud of you."

"Taylor."

"I just don't get it," Taylor continued. "What are these people giving you? What are you gaining from a relationship with such nasty individuals? Because all I see them giving you is bad habits and spreading their toxicity."

"They care about me," I said. "That's what I'm gaining. They're my friends. They like targeting people a little, but who doesn't? Everyone has people they don't like, and I don't want to be one of their disliked people. I like having them as my friends."

"What'd they get you for your birthday? Taking away the fact that none of them know that you love to draw and how good you are at it, or any of your other secret hobbies that shouldn't be secret, did any of them get you anything they thought you might like? A football? New gloves? Polish for your helmet? New grips for your bats?" I didn't say anything, because there was nothing to say. They hadn't gotten me anything. I suspected Hannah probably did and was going to give it to me at a different time, but apart from her, nothing. "Exactly."

"I don't know what you want from me," I said.

"Fuck what I want," Taylor said. "You should want better for yourself. You should want better for Aria. She's a good person and she didn't deserve that." He took a deep breath in and then out. "I love you, Tris, but I didn't think it was possible to be *this* disappointed in you. You're my brother, yes, but this behavior makes me ashamed to call you my friend. I don't want to be associated with someone like that."

Ouch. That cut deep. "I'm sorry."

"You don't have anything to apologize to me for. It's yourself and the good people in your life that you're hurting." He stood up straight. "I'll let you go back to your friends. Hopefully they aren't talking shit about *you* behind *your* back, but knowing them, they probably are." He gave me a final, frustrated look, then walked around me and back into the house.

I spent the next twenty to thirty minutes just standing in the garage, trying to decide if I should call Aria or not. She probably hated me after hearing me say such horrible things about her and the gift she got me. Maybe it would be enough just to double down on my appreciation of her present and tell her again that I loved it, but would she even believe me?

Whatever I was going to do, I was going to have to wait until I could look her in the eyes at school on Monday. She deserved an in-person apology at least.

After a while, Sherelle came and found me to remind me I had an entire home of guests to entertain, so I begrudgingly left the garage and mingled my way around the party. I spent some additional time with my friends, but being around them just reminded me of what I'd said about Aria, and it bummed me out. I did what I had to do to not elicit too many questions, and otherwise stayed quiet and let the party pass by.

It'd officially been soured for me, and I had no one to blame but myself.

After what felt like weeks, people eventually started to leave. I took my place near the door to hand out hugs and appreciation for coming to my party. Some people lingered, wanting to talk or try and squeeze the last bit of fun out of the festivities, but finally even Ceradi and all my other friends said goodbye, assuring me that my party was a blast, and left.

I let out a sigh of relief as I sunk down onto one of the couches pushed against the wall in the living room. Hannah, the only of my friends remaining, and the only one I didn't mind still being there, sat down next to me.

"You've been down in the dumps for the last three hours. What's going on?" she asked.

"Apparently, Aria overheard us talking about her and her gift. Taylor too. He's really upset," I explained, letting my head fall against the back of the couch. "I feel like shit."

"Oof. That's rough. We were *not* being very nice."

"No. We weren't." I let out an irritated growl. "I can't believe I let them suck me in to all the trash talking."

"What choice did you have?" Hannah asked. "If you hadn't, Ceradi would have turned on you quick. She may have even thrown the pad and pencils in the punch. You made the best decision."

"Right?!" I yelped. "I keep trying to explain it to Taylor, but he doesn't get it. He thinks it's easy to just not give into it."

"I mean, no offense to him, but he wasn't popular in school, right? He just doesn't get it. He doesn't know the pressure we're under to maintain the status quo. People like you and me, we're either at the top or we're at the bottom. There's no middle. We've been given a rare chance to buddy up to Ceradi and the others instead of being her victims. We'd be stupid not to do what it takes to cash in on that opportunity."

Everything that Taylor struggled to understand when I said it, sounded so succinct and reasonable coming out of

Hannah's mouth. Maybe I needed *her* to explain it to him, and then he'd get it. I just wasn't as eloquent as her. I felt terrible after talking to Taylor, and I was still sad knowing that I'd hurt Aria's feelings, but Hannah was right. I just got dealt a shitty hand, that was all. A stroke of bad luck.

"Anyway," Hannah continued. "Can I give you *my* gift now?"

I looked over at her. "You got me one?"

She smirked. "Of course I did. Be right back."

She got up and walked out of the living room, and I heard the front door open and close. I watched through the big bay window in the front as she walked down to her car, opened the door, and pulled out a wrapped box. She shut the door and walked back towards the house, until I heard the front door open and close again. She returned to the seat at my side and set the box in my lap. It was thin, but wide, and was wrapped in a shimmering orange wrapping paper.

"Happy Day Before Your Birthday."

I smiled. "Thanks." I clawed into the wrapping paper, tearing it free from the box, to reveal a set of charcoals I'd eyed when Hannah and I went walking around the mall the last weekend before school started. "So this is why you kept swatting my hand when I tried to get them?"

"You're so annoying. Don't you know the rule that you can't buy anything for yourself within a month of your birthday? I'd already bought and wrapped them when you saw them," Hannah explained.

I wrapped my arm around her and pulled her snug to me. "Thanks Hannah."

She patted my stomach. "Of course. You deserve it."

"Although I do wish you'd given it to me a little sooner. It probably would have cheered me up some."

She scoffed. "Why? So those guys could do to me what they did to Aria? Pass."

It knocked the wind from my sails. "Yeah I guess that makes sense."

"Their mocking aside, that stuff Aria got you was really nice and super expensive. Especially if she bought it on her own. She probably spent close to an entire paycheck." I started to glare at her and she recoiled. "What?"

"Are you trying to make me feel worse?" I asked.

"No, of course not. Just making an observation." She poked my cheek. "You shouldn't feel bad anyway. This is a good thing."

I raised an eyebrow at her. "Uh. You know, I'm failing to see how that could possibly be the case."

"This whole thing was a bad idea from the start. We shouldn't co-mingle. She'll go on with her life now and you can go on with yours. Continuing on with Aria was a fast track to the bottom of the food chain. I was there, and trust me, you'd much rather be up here."

Hannah stood up after that, likely sensing that it was time to put a period on that conversation. I walked her to her car, gave her a huge hug, and waited while she pulled out of sight. I retreated to my room after that, even if it was a fruitless effort. I knew I wouldn't be getting much sleep that night.

10

TRISTAN

My night was a continuous stream of lying awake for an hour, flipping over and falling asleep for twenty minutes, then waking up again to start the cycle all over again. I didn't dream, but the constant mental reminder of the way I'd hurt Aria may as well have been a nightmare. I kind of wanted to call or text her in the middle of the night, but then Hannah's words came back into my mind.

We shouldn't co-mingle.

Taylor would probably tear me to shreds if he knew I was considering actually turning my back on Aria for that reason. I got where he was coming from, I really did, but it didn't change the fact that I didn't want to go back to being bullied. I could barely handle it when I was a kid, and that was when the worst anyone could say to me was that I was stupid and scratch me with sticks. Teenagers—people just a handful of months away from being considered legal adults —could do much worse, and I didn't want to be a part of it.

Besides, I really did feel like Ceradi and the others *were* my friends. They were the pickiest people in the entire world, and though they could choose to hang out with anyone at any time, they chose to hang out with me and that counted for something. Did that truly mean that I had to remain totally uninvolved with Aria? Maybe the situation just required more finesse. If they could just see what I saw—how absolutely astounding she was—there wouldn't be an issue. They just wanted beautiful, cool people to hang out with, and Aria was both of those things.

At least I thought so.

Eventually, the smell of bacon frying and fresh spices filled the air. Molly was already hard at work cooking breakfast to celebrate my *actual* birthday. For as excited as I had been for my party, between what had actually happened and the obstacles I knew the day was going to bring me, I found myself wishing I could just stay in bed. My stomach growled though, begging me to head in the direction of the food, so I threw back my covers and trudged downstairs. I eventually made my way into the kitchen where Molly and Sherelle were both working on different aspects of breakfast, dancing to some music playing over the smart speakers, and laughing at one another's horrible performances.

Sherelle was to Molly what I was to Taylor, so seeing them cheery and bubbly just reminded me of how unhappy with me Taylor was. I never liked disappointing him, but yesterday was the angriest I'd ever seen him get with me.

"Happy birthday to you," Sherelle started.

"Happy birthday to you," Molly joined in.

"Happy birthday to Tristan…" They both dove under the counter and brandished silly string canisters. "Happy birthday to you!"

At the exact same time, they both fired off, covering me in mint-smelling foam strings. Both cans hissed as they closed in on me, spraying more and more of the silly string until the cans were blowing nothing but air. For good measure, Molly tapped her can against my head a few times.

"That's not going to help the silly string regenerate," I barkcd.

She giggled at me. "You never know. Stranger things have happened."

I pulled the strings that were already matting into clumps all over me off and dumped them in the trash. Both of them returned to what they were working on before I entered the kitchen, still laughing at their antics as they went. I opted to move over to the kitchen table and wait for the rest of breakfast to be done.

The table already had a few things on it, alongside the empty plates and glasses. There were different bowls filled to the brim with fresh ingredients like bacon, sausage, ham, green onions, mushrooms, and peppers. Sherelle was making pancakes and Molly was working on some fresh squeezed orange juice. Molly had asked me what I wanted for breakfast and I told her that I wanted my favorite thing that she made, her omelettes. Seeing and smelling the savory ingredients to be mixed in, my excitement for the meal was already going. I couldn't wait.

"Alright kid," Molly said. "Take one of those empty bowls and fill it with what you want in your omelette and I'll get started."

I smiled. "Aw, yeah." I grabbed a spoon and started to add in a combo of meats and veggies and then brought it over to Molly. She already had a few different kinds of cheeses freshly shredded and sitting next to the pan she was heating. "I'll just have all the cheese too, please."

Molly giggled as she took the bowl from me. "You got it."

I returned to my seat and started to flick through my phone, seeing all the photos everyone had posted of my party from the night before. Despite how shitty I felt for most of the night, I looked perfectly happy in all the selfies. If Aria saw it, it would probably make her feel worse. Maybe it was a mistake waiting to call and apologize to her.

No. The mistake had been saying that stuff in the first place.

"Where's Taylor?" I asked, as Molly started on my omelette.

"He went out for a run," Molly replied.

I winced, already knowing the answer to my next question. "Is he still pissed?"

Molly scoffed. "Yeah. He was ruminating all night, and I don't think he slept very well."

Sherelle looked up at me as she stacked more pancakes on a platter. "Literally. He went on and on about it." She carried the pancakes over to the table and set it down. "I don't get it, Tristan. Why even be friends with those guys? When Taylor told us the stuff he overheard you saying, I didn't believe him at first. It didn't even sound like you. You're such a good guy. Wouldn't you want friends who have your same energy?"

"Hannah's not even that bad," Molly said. "I overheard you two talking last night. It's so strange. It's like you guys get it, but you don't. Where does this pressure come from to impress people who are unkind to you?"

Just like that, all that sense that Hannah made last night

suddenly made less sense. "From the outside, yeah, they look like awful people. I get why you guys think that, but there have to be things about you guys that you all think are fine but other people think are terrible, right?" Molly and Sherelle exchanged looks and remained silent. "See? Exactly. Everyone's different, and no, I don't like the things they said about Aria, and I don't like the things I said even more. People fear things that are different from them, and my friends are big on confidence and all that. I just think they don't understand how to take someone in who is so confident in themselves when they haven't put in the level of effort that people like Ceradi have." I threaded my hand into my hair. "I get it. I know Taylor is disappointed in me, but I don't know what he wants from me. It was either that, or lose all my friends and become the victim out of spite."

"You don't see the problem with that?" Molly said. "That standing up for someone you really care about would cost you all your friends?"

"Life isn't black and white," I said. "I don't want to talk about it anymore."

Molly shook her head. "Fine, but just take it easy with your brother. We have a full day ahead of us and the last thing we need is the both of you in a bad mood."

"Yeah," I said quietly. "I will."

Not long after that, the front door opened and shut, and a few minutes later, Taylor passed by the kitchen down the hallway towards the stairs. He glanced in, and our eyes met briefly, but then he just kept going without saying anything. Molly was just finishing up my omelette and Sherelle was serving Molly's fresh orange juice when Taylor walked back into the kitchen, changed out of his running clothes into a simple nice button-up and slacks.

"Happy birthday," he grumbled at me.

"Thank you," I replied, tracing him with my gaze even though he wouldn't even look in my direction.

He walked over to a cupboard in the kitchen and opened it, revealing a handful of colorfully wrapped gifts. He shoveled them over to the table one by one and set them in the middle of the table, at which point Molly brought over my omelette and gave Taylor a kiss for good measure. I was grateful for her, because I knew she'd do whatever she could to lighten the tension.

"Pick out what you want in your omelette baby, and I'll make it for you. Sheri, you too."

Both Taylor and Sherelle grabbed two of the small glass bowls from the table and stacked ingredients in them, then Molly started to make them in two separate pans, clearing her own out of the second pan from the one she made mine in and then beginning theirs.

We all sat in silence at the table while Molly finished the remaining omelettes, then when everyone was served, Sherelle poured syrup over the tall stack of pancakes, then topped them with whipped cream and sprinkles and stuck a candle in the top. She lit it and presented it to me to blow, giggling.

"We sang the birthday song too early," she said, removing the candle in order to dole out the pancakes.

After finishing my omelette and pancakes—quickly, because of the fact that we were all sitting in a painfully awkward silence—Molly pushed my gifts towards me to coax me into opening them. There were a few from Taylor, a couple from Molly, and even one from Sherelle. I started with Sherelle's, delaying the inevitable, and it was the newest release of a game we liked to play together.

"It has a new battle royale game mode," Sherelle said. "I can't wait to kick your ass."

I laughed at her. "Yeah. You wish."

Molly got me a new jacket that I'd been looking at, and a new pair of baseball gloves, as the ones I'd been using were little more than two pieces of unsewn fabric after so much use. Taylor's gifts were unbelievable, as expected. He got me a brand new digital camera for taking pictures to draw from, and a folding, metal-frame easel. The last gift was a photo album of the pictures we'd taken in the past ten years. He always took me with him on vacation every year, and we often had what he called 'Brother Days' where we would just go on a random adventure.

It made me feel lower than dirt.

Taylor had always taken such wonderful care of me, and yesterday I let him down. I hated that.

"Thank you," I said. "All of you. These gifts are incredible."

"Sheri and I actually have one more for you, but we'll give it to you later at your dad's," Molly said. "Your dad wants us there at around two, right? The rest of the family will be there at four?"

"Well, you and Sheri will have to go separately. Tristan and I have a visit first," Taylor replied.

"Right," Molly said. "I almost forgot. Well that's not a problem. We'll clean up around here and, Tris, if you wanna leave a majority of your stuff, we'll take it to your dad's when we go."

"Really? I'll take you up on that. Thank you."

Molly nodded and smiled at me. "Of course."

I couldn't help but smile back at her. Taylor was really

lucky to have such an awesome girlfriend. It made me jealous all over again.

"If you're done, you should go get ready to leave," Taylor said, still not looking at me.

"Yeah. Okay." I reached out for my plate, but Sherelle pushed my hand away and collected it, stacking it on top of her own before grabbing a few more empty dishes and standing up from the table. "Thanks," I murmured, then stood up and trudged off.

After getting dressed and packing up my stuff for Molly and Sherelle to transfer back to my dad's house, I met Taylor in the garage so we could leave. Since I'd driven and Molly would be driving to my dad's house, we decided to take my car, but I let Taylor drive as he knew the way much better than me. He got into the driver's seat and opened the garage, and we were off.

In a terrible, poisonous silence.

I was too nervous to even play some music using the aux cord, but given how long the trip was, I knew we would never be able to survive that way. So as scary as it was, I finally cleared my throat.

"I need you to say something or do something or… something," I snapped. "I can't take you being mad at me. I can't deal with it."

"I'm not mad at you," Taylor said. "I'm frustrated. I knew that you had those nasty friends, and I assumed you had to be falling into their antics a little bit in order to be their friends, but I had no idea you were *that* bad. I mean… I hated guys like you in high school. And you should have seen the look on Aria's face. She was crushed. I just didn't think you were that guy."

"I'm not that guy," I replied.

"You are that guy. I saw it with my own eyes. I heard what you said with my own ears."

I stared at him with desperation. "I didn't have a choice."

Taylor shook his head. "You always have a choice, Tris. It's just a matter of what's important to you. Obviously Aria isn't."

"Aria means a lot to me," I said. "But my friends do too."

Taylor and I went around and around in circles for longer than I was happy with. For every argument I posed, he posed an opposite one, and it felt like neither of us was going to give ground. Eventually, we ended up just sitting in silence again, and I could tell I'd lost Taylor's respect even further for trying to argue that I had done the right thing in the moment. I probably should have just admitted defeat.

Or maybe I should have just stayed quiet.

Eventually, we got to the place I most dreaded to visit, our city's penitentiary. Taylor turned in and I felt my stomach give out. If I never had to visit the place again, I wouldn't, but I understood the importance of it and went along with Taylor once a month. This month, however, I agreed to go twice, once for our regular visit and once for my birthday.

It was the only way I ever remember seeing my mom.

By this point, Taylor and I had the routine memorized. We left all of our important items apart from my keys in the car, and both of us had been intentional about wearing articles of clothes with little or no metal. We walked inside, collected our visitor's passes, and went to stand by the metal detector where a guard eventually came to get us and usher us through.

After the amount of time my mom had served, she'd been moved down to a minimum security prison that allowed for visits most days of the week, and at a table where we could actually sit with her and even touch her if we wanted, though it was generally forbidden. We were allowed a couple of hugs without the guards getting too angry, which was a far cry from when she was in maximum security. There we could only talk to her via a phone and we could barely see her on the other side of multi-inch thick, foggy plexiglass.

"My boys!" We heard my mom's voice before we saw her. We looked over and a guard had opened the door to the visitor's room. My mom came walking through. She waved with a wide, bright smile. "Or should I say my adult men!"

Taylor and I stood up as my mom walked over, both of us tucking away our earlier argument for her benefit. We'd both gotten our dad's dark hair and eyes, but my mom had long, frizzy blond hair that had grown even longer in the years she'd been locked up. Her eyes were a golden color, and sparkled more and more with each visit. When we first started to visit her around ten years ago, she was emaciated, but getting clean and healthy behind bars had helped her pack on a little bit of weight. It looked good on her. She looked happy.

Hopefully another ten years would only continue to help her.

"Hey mom," Taylor said, holding out his arms. My mom walked into them.

She gave a quick hug at first, but then one of the guards called over, "Go ahead, Diane. It's your boy's birthday, right?"

My mom smiled. "Yes, it is. Not this one though." She gave Taylor a firmer hug still, since she had permission, then she turned to me. She set her hands on my face and gave me a bright, warm smile. "Tristan is eighteen now. A young man. Happy birthday, sweetheart."

"Thanks mom," I said, relenting when she pulled me in for a big bear hug.

"Oh, I wish that things were different so I could celebrate with you in a better way. It's your birthday and you're spending part of it in a prison. Some mother I am," she said.

I shook my head as I pulled back. "It's okay. I'm just glad I got to see you."

It was only partially a lie. I never liked visiting the prison, but it did make me happy to see my mom and to witness for myself that she was doing better. We sat and Taylor engaged her in conversation as he normally did. They were much closer than I was. I was still fairly young when she got arrested for bingeing on drugs and attempting to kidnap us. I most remembered the woman I'd seen behind bars.

I never would have made it through all of that if it weren't for Aria. When all those kids were making fun of me, Aria stood up for me. When one of them pulled out a sharp stick and scratched me, simply because he knew I couldn't defend myself, Aria went toe to toe with him, tussling until they were both covered in dirt and Aria's dad had to come drag her off. All the bullying pretty much came to a stop after that, because a lot of the kids feared Aria's strength and headstrong attitude.

She was truly my hero.

Taylor tapped into his almost supernatural ability to

read my mind when we got back into the car. He didn't start it up, but just looked at me with that sad, disappointed expression. "You were thinking about her?"

I nodded. "She saved me back when all this shit went down. I probably wouldn't have made it honestly."

"It would have been so much easier for her to leave you to the wolves, but she risked herself to stand up for you. When you had the chance to do the same, you didn't." A lump of emotions rose to my throat as I looked at Taylor. "You need to think long and hard about the kind of person that makes you, and if you don't want to be that person, then something has got to give."

11

ARIA

After an incredibly restless night, my alarm went off, coaxing me out of sleep just a little before noon. My stomach growled almost as soon as I opened my eyes, but I ignored it because lunch wasn't too far off. I peeled my eyes open and just sat staring at the ceiling. Hazelnut was laying in my bed as she always was, though curled much closer to my face than normal. She'd unexpectedly spent the night consoling me. In a strange way, I felt like she knew how I was feeling. They say that dogs can sense strong emotions, and the way Hazelnut stuck extra close to me, showering me in kisses and distracting me by turning up her belly and begging me to play with her, I was willing to believe it.

I petted her head to let her know I was about to move, then I dragged myself out of bed. Part of me just wanted to stay in bed and lock myself away. But following the plans that Arden and I had loosely made before I left the party, I made a formal plan between her, myself, and Lucky. She was clearly going to be my closest friend at my new school, so I figured I should introduce her to my best friend from my old one.

The idea of spending time with my closest friends was enough of a promise to improve my mood that I was able to shower and get dressed without issue, then I went downstairs so that my mom could start her motherly duty of checking on me to the point that it made me sad all over again.

"Good morning, sweetheart. Or afternoon I suppose," my mom said with a smile. She was working on her laptop at the kitchen nook. "Do you want me to fix you something to eat?"

"No. I'm meeting up with Arden and Lucky for lunch today," I said. "Thanks though."

"Oh. Going to introduce your old friend to your new one, huh? How do you think that's going to go?"

That was a strange and unexpected question, but if that was the path she wanted to take instead of talking more about Tristan and the party, then I'd take it. "Uh. I don't expect it to go poorly, if that's what you're wondering."

My mom shrugged. "I don't know. I like Lucky, you know that, but I've often felt like he's a little possessive. I just wonder how he's going to take to meeting your new friend. He may get jealous."

"If he does, I'll tell him to get over himself," I spat back. "Arden is awesome, and she goes to my current school and he doesn't." My mind drifted back to when I first told Lucky about how my first day had gone and how strangely he behaved about it. That felt more like loneliness than jealousy. "This is *why* I want them to meet. I want Lucky not to feel threatened like he's being replaced. I want Arden to know who I'm talking about whenever I refer to

Lucky, and, in general, I feel like I need them both to feel better."

For a brief minute, my mom looked at me with concern, but then she wiped it away and offered her same, comforting smile. "Well, I'm sure it'll go okay."

"I don't have the mental or emotional capacity for it not to go well, so hopefully it does." I walked over to her and kissed her on top of her head. "I'm meeting them at twelve-thirty, so I gotta go. Love you."

"Love you too, sweetheart." There was an uncertain tone in her voice that echoed with me as I left. I didn't like it, but I just had to pray that Arden and Lucky would get on just fine.

The restaurant we picked was one Arden suggested, since I still didn't know my way around this part of town. It'd be more of a jaunt for Lucky, but he didn't seem to complain when I sent him the address the night before. It was an Italian restaurant with a laid-back atmosphere, and as soon as I walked in, Arden was already there in a booth. I walked over to her and gave her a huge hug, and not long after that, Lucky arrived.

"Lucky!" I waved my arm to flag him down. "Over here!" He walked over and I gave him a huge hug before holding a hand out towards Arden. "This is my new friend Arden, the one I was telling you about from debate club. Arden, this is my best friend Lucky."

Arden stood up from the booth and held out a hand. "Hey! Nice to meet ya!"

Lucky was briefly hesitant, but then smiled and extended his hand to take Arden's. "Nice to meet you too. Thanks for taking care of this weirdo."

"Oh, hey, no problem. She's kickass, so it's nice to hang

out with her," Arden said, and it actually brought a smile to my face. "Sorry I let you down last night though."

Lucky frowned as we all settled down into the booth. "Uh. Did something happen?" He looked at me. "At the party?"

"Oh, you haven't told him yet?" Arden said. "Sorry."

"No, it's okay." I looked at Lucky. "Yeah. Shit sort of hit the fan last night."

"Why didn't you tell me?" he asked. "You texted me to invite me here."

I frowned. "Because I was a mess and I didn't want to talk about it."

"Yeah. She didn't even really talk to me about it, only confirmed my fears that things would go poorly," Arden said. "She wouldn't talk to me about it either."

This seemed to settle Lucky's frustration that was clearly growing, and he smirked at Arden. "So I'm guessing you're learning that this one doesn't deal well with her emotions."

Arden raised an eyebrow. "Yeah, so I see. But you know, I have a shaky relationship with my emotions at best, so we're two peas there."

A waiter came over and took our orders and brought us some drinks, then I settled into the story while we waited. "I mean, at first, everything went really well. I gave him the present and he was really grateful. We even…" My face got a little hotter. "We made out a little bit."

Arden's jaw dropped. "Wait. Seriously?"

Lucky was looking at me as though I'd just revealed serious medical news. I flicked a gaze between him and Arden. "What? Am I *that* much of a loser that you guys just can't imagine he would even kiss me?"

Lucky didn't respond, but Arden snapped to attention.

"What, no! You're obviously a babe. Right, Lucky? Back me up. You have eyes."

"She's right, Aria," Lucky replied. "You're stunning, and obviously someone would want to make out with you."

Arden set one of her hands on top of mine. "It's not shocking because of you. It's shocking because of him. I would have assumed that his handlers would have such a tight leash on him that he would never risk it. You're incredible. I guess he thought you were too good to pass up."

"Yeah, well, it was all for nothing," I said. "He walked away to greet his friends and when I found him later, they were all trashing me, him included. He called me fat and made fun of the gift I gave him."

"What an asshole," Lucky said, though he said it with something like a smile. "Hopefully you're done with him."

"Of course I'm done with him," I growled. "Why are you smiling?"

"Yeah," Arden said. "It shouldn't make you happy that someone hurt her."

Lucky shook his head. "What? Of course it doesn't. I'd kick that guy's ass if I felt like I was even marginally capable. I just didn't like the sound of him from the beginning, so now that Aria has seen his true colors, she can move on."

I gave him a warm smile. "Yeah. You did have issues from the start. Both of you did, and I didn't listen. I'm sorry."

"Hmm," Arden said as she took a sip of her drink. "I mean, you seemed to really like him, so I'm sorry it didn't work out."

Next to me, Lucky shifted, almost puffing out his chest in defense. "Yeah. It would have been cool if it would have worked out, because you would have been happy. But I'm glad to know that you aren't going to end up wasting all of your time and *then* finding out he's a jerk. Better at the beginning right?"

Arden shrugged. "I suppose."

"You're right," I said. "Thanks, Lucky."

He smiled at me. "Of course."

We avoided the subject for the remainder of the meal and instead talked about different things that each of us were into. Arden dominated the conversation talking about her latest invention, but Lucky seemed fine to let her talk as he sat next to me, damn near glowing. If I felt like getting into an argument with him about it, I would have said something, but instead, I just allowed my brain to be carried away on the gadgets and gizmos of Arden's imagination.

The meal came to a close and when Arden saw that I didn't eat much, she hit me with what she called her 'make sure friends eat when they're sad' clause, and made me take both her and my leftovers home for later consumption.

"And I *will* be doing a fridge check. So don't even try to get out of it," Arden said. "Arden knows all."

I laughed at her. "You don't have to worry. I was torn between the fettucini and the stroganoff anyway, so now I get both."

She punched my arm. "Hey, there you go." I gave Lucky another huge hug and then he waved goodbye to Arden before getting into his car and pulling off. Arden kept a bright smile on until he was well clear of the parking lot, then she crossed her arms. "Um, so how long have you two been friends?" she asked.

"Oof," I said, tilting my head towards the sky as I

thought backwards. "Uh, we met in middle school and have been friends ever since then. Why do you ask?"

"I don't know. Maybe my spidey senses are tingling for no reason, but his vibe feels a little off to me. Have any of your other friends ever told you that?" Arden asked.

I laughed. "*You're* my other friends."

She laughed back at me. "Okay, let me rephrase. Has anyone else ever told you that before?"

"My mom thinks he's possessive, but she likes him just fine," I explained.

"That's good," Arden said. "We're new friends, so I'm not trying to cause problems between you and your bestie. It just seems like he may have a chip on his shoulder about something, you know? It was almost like he was legitimately happy to hear that you weren't having a good time. Has he ever hit on you?"

I recoiled heavily at that. "No. Things have only ever been friendly between us."

"Okay," Arden said. "I'll drop it then. My gut has gotten me into trouble before. Maybe I'm just tired."

I furrowed my brow at her dismissal. Arden clearly felt some type of way about Lucky, but I didn't want to press the issue. I had enough mess to deal with for one weekend. "Well, anyway. I gotta go. I'll see you at school tomorrow?"

Arden pinched my cheek before giving it a little slap. "You know it, girl. Take care."

I was hoping that my meal with Arden and Lucky would have left me feeling a little more hopeful, but my mom's concerns blended with Arden's left me unsteady to say the least. I distracted myself with all of the homework I'd neglected over the weekend between work and the party, but by the time I was laying down in bed for the night, it was to spend the next eight hours tossing and turning, and having mixed, hazy dreams of Tristan mocking me and Lucky laughing at me.

I typically held on to a few "fake" sick days for later in the year, but when morning came, I was considering cashing one in early. After the weekend I'd had, my mom would understand, and not having to look at Tristan all day could only benefit me. However, when I picked up my phone to text my mom and fake being under the weather, I had a text from Arden already waiting.

Hey girl! I'm stopping to get you a coffee and bagel on my way in. What are your faves?

I smiled at the message. It filled me with warmth and made me feel supported. It wasn't like Lucky was a bad friend, but I was always the one doing more of the supporting in our relationship. It was nice to have a new friend that I could lean on a little bit. I was unused to it, but I could quickly develop an affinity for it.

I'm a matcha tea latte girl and a plain bagel with strawberry cream cheese.

Omg! I swear, I'm not lying. That's exactly what I

was planning to get.

No way!

*It's a match-a made in
heaven! ;)*

With Arden having my back, I no longer felt like I needed to fake sick. I climbed out of bed and started to get ready, excited to get to my new friend and forge a new path through this high school that didn't involve Tristan at all.

After snickering as I opened my locker, I loaded my things in and started to pull out the things I would need for my first few classes. A few people were keeping a close gaze on me, for a reason I didn't quite understand until I closed my locker door. Tristan was standing there waiting. He had a pair of purple tulips wrapped up in some tissue paper, and it irritated me that he remembered both my favorite color and my favorite flower.

I looked between them and him a few times before completely turning my back on him and walking away. I half expected him to not even know that I was upset, but Taylor must have told him. Whatever the case, it didn't matter much to me. Nothing good would come from looking at his face or giving him any sort of sympathy, so I tried my best to walk away.

But he was a little more persistent.

"Aria," he called out, running up until he could cut in front of me. He held out the flowers and looked at me like a puppy that had just been scolded for getting in the trash. "These are for you."

"I don't want them. Move," I growled.

He slumped a little bit. "Aria, I'm sorry. I never should have said that stuff. I didn't even mean it, I just got caught up in the moment."

"Somehow that makes it worse," I said. "Apology not accepted." Then I walked around him and tried to keep going, but he reached out and grabbed my arm. I whipped back towards him, looking up into his truly anguished gaze, and feeling my heart crack a little bit. "Let me go. You don't get to look at me like that after what you said. You mocked my gift. You mocked my weight. Do you have any idea how it feels to be made fun of like that?"

"I do, remember?" he said.

"Yeah, I remember standing up for you. Thanks a lot for doing the same for me." I tried to pull my arm back, but Tristan held on tight. "Stop. Let me go."

"Aria, I know you felt the same stuff that I felt back at my house. I don't care what other people think. I like you. I'm sorry, I fell into a bad habit. Let me make it up to you."

It would have been helpful if he wasn't so gorgeous, or if my body wasn't warming at the memory of his hands on me. I stared into his eyes and could see how genuine he was. If he was under pressure to present himself in a certain way, I could see him giving into that pressure. Maybe if he could change going forward it would be okay.

"If we're going to do this," I said, bringing a little light to Tristan's eyes, "we can't—"

"Tris?" Without even seeing who had called his name, Tristan let go of me and jumped backwards like I was a boogeyman. I looked over and saw some of Tristan's friends standing off to the side, looking in our direction. It must have been Hannah who beckoned to him, because she pressed on saying, "Let's go so we aren't late."

He backstepped, almost immediately about to follow them, but then hesitated and looked at me with desperation. He was begging me for permission to go.

And he would get it.

"Don't let me hold you up," I hissed. "This is proof positive that nothing good can come from being with you."

"Aria…" Tristan said.

I shook my head. "Don't say my name. In fact, don't speak to me again."

TRISTAN

For a year that I thought was going to bring a big and exciting change to my life, by the end of the first month I was toeing the line just like any other year.

Well, no.

I felt worse than I normally would.

In years past I'd been doing relatively okay. Enjoying playing sports, having fun with my friends, getting through classes just fine. In general, I'd liked going to school every day for the past few years, but now showing up meant I was blasted with pain out the gate every single day. It wasn't just that Aria and I had the same first class, which meant I had to see her first thing every day, but while I was sliding down a slippery slope, she was blossoming.

Aria had always been that way.

She never even gave me so much as a second glance after telling me not to speak to her the Monday after my party, and we hadn't interacted at all in weeks. She and Arden seemed to be getting closer and closer and were nearly inseparable, which made it even more difficult because Arden and Hannah had history that made Hannah's views of the entire situation even more sour.

I pretty much kept to myself, only really interacting with Hannah when I needed a friend, but Aria's circle was growing more and more. Most kids just liked her, not that it was all that shocking, and it seemed she was developing a solid group of friends with her fellow debate club members. Sometimes, I would walk into the lunchroom and see her sitting there with them, laughing and smiling, and would give anything to just go sit next to her and join in.

Hannah kept trying to tell me that this outcome was for the best, but then why did I feel sick to my stomach every day?

But at least Aria was happy. All my ambivalence could have ruined her senior year and I was glad to see that it hadn't.

"Focus," Hannah said, pushing me forward towards the lunch line. "You're gonna trip and hurt yourself."

"Sorry," I grumbled.

"And quit staring," Hannah said. "People are going to talk."

I wanted to say "So what," but knew why I couldn't do that and just grunted out, "Fine." I dragged my feet all the way through the lunch line and eventually over to my table where Ceradi, Josh, and Milton were already sitting and chatting about a variety of unimportant things.

"Hey," Ceradi greeted. "I always did love red on you. It looks good."

I looked down at my t-shirt and furrowed my brow. If someone had given me a pop quiz and asked me what color shirt I had on before that moment, I would have had no idea. I'd been going through the motions so much lately, that I barely even knew what day it was. "Thanks."

"What's up with you lately?" Josh asked as I sat down. "I mean, you've been a real grump lately. Your stepmom at it again or something?"

"I know what it is," Ceradi said, and I shot my head in her direction, nervous that she had me figured out. She looked at me, gingerly propping her head up in her hand and smiling at me with a raised eyebrow. "You're afraid that *whale* is going to ask you to Sadie Hawkins?"

"Uh. Oh…" The Sadie Hawkins dance was a dance that happened every year the weekend before Thanksgiving break which turned the dumb guys-ask-girls sterotype on its end and instituted an equally dumb girls-ask-guys tradition. Every year, girls clamored for who between myself and the other athletes and popular guys they got to ask, but I typically just ended up going with Hannah as a friend. "Y-yeah. I guess."

As if Aria would even look in my direction for that dance. If she did, I'd be hard-pressed to say no. If Aria was willing to talk to me at all, I wouldn't turn her down.

"She'd be dumb to ask by this point," Milton said. "She *has* to know you're not interested by now."

"I don't know. Fat body, fat skull," Ceradi said.

There was a part of me that burned to punch Milton in the face and pour Ceradi's juice down her bright white shirt, but I abstained. Not just because I didn't want to start trouble, but because when I opened my mouth to respond, Hannah kicked me under the table. I locked eyes with her and she shook her head. Just as much as I didn't want to start up with Ceradi, I didn't want to hear more lectures from Hannah.

"Well, I hope not," I bailed.

Ceradi filed down her nails as she continued. "Are you actually gonna accept someone's offer this year, or just bail with Hannah?"

I looked over at Hannah. "If she asks me." It was a joke when I said it, but Hannah was looking back at me with a borderline shy expression.

"Um… I'm actually already planning to ask someone."

This got the attention of everyone at the table. "What?" I said.

"Who?" Ceradi yelped.

"He goes to a different school," Hannah said. "Just someone I know."

I lowered my eyebrows at her. Why was she allowed to invite someone outside our friend group and I wasn't allowed to go with Aria if she asked? "Pretty cool, this guy?"

"He plays football at his school. He's popular," Hannah explained.

"Plus you get the added allure of having him be from a different school," Ceradi said. "The mystery is so enticing."

"What's his name?" Josh asked.

"You'll find out when you meet him," Hannah quipped back.

I was beginning to think the guy was just made up just to get out of going with me, but Hannah and I had gone as friends in the past, so why would she suddenly not want to do that now? If she didn't want to go with me, she simply didn't have to ask me. It wasn't like it was a huge deal.

"Who are you asking, Ceradi?" Hannah asked, not subtly, to shift the subject.

Ceradi looked across the table at Milton, who puffed

out his chest and smiled brightly. She smiled back at him and said, "Hey, Mil."

"Yes?" he sang, starry eyed.

"Do you know if anyone has asked Tanner yet? I was thinking he might be fun to go with."

Milton deflated. At this point in time, anyone else would bail and say they were kidding, but Ceradi wasn't just anyone. She stayed staring at Milton, batting her eyes, and waiting for an answer. Milton was clearly waiting for her to back out, but when a handful of awkward minutes had passed, he took his tray and stood up from the table.

"No. No one's asked him yet," he said.

Ceradi winked. "Great. Thanks!"

Milton stormed off, and though Josh started laughing, Capito and Hannah both remained mostly quiet, as did I. Ceradi looked around at our concerned gazes and waved her hand. "Oh stop. I'm obviously gonna ask him. I'm just having a little fun."

Josh held up a hand for Ceradi to high-five, which she did. "Classic."

She giggled. "What can I say? I'm a prankster."

More like a sadist.

My first class after lunch had Aria, Arden, Hannah, *and* Ceradi in it, which meant it was always prepped and primed to be a trainwreck. When I walked into the class, there were several people standing around Aria as she told a story that was eliciting a bunch of laughs. I smiled at the way she shimmered under the attention and was glad she was getting it from someone, since I couldn't give her the attention she deserved.

For whatever reason, my entering the room drew her attention and she turned to look at me. I expected her to look away right away, but she held my gaze for a little bit, and I could see the longing in her eyes that matched my own. I took a step forward, and when she didn't look away, it gave me some confidence. When I attempted to apologize to her before, she almost gave in until I let Hannah scare me. Maybe all she was waiting for was for me to apologize again.

Maybe I wasn't as far from her as I thought I was.

I held up my hand and led with a smile, but someone snatched my hand and whipped me back. I turned and saw Hannah standing behind me with a wild, panicked looking expression on her face. "What are you doing?" I hissed.

"What are *you* doing?" she snapped back. "We've been through this."

"I just want to apologize," I growled back.

"Just let it go."

Before I could fight further, Ceradi walked into the room, swinging by my desk as she did so. "Don't worry. I'll make sure the narwhal knows to leave you alone."

"What?" I said. "No, it's okay."

But she was already off. I watched, terrified, as she walked straight into the group of people surrounding Aria, and everyone scattered, apart from Arden. She looked down at Aria with an evil grin on her face.

"Hey," she started. "Have you heard the joke about the *cow* who walked into a bar?"

My heart broke. Aria didn't deserve that treatment when she'd done nothing wrong. I moved to try and stop it, but Hannah maintained her grip on my arm and held me back. I wanted to avert my gaze so badly, but I also couldn't bring myself to look away.

"No," Aria replied. "But I imagine it ends with a Tik Thot who thinks seven likes on her post is a big deal."

The entire room erupted with laughter and jabs, and I had to put my hand over my mouth to keep everyone from seeing the way I was smiling. Ceradi took in the stock of the room and decided it was in her best interest to back off. She probably could have done some serious verbal damage if she chose to stick it out, but I could also see that she was embarrassed. People didn't typically talk back to Ceradi, and as she swiped all of Aria's things off her desk before storming away, it was evident.

"Nice!" Arden yelped, giving Aria a fist bump before helping her pick up her things.

"Thanks," Aria said. "I only spoke the truth."

Arden snickered. "Hell yeah you did."

"Holy shit. Does this girl have a death wish?" Hannah asked. I turned around, expecting to see her angry or at least concerned, but she was fighting back a smile. "Ceradi got like nine likes on her last post and didn't stop talking about it for like three days."

I couldn't stop myself from staring at Aria with a smile. Suddenly, I was beginning to think Hannah was right, it was a good thing I was leaving Aria alone. Not because it was good to maintain the status quo, but because Aria deserved someone much, much better than me.

13

ARIA

I gave Arden a high-five as she passed me on her way back to her seat. It shouldn't have surprised me that she'd be able to throw together one hell of a science project, but even I had to gawk at her beautifully organized tri-fold display and self-functioning, rotating mobile of rock formations. The teacher looked like she was watching a professional perform a dissertation.

She was gonna get an A for sure.

Students had the option to do this particular project alone or in pairs, but Arden and I were just starting out, so we both opted to go it alone. About a week into the project, however, we realized our mistake and started working on our individual projects together. I was glad to have her because while I could research my ass off and create a beautiful written report, I wasn't creative at making things look nice, and that was where Arden excelled. Thanks to our collaboration, we'd both be getting high marks on the assignment, which was good, because I was generally pretty garbage at science.

"Well done, Arden," the teacher, Miss Piotte said. "I believe that just leaves Tristan and Hannah." She motioned out and Tristan and Hannah slid out of their seats and started setting up their project in the front of the classroom. "Oh. A Powerpoint. I do love it when you all make the best use of our school's incredible technology. It certainly costs enough."

This pulled muted chuckles from the class, but I was too busy trying not to get caught up in staring at Tristan to respond one way or the other. His chosen outfit for the day was a plaid shirt in different shades of red, with the sleeves rolled up to three-quarters length, a pair of black jeans with designer rips, and a pair of black, athletic shoes. His hair was a little more unkempt, but it gave him a rugged, laid-back look that, alongside his knockout smile, had me a little gut-punched. Hannah made a joke as he was loading their presentation and he chuckled, tightening up my stomach.

Could he just look *bad* for once? That'd make getting over him much easier.

Hannah stood next to him in a pair of maroon leggings, and a sweater dress that drifted down to mid-thigh. Her blond hair was hanging in loose waves on either side of her face and her makeup seemed like it had been done by a professional. She hovered near him with a comfort I was jealous of. I'd heard from Arden and a few other people that they'd dated in the past and I wondered if she still liked him.

Did he still like her?

They were so close, and whenever Tristan was most trying to avoid me, it was with Hannah at the crux of it. It was possible that maybe the way he treated me suddenly had nothing to do with my appearance at all, and had everything to do with the fact that he was hoping I could be a secret side-girl while he was with Hannah more publicly.

Not that it made him that much better of a person, but at least I'd know he didn't really think I was fat and ugly. Then again, the way he made out with me at his party already seemed to suggest that. Every time I thought about it, my body tingled all over and I wished I could just take a quick trip back to that moment. I'd skip all the stuff afterwards—it wasn't pain I needed to suffer through again— but at least I could have his lips on mine again, if even for just a few moments.

There was a flick at the back of my neck and I knew it was Arden who'd caught onto me staring at him longingly. I shoved my hand behind my head and held up my middle finger, and Arden snickered. She was just trying to be a good friend, I knew that, but it wasn't like I could just drop Tristan as if there was nothing between us. Maybe if he hadn't been so excited to see me again when we first reconnected or if we hadn't fallen so easily into each other in the basement at his party, but I'd been allowed to indulge a little bit, and just like most drugs, though I knew it was bad for me, I wanted more.

"Well, saving the best for last, Hannah and I focused on astronomy and did a study on how the stars can be used to track everything from directions to the tides," Tristan began with a smile. His eyes gazed over the room and eventually landed on mine. He gave me a warm smile that sent a shiver down my spine. I smiled at first, but then averted my gaze.

Stop it, Aria. Tristan was a popular asshole concerned with appearances. He openly mocked me to his friends.

What was wrong with me? Why couldn't I just write him off like other people?

I'd give anything to remove the stop gap, even if it involved invasive surgery. I just wanted my own thoughts back and to not have him on my mind all day every day.

Hannah flicked to the next slide and I kept my eyes off of Tristan as much as I could. In spite of this, I frequently felt his eyes lingering on me, and would occasionally lose myself and flick up to meet him. Each time it happened, it was like I was walking into a trap and only just *barely* managing to back out every time I had to force myself away.

There was a tap on my shoulder and I looked back to see Arden holding out a small piece of paper. The teacher was fairly engrossed with Tristan and Hannah's project, so I reached back and grabbed it, before unfolding it as close to my body as I could for subtly.

Don't be stupid, Aria. You're too beautiful for that.

I knew that already. Didn't she get it? I knew it was a mistake to hang on to Tristan, I simply didn't know the way out.

"Oh my gosh!" Miss Piotte said.

I looked up and saw that they'd flipped to a slide that had a hand-drawn, unwrapped globe with different constellations all over it. Thanks to the large projector, the drawing spanned the entire wall like a beautiful mural. It was like being in an observatory, even more so when Hannah started to scroll the mouse over different info-nodes on the powerpoint and started talking about each of the constellations that were detailed there.

One of the kids leaned forward and noticed there was a small signature in the bottom, left hand corner of the drawing that was indisputably Tristan's signature. "Hey, did you draw that, Tristan?"

I studied the lines of the drawing and they put me in the same mind of the sketch of me that Tristan had done. There was no doubt in my mind that it was his work.

"You drew this?" Miss Piotte asked. "It's marvelous, Tristan."

At first, Tristan seemed flattered, but then one kid further back in the room started to laugh. "He's been talking like a real poindexter this whole presentation too. Captain of the football team, or underground nerd?"

A girl sitting next to him cupped her hands around her mouth. "Yeah! Do you draw nerdy comic books too?"

I sneered at them both, and when they caught my gaze, they both slunk further down in their desks. Miss Piotte attempted to quiet them, but it was too late, the damage had been done.

"What?" Tristan said, pulling attention back to himself. "No. I didn't draw this. My name's just down there because I worked on the presentation. I just memorized what Hannah told me to say. I need that grade for football, you know. How else are we gonna *smack* Southwest next week?"

A few kids cheered and I watched as the light faded from Tristan's eyes. Arden sighed behind me and whispered, "Jeez."

Next to Tristan, Hannah nodded. "Yeah. We just got the pictures off the internet. I thought this one looked nice and easy to attach the info-nodes to."

Miss Piotte frowned. "Oh. Well compliments to the true artist. It's quite the masterpiece."

It left a sick taste in my mouth to watch Tristan deteriorate after that. All the pictures that came up after that which were clearly drawn by him, he started to mock and laugh at them, with Hannah's support as she continued to posit that they'd just ransacked some free-to-use image site. His speech got less intelligent as well, and he started to trip and stumble over all of the information, clearly on purpose.

He was lowering himself to meet the standards of the idiots in the back of the classroom.

Miss Piotte seemed to check out, and eventually Hannah and Tristan reached the end of their presentation. They returned to their desks with Tristan slinking defeated into his seat, and it just made me angry. What was the point? If it made him feel so shitty, he shouldn't do it. Why deny such beautiful artistry? Why pretend to be less intelligent than he really was? Those weren't bad things. He should be embracing them.

"Alright everyone. I'll be grading the assignments over the weekend and your grades on them will be on the portal by next Monday, but overall I'm pleased with your collective performances. This is shaping up to be a spectacular year." The bell rang and she waved her hand. "Go on, have a good rest of your day. I'll see you tomorrow."

"You have a study period next, right Aria?" Arden asked.

I looked over my shoulder as I picked up my stuff and prepared to head out. "Yeah."

"I'm gonna ask if I can join you. Can you help me with this calc? I'm struggling."

I laughed at her. How an aspiring inventor struggled

with math, I had no idea, but I'd seen her tinker and she really just threw things together until they started to work. She switched math with just forcing it.

I couldn't entirely blame her for that.

"Yeah, of course," I said. "I have math homework to work on too, so we can get it done together."

Arden threw her bag over her shoulder and sifted into the students leaving the classroom, and I fell in line behind her to follow her out. As I was passing Tristan's desk, I looked down. He was so dejected from how the presentation had gone that he wasn't even attempting to move. It broke my heart and made me angry.

I simply didn't understand.

"You know." I stopped and turned around to look at Tristan. He looked up at me, briefly lighting up at the fact that I was talking to him, but then noticed how frustrated I looked and deflated. "I'm sad for you. I don't get how you can just stand up there and be ashamed of who you are."

"I'm not as brave as you, Aria," Tristan replied. "You have no idea what the fear of being ridiculed is like."

I scoffed. "*I* have no idea?" I yelped. "Please, tell me, the fat, unpopular, debate dork more about the fear of being ridiculed. That's something I've never experienced before."

"Are you hoping to gain something here?" I looked up and Hannah was standing defensively over Tristan's back. "What are you trying to do? Just leave us alone."

"You should be ashamed of yourself," I snapped at Hannah. "You're supposed to be his friend. I could see in your face that you knew those drawings were his and the stuff he was saying was his natural intelligence. If you really cared about him, you wouldn't let him shove his real self down like that."

Hannah frowned. "Don't lecture me about stuff you don't understand."

"Aria, let's just go." Arden appeared next to me and put her hand on my back. "This conversation isn't going to lead anywhere." She glared at Hannah. "Trust me, I know."

Hannah looked back at Arden as though she'd stabbed her in the face, but didn't say anything. Tristan was staring at me sadly, but I struggled to find sympathy. It was clear that I'd developed a crush on him, but even if my standards didn't make me leave behind someone who would publicly make fun of me, they definitely wouldn't let me screw around with someone who was embarrassed of themselves. I'd spent too much time learning to love myself to deal with that.

"Bye Tristan," I said. "I hope you figure things out."

With that said, and my heart breaking more, Arden and I left.

14

TRISTAN

*N*either Hannah nor I was able to bounce back after the altercation with Aria and Arden. Hannah and Arden had history as well, though she'd told me very little about it, and the combo of them both staring us down with disappointed gazes and telling us that the way we were choosing to live our lives was problematic, broke us both. I'd even found Hannah sitting and crying a little bit outside the lunchroom.

I slid down the wall and sat next to her. "You feeling like shit too?"

"And it wasn't even Ceradi bullying us," Hannah whimpered back.

"Let's ditch," I said. "I don't want to be here anymore. I probably wouldn't make it if I had to look at Aria again, and all of my classes after lunch are with her."

Hannah looked over at me through red, puffy eyes. "Yeah. I wanna leave."

I stood up first, grabbing Hannah's hand to help her stand up, then we made our way out to the parking garage.

It wasn't difficult to leave, given that seniors were technically allowed to leave campus for lunch, but it was an option few students took since any reasonable food place was too far to get back in time. Still, it was the window we needed to escape given that both Hannah and I knew we had no intention of coming back. She climbed into her car and I got in mine, and we drove to a cafe not too far from school that we liked to go to.

A few of the adults inside recognized us right away, figuring we were students on the run. No one said anything though, and after giving us some judgemental glances, they returned to their coffee and laptops and left us to our business. Hannah found a table for us to sit at while I went up to the counter and got us each a cup of coffee and one of their freshly made ham and cheese sandwiches. I knew exactly how to make Hannah's coffee so that it was to her liking, so I mixed in some cream and sugar into both cups and then carried everything over to the table and sat down.

"I mean, that's totally unfair, right?" Hannah snapped as I sat down. "Trust me I know," she said in a mocking tone. "Arden doesn't know anything. She doesn't get it."

"Yeah. Aria's always been comfortable with herself. She can't just hold people to that same standard surreptitiously and get angry when people don't meet her at that level."

Hannah got quieter then. "Well…"

I furrowed my brow. "What?"

She shrugged as she picked at the edges of her sandwich. "It's not a horrible thing that she expects people to be their best selves. Some might even consider that a virtue."

"Are you taking her side all of a sudden?" I asked. It was a far cry from the woman who'd been relentless in keeping me totally unattached to Aria at all costs.

"No, it's just…" Hannah stared so far down at her sandwich that I could barely see her face. I watched her curiously until all of a sudden I saw tears darken the napkin in front of her. She looked up at me with anguish in her gaze. "Am I a terrible friend?"

"What?" I said. "Of course not."

"I am." She sniffled in. "Aria's right. You're such a talented artist and you're so smart. If I was really your friend, why would I let you hide those things about yourself?"

"Hey." I reached across the table and wiped the tears off of her face. "You're a wonderful friend. We've been through this, we have a certain image to maintain."

"Yeah, but we weren't maintaining an image there. I don't care what those idiots think. I should have stood up for you. Why can some girl just come along and fight for your real self better than me when I've been your best friend for years?" She started to sob a bit harder. "It was the same thing that happened with Arden."

"Arden?" I said.

She nodded. "I didn't think you guys would accept her." She used one of her napkins to wipe her eyes. "We used to be best friends. Like way back best friends. Our mothers were best friends too. We'd been inseparable since birth."

"Wow," I said. "I knew you guys had history but I didn't know it was like that."

"Then I got my braces off and my boobs finally decided to show up and it was like you guys were interested in me all of a sudden. Arden was so unique. Her dyed hair and piercings. I told her that, maybe if she toned all that down, she could come be friends with all of you guys with me, but she said she wasn't going to sacrifice herself and we started to fight about it a lot. Eventually I just started to distance myself from her. I thought I was doing the right thing. It would only hurt us both for us to drag that cart with only one wheel."

"That's why she said Aria's argument with you was pointless," I said. "She'd been there before."

Hannah buried her face in her hands. "Now I'm doing the same thing to you. I think it's better for you to be some cookie cutter jock than the amazing guy that you are? What's wrong with me."

"Hannah." I set my hands on her shoulders. "At least *you* know the real me. That's all I really care about. What do I have to gain from someone like Ceradi or Josh knowing that stuff? I'd rather just toe the line with them. Once school is over, it's not like I'm going to be dealing with them anymore anyway." Hannah looked at me and blinked a few times and the same realization that must have hit her struck me at that exact same time. "Oh," I said. "We're wrong. We're just all the way wrong."

I didn't give a damn about Ceradi, Milton, Josh—any of them. Hannah was my best friend, and the rest were just friends I kept around for the status. I didn't really care what they thought about me ultimately, I just didn't want to cause problems.

Hannah nodded. "Yeah. Any way you look at it, Aria and Arden are right to hate us. We're shitty."

I slumped back in my chair, feeling defeated. "What's that saying? The first step is acknowledging it."

Hannah took a giant gulp of her coffee. "Yeah, but there's nothing we can do. Knowing what we know doesn't make any difference. We're still in the position we're in. If we were to try and make some monumental change now, it wouldn't just affect us, it would affect everyone around us. For better or for worse, we chose to stick with the popular kids, so we have to ride this train out."

"I get what you mean now. How it's better for me and Aria if I just leave that distance there," I said.

Hannah frowned. "That's what I did with Arden. I didn't want to see someone I cared about so much get mocked."

"She doesn't really seem like the kind of person who would be easily ruffled by something like that though," I said. "Just like Aria."

"She's not," Hannah said. "Her and Aria are a good pair."

We sat in a frustrated silence for a while then, just working on our sandwiches and coffee and trying not to feel as shitty as we did. Every time one of us opened our mouths to say something, we stopped short and didn't. Was that really it? I had to just give Aria up even when I knew what I was fighting for was meaningless?

What kind of life was that?

"Why do I suddenly feel like a bad guy?" I asked.

"I think we've always been the bad guys, we're just finally realizing it," Hannah said. "Whatever. It's better than being the victim."

I glanced up at her. "You *do* realize that's a lot of supervillains' logic, right?"

Hannah looked across at me in pained seriousness. "I guess we'd better pick out our supervillain names then."

Sleeping on the information Hannah and I had unearthed at lunch was not an easy task. Every time I fell asleep, it was only to find myself face-to-face with visions of myself as an evil guy dressed all in black with a curled mustache and Aria looking like a damsel in distress. At the last minute, when I was finally about to defeat her, she'd stand up for herself and send me falling into a black, endless void. Sometimes Hannah was there as an evil partner, or Arden would show up like a knight in shining armor.

Could I really just be okay with being the bad guy in Aria's story? I wanted to be the love interest. The one who swept her off her feet and carried her off into the sunset. Was this really how our tale was going to go? A guy too spineless to admit when he was wrong and just let the possible love of his life slip through his fingers.

No. I wasn't okay with that.

It took seeing Aria and Arden all day for me to muster up the courage, but finally when school was out and I saw them headed to debate, I ran up and stepped in front of them.

Arden wrinkled up her nose at me. "You're awful."

"I deserve that," I said. "I just wanted to say I'm sorry, to both of you. Without going into too much detail, Hannah and I spent most of yesterday lamenting the people we've become and that we let you down. I can't speak for her, but for me, I just have to say from the bottom of my heart... I'm sorry." Aria and Arden exchanged glances, clearly not expecting that. Aria gave me a curious look, and I could see the interest, wondering if this was a step in the right direction, and I was hoping that it could be. "Um, Arden, would it be okay if I spoke to Aria alone for a few minutes?"

Arden looked at Aria, who nodded, then she looked back up at me, taking a menacing step forward. "Fine, but if you hurt her *again* I'll hurt you, and I will leave scars."

I swallowed hard. "That's a terrifying threat. I'll be good."

She narrowed her gaze at me before rolling her eyes and walking around me to head into the debate room. I wanted to step closer to Aria, but resisted the urge. This was going to require finesse. I needed not to rush things. "Arden seems like a good friend."

"She is," Aria responded.

"Listen, uh, I was wondering if—"

"Aria!" I looked over Aria's shoulder and one of the guys I'd seen her and Arden hanging out with a lot, a guy named Devario, walked up to us. He looked me up and down first, almost like he was sizing me up, then he stepped right between us and turned his attention to Aria, holding out a couple of comic books in her direction. "After we talked about Poison Ivy the other day, I thought you might want to read this. They *are* limited editions, but I trust you."

"Whoa!" Aria yelped, her face lighting up. "Thank you. I'll be careful with them, I promise."

"Maybe when you're done reading them, I can buy you dinner and we can exchange notes," he said, and the flirtation was obvious.

It was probably stupid of me to assume that Aria didn't have anyone else looking in her direction, but I thought it was a safe assumption that she hadn't moved on yet. But she looked up at Devario with a romantic smile on her face and her eyes batting like a girl from a movie and my heart shattered.

"I'd really like that," she replied.

"What?" I said.

Devario looked back at me briefly, 'back off' shooting across at me from his steely gaze, but then returned to

Aria's attention. "Great. Let me know when you're all done."

"Okay," she responded.

Devario seemed rather proud of himself as he turned around, gave me a final glare, and then walked off towards the debate room.

I watched him go, not necessarily wanting to face the answer to the next question I couldn't stop myself from asking. "So…" I looked at Aria, praying that she gave me better news. "You and Devario… Is that a thing, or…?" The jealous sludge in my stomach threatened to turn it inside out.

"What does it matter to you?" she asked.

"Well… what about me?"

Aria crossed her arms. "What about you? Your friends have already made that call."

"I'm sorry," I said.

"And I accept your apology, but that changes nothing," she replied. "I told you nothing will happen between us, and I meant it."

She gave me a quick, saddened look, then walked around me, leaving me standing in place shocked and hurt.

Nothing would happen between us ever?

Why did I feel like my heart would never recover?

I'd severely underestimated the strength of my feelings for Aria, and hearing her say something so definitive hurt me far worse than I ever could have prepared for.

15

ARIA

It was difficult holding back tears, but I managed to do it until I got into the debate room. I bolted straight back to the last row, past Devario and my other friends, and dropped down into one of the seats and buried my face against the seat in front of me to hide my emotions.

"What happened?" Arden's voice filled my ears before her hand rested on my back. "I'm gonna kill him."

"No," I whimpered. "It wasn't him. It was me."

"What do you mean?" Arden asked.

I sniffled in my pain, trying to get it to leave my face alone before debate was truly underway. "Devario kind of asked me out… right in front of Tristan."

"Oh, a power move. I like it," Arden said. "Did you say yes?"

I nodded against the seat. "Yeah, but Tristan looked like I'd just reached into his body and ripped his heart straight out of his chest. He was clearly heartbroken."

"What does that have to do with you?" Arden said. "He had his chance and he blew it."

"Yeah," I whimpered. "I pretty much told him that. It just hurt. When I think of Tristan… I think of the future, ya know? I can't shake this feeling in my gut that he's… ya know… the one, or whatever, but that's so stupid." I looked up at Arden. "Why are my feelings so strong? We didn't go out or anything."

Arden slipped down into the chair next to me and wrapped her arm around my back. "I mean it's not like you've just had these couple of months, there's a lot of history behind you two. Sometimes those feelings are just there. You can try and try to get rid of them, but they never really go away."

I looked at her. "You sound like you're speaking from experience."

She threw on a phony smile. "Me? No. I'm a roamer. A nomad. I don't dedicate my heart to just one woman. Where's the fun in that?"

"You're not a very good liar," I grumbled, feeling dejected.

All the fake confidence in Arden's shoulders melted away. "Thanks for bringing me down with you."

"Sorry," I hummed.

"Look, you gotta put that stuff with Tristan out of your mind, at least as much as you can. People like him and Hannah, they're not used to people not falling at their feet. They just don't know how to take no for an answer."

"So it's Hannah?" I asked.

Arden recoiled then lifted a finger and stabbed it against my cheek until it stung. "Hey. What are we going to do if we're both caught in depression's well-spun web? What are you doing? Let me stay afloat at least so I can carry you."

Her phrasing brought a little smile to my face. "I'm glad I met you."

She pulled her hand back and smiled at me. "Aw, you jerk. You know just what to say." She pulled me into a hug, squeezing our cheeks together. "Don't worry, Ari. We'll get through this together."

I hugged her back. "Thanks. I'll take all the help I can get."

At Arden's suggestion, I excused myself from debate for the day and went home early. Fortunately, my mom was working late, so I didn't have to try to explain to her why I was in such a terrible mood. I made myself an early dinner, feeding Hazelnut as I went, and then headed up to my room to eat. Once I was done, I ran a nice, hot bath for myself, complete with some bath salts to hopefully relax the pain away. I leaned my head back and closed my eyes.

If I tried hard enough, I knew I could forget all about it. "Aria?"

I sat up in the water and looked around. The voice I'd heard echoed in my ears clear as day, and it was definitely Tristan.

"Tris?" I called out, but there was no response.

I leaned my head back and closed my eyes once more, but the voice called out to me again. "Aria?"

That time, instead of just sitting up, I climbed out of the water. Droplets hit the tile floor as I stepped lightly to the rack where my towels hung and pulled one down. I wrapped it around my body, making sure everything was sufficiently covered, then opened the door and walked out into my bedroom.

Except it wasn't my bedroom.

It was Taylor's basement, where Tristan and I had

made out. When I looked down, I was terrified to find that I was still wrapped in a towel. I looked behind me, to see if I could run back into my bathroom at least, but the only door there was the doorway that would lead me back to the upper floor of Taylor's house, where I'd be far likelier to cross paths with someone I didn't want seeing me like that.

What I was supposed to do, I wasn't sure, but without any real instruction from my brain to do so, I opened my mouth and called out, "Tristan?"

And that time, I got a response. "Aria? Where are you?"

His voice was omnipresent, so I didn't look in any particular direction as I replied, "Taylor's man cave!"

It wasn't like I was afraid, more confused, and as frustrated with Tristan as I was, if he could get me out of his brother's house and back to mine without anyone seeing me damn near naked, I'd take it.

"There you are. I've been looking all over for you." His voice was directional that time, and came from behind me, so I turned around and saw him in the same outfit he'd been wearing at his party. He looked really good, and my heartbeat was already starting to hasten at the memories of what we'd done last time we were down there together. "I see you really dressed up for the occasion."

"Clothes seemed like a waste of time at this point," I replied. It wasn't at all what was in my head, but when I said the words, Tristan's eyes flashed with excitement.

"Oh?" He took a few steps towards me, backing me up. "Making my job a little easier?"

"What can I say?" I said, grabbing the part of the towel where one flap was tucked into the other. "I'm a woman of action."

Then I unwrapped the towel and let it drop to my feet.

What in the hell was I doing? It was an out of body experience, but I was in my body. It was like the logical part of my brain had been possessed by the part that had developed a desire for Tristan at the party that night that had been growing and growing without my knowledge.

Tristan closed the distance between us, setting his hands on my waist, and lifting me with ease up onto the pool table. My legs parted naturally, and he stood between them as his lips found mine. Alarm bells were going off in my mind, or at least the sane part of it, but the Aria that had the controls was all in, as I wrapped my arms around Tristan's neck and pulled him closer to me.

He worked his way from my lips, down my neck, and across my chest. Even as he got lower and lower, I wasn't stopping him, until he was just about to latch over one of my nipples. He stopped just short of it and looked up at me.

And barked.

I hunched my brow and looked at him like he was insane. "Did you just bark?"

The only response I got was another bark, then another, then another.

With one final, loud bark, I shot straight up in the bathtub, moving so fast water splashed out over the basin and drenched the floor. My heart was pounding so fast it felt like there were four in my chest.

It was just a dream?

Another bark pierced the silence, and I immediately recognized it as Hazelnut, not Tristan. All the bubbles that had been in my bath when I started, were gone, and the salts had all totally dissolved. Quite a bit of time had passed, and Hazelnut was likely barking because she was ready for bed, but my bedroom door was closed.

Was I happy or angry that she disrupted my dream? Even if it was just in my mind, having Tristan's hands on me again was beyond welcome. I wanted him to keep going. To devour me to his heart's content.

But why dream of something that could never be?

As long as I continued to dream about Tristan and imagine us in these scenarios that would never come to pass, I wouldn't get over him. I *had* to start putting him out of my mind.

It was a feat much easier said than done. All manner of spicy dreams plagued me that night, which meant I was a wreck as I walked into work the next morning. It was my hope that I could hide it behind makeup, but Lucky's eyes narrowed the second he saw me. I managed to avoid his questions as I kept myself busy with the morning soup kitchen rush, but as soon as that slowed, Zameera sent Lucky and I on break together, something I might have liked in the past, but now just made me anxious.

"Hey," he huffed as he trudged into the break room behind me. "You seemed exhausted when you first walked in, but you've been going like the energizer bunny. Is everything okay?"

Arden and my mom's concerns skidded across my brain and made me nervous to share. I'd talked about crushes before with Lucky and it was never an issue, but Tristan seemed to be the exception.

"Nothing. I'm okay," I replied, grabbing a bottle of water and my lunch and sitting down at the table.

Lucky frowned as he sat across from me. "What the hell is that? I'm your best friend, so I know you're lying. What, you can't talk to me anymore? New bestie officially replacing me?"

"What? No. I just… Didn't wanna bore you," I said.

"First of all, you once spent like two hours explaining the antics of a dart frog to me, in *insane* detail. Second of all," he tossed an irritated gaze at me, "is it about Tristan and that's why you don't wanna tell me?"

My cheeks burned with embarrassment. "Um…"

"Aria, just tell me. What's with all the secrets?"

It made me feel instantly guilty. He was right—he was my best friend. There had never been secrets between us before. Sure, he was being a little weird about Tristan, but that was probably just because he wasn't there to see it all in person. Lucky had always been overprotective of me, and it likely just bothered him that he had to wait and get everything secondhand and couldn't be there in the moment for me like Arden could.

Second guessing things with Tristan had me second guessing things with Lucky, and that was *not* what I wanted.

"You're right, I'm sorry. I think all of this stuff just has my brain muddled. Go get your lunch and I'll explain."

Lucky did just that, and I told him about how things had gone with Tristan for the past couple of days, from the argument after his presentation, to my night of heated dreams. He listened intently, taking everything in, and didn't seem bothered or annoyed at all. It was just what I needed. Having Arden was nice, but talking to Lucky just felt comfortable and familiar and really helped lift the weight some.

"Anyway, I know that's a lot, but it's basically it," I finished. "I'm just frustrated. I don't know where these intense feelings are coming from. I'm not some protag in a rom com."

"Are you in love with him?" Lucky asked straight up.

It felt weird to hear it put plain like that. Even weirder to consider. As much as it felt like it *shouldn't* be love, it also felt like that was what it was. I was crazy about everything about Tristan, from the way he looked to the person he was —the real person, not the fake one he showed his "friends."

"I think I could have fallen in love with him. Probably pretty quickly too, but it can't happen. I won't do that to myself."

"You mean it?" Lucky asked.

I nodded, smiling at my best friend's concern. "I mean it."

"Then…" He poked at the empty wrapper where his lunch used to be. "What about me?"

My heart came to a stop. "Wh-what about you?"

Something Lucky read in my reaction had him retreating quickly. He tossed all of his trash back into his lunchbox and stood up from the table. "Nothing. Never mind."

My mouth hung slightly open as he rushed to his locker, shoved the bag inside, and then raced from the room muttering something about the bathroom.

Was he asking if I had feelings for him?

"Definitely!" Arden said when I video called her after work to talk about it. "He was trying to confirm that Tristan was a no-go and then tried to wedge himself into that spot."

The thought that it was actually what Lucky was doing had me in a tailspin. I had enough going on trying to navigate things with Tristan, now I had to be worried that my best friend had feelings for me too? It was clear that Yunmir and Devario had crushes on me too.

What the hell was going on?

"So for the first seventeen years of my life, I couldn't *pay* a guy to look at me, but now I'm beating them off with sticks?"

Arden laughed. "I told you you're a hot item."

"I don't see it," I grumbled.

"The good ones never do, Aria. The good ones never do."

"Well what do I do now? I don't have feelings for Lucky, but if I tell him that and it breaks his heart, I could lose him." I dropped my head into my hands. "I'm certain you wanna say 'I told you so.'"

"I'd rather just tell you to be careful. What you say and do with these boys has to be done very mindfully so they can't take advantage of you. That's a good rule of thumb for people in general. Everyone always has an ulterior motive." She slapped on a mischievous grin. "For example, you're only sticking with me so that you can have a slice of my billions when I invent the next big thing, and I still haven't *totally* given up on making you my trophy wife."

I laughed and Arden laughed with me. "Hey, there you go."

She always knew the right thing to say to make me feel better. "Well, who knows about Tristan or Lucky, but I know one thing for sure. I *definitely* love you."

Arden's smile grew. "It's like music to my ears, gorgeous."

"Be more careful, huh? Any chance they'll just both leave me alone?"

"With how amazing you are, I wouldn't count on it, but just know whatever you decide, I've got your back."

"Thanks Arden."

"No problem."

At least in the midst of all the chaos, I'd gained a really amazing friend. Now if I could just figure out how to find romance in a reasonable place, I'd be back on the road to sanity.

16

TRISTAN

*H*annah took in the sight of me with disgust as I dragged myself towards her. "Let me guess," she said. "Drill Day is also the day that you're choosing to try out your simpleton look?"

I looked down at my gray sweatpants, black t-shirt, and black shoes with pursed lips. "What? Less is more."

"Less also means you're still doing the bare minimum after the whole Devario fiasco, which was weeks ago by the way. I mean, when are you going to get over Aria? You're wearing it like a break up and you guys never even went out. Ceradi and the others are starting to ask questions."

"So?" I grunted. "I told Josh yesterday to mind his own fucking business and I'll tell the same to Ceradi."

"Okay, sassy," she replied. "I heard that they went out and it didn't even go that well."

That wasn't what mattered to me. It wasn't the fact that Aria was willing to go out with Devario that bothered me, it was the fact that she said nothing would ever happen between us.

"Is today really Drill Day?" I asked, desperate to change the subject.

Hannah hooked her arm through mine and started forcing me in the direction of homeroom. "Yes, it's Drill Day. They announced it like four times yesterday. Where was your head?"

"Halfway up my own ass," I admitted.

Drill Day was something that happened at our school twice a year—once in the fall and again in the spring—where the school practiced all the possible emergency drills that could happen, from tornado, to fire, to a shooter lockdown. In the past, they tried to do them interspersed with classes, but students got so distracted and excitable waiting for the drills that it made all their classes a crapshoot. My freshman year was the beginning of the new system, Drill Day, when classes were cancelled for the day and students spent the entire day in their homeroom classes. The teachers typically had a place they could send students if they wanted to study or work on homework, but they would also occasionally ask for help doing things around the room or play movies and games.

It was bad news for me because it meant I had to spend the next several hours in the same classroom with Aria, as opposed to a typical day where I'd be able to break it up with the few classes we didn't have together. If Ceradi and my other friends weren't around, I would maybe try and use it as an excuse to try and spend a little more time with her, but with all the watchful eyes on me, I'd have to just grin and bear it.

"Good morning," Coach H greeted as we walked in. "Sit wherever you'd like. We won't be in our assigned seats for long anyway."

Ceradi held up a hand and waved us down to the corner of desks they'd seized control of near the window. Hannah and I walked over and sat down and I could see that Aria was sitting with some of her friends near the front of the room. Her eyes looked as sleepless as I felt, and somewhere in the back of mind I wondered if her restlessness was for the same reasons as mine. She had feelings for me, that was obvious. Was she really going to continue ignoring them?

If only I'd done a better job of proving to her that I was worth the risk.

Once the bell had rung to signify the beginning of the day, Coach H got up and stood at the front of the classroom. She clapped her hands to bring attention to her and the murmur in the classroom died down. "Alright everyone, we all know that Drill Days are just us sitting around waiting for the next drill to come around, so I've set up a few different options to keep us busy today. The first is, any of you who want to use this time to study can go to the lunchroom where a few different teachers are going to be taking attendance. You'll check out here and check in there, and if any drills happen while you're there, those teachers will make sure you're accounted for and get that information to me."

Ceradi raised her hand. "Can we stay there the whole time?"

"Yes. You'll be released briefly to come back here before lunch and then you can go back afterwards if you'd like," Coach H explained.

Milton snickered next to me. "Leave the lunchroom to come back here, go to the lunchroom, then come back here, just to go back to the lunchroom."

Coach H pinched the bridge of her nose. "I'm aware of how silly that is, but it's the only way for us to keep track of you, so just deal with it." She paused to see if there were any other questions, but when no one else raised their hand, she kept going. "Great. Mr. Sung will be showing movies all day in the auditorium, so same routine there if you'd like to go there, or you can go to the gym for games. Anyone who wants to stay here, I'll be cleaning and organizing the room and I'd love the help. I know it's not much but anyone who stays to clean will have their lunch accounts loaded with enough to cover a few meals, so you're technically getting paid."

Ceradi sighed. "My—"

"I know," Coach H cut her off, sounding annoyed. "I know money isn't a struggle for you. Feel free to take another option."

Ceradi gave her a cocky smile. "I will, thank you."

"Alright, let's split up. Who is going to take the study option?"

Ceradi immediately raised her hand, and everyone in our little friend group followed suit, apart from me. Hannah looked over at me and raised an eyebrow. "You're not going?"

"Come on, Tris. Let's go slack off," Ceradi said, making no attempt to hide her words from the teacher.

"I'm thinking of going to the gym. You guys go ahead," I said.

Ceradi shrugged. "Suit yourself."

Hannah, Ceradi, Milton, Josh and a few other students in the class signed out and left, bound for the lunchroom, and I looked over at Aria. Whatever she decided to do for the day, I'd do that too. I had to try at least one more time to earn her forgiveness. We were meant to be together. I didn't want to just give up.

Coach H released the students who wanted to go to the auditorium and the gym, and then smiled at the handful of students remaining to help her clean. "You guys have always been my favorites. I know you think I'm just saying that, but I'm serious. I had a feeling you all would be left. You're the good ones."

I glanced over at Aria and we locked eyes for a moment before she looked away, but not before I saw the light blush rise to her cheeks. There was something there, I just had to prove that she could trust me not to hurt her.

Coach H picked up a clipboard and set it down on her desk. "Here are all the things I want to try and get done, in order of priority, so please fill in from the top down. What I didn't tell the others was that lunch is on me today for your help, too, so please write down what you want from Stone and Sandwiches as well. We'll enjoy a nicer lunch since you were willing to help me."

There was a small round of cheers and then people started to get up one by one and head up to the clipboard. I lingered until everyone had gone up, and when everyone had returned to their seats, I stood up and walked over to the list. I scanned it and saw that Aria had signed up to deep clean and organize the supply closet, and there was no one else signed up to help. Praying it wasn't a mistake, I added my name near that task, wrote down what I wanted for lunch, then returned to my seat.

Once everyone had signed up, Coach H took a look at the clipboard and smiled. "Cool. Thank you guys so much for the help. Denver, Shane, I'll go collect the broom and mop bucket for the floors, but you can start by shoving the desks to the sides. Mary, Cait, Anna, if you guys want, you can get started with the markers. Then when we know how many are dead and have to be thrown away, we'll move on to taking an inventory of everything. Tristan and Aria, your job is arguably the hardest because I have no idea what's in that closet, but I'll get you a big garbage can because I'm assuming most of it can be thrown away."

Aria turned her head to look at me, and I gave her a weak smile, getting a deep eye roll in response. She wasn't thrilled with my antics, but that was okay. I didn't think she'd be that excited at the outset, but this was the most time we'd had to talk since my birthday. I just had to explain myself honestly and promise her that I wouldn't hurt her again. Everything would be okay as long as I didn't shove my foot in my mouth again.

"Let's get started. I'll put some music on," Coach H said, then everyone jumped to get started. Aria and I collected near the supply closet in the back of the room and Coach H came over to unlock it. "I was certain no one would sign up for this. You two are saving my life."

Aria smiled. "I always organize our storage spaces at work, so I'm kind of a pro."

Coach H just shook her head. "I might have known. Do literally whatever you want, just run anything by me that you're thinking of throwing away. I'm gonna go get some cleaning supplies too, so if you come across anything that is spilled or needs to be cleaned that'll be here for you." She tapped me on the back. "Thanks, Tris."

I nodded. "No problem, Coach."

With that, Coach H walked out of the room to go and get the cleaning supplies and Aria stepped by me and into the closet. "You didn't have to sign up for this too."

"I wanted to help," I replied. "And spend a little time with you."

She looked back at me. "We're cleaning, and that's it."

It deflated me a little, but I didn't let it discourage me entirely. "Yeah, cleaning."

She tossed me a narrowed gaze, but then sighed and turned her attention to the closet. "Let's just get everything out first, then we can go over it all and figure out the best way to organize it."

"Okay."

Aria started handing me things out of the closet, and I started to stack them on a nearby desk. I kept everything in as organized piles as I could, setting everything that I assumed we'd eventually be trashing off to the side on a different surface. Every time she bent over in front of me, my eyes immediately drifted to her curves, but I begged my mind not to get distracted. Yes, Aria was hot, but letting that muddy my mind while I was just trying to get her to deal with me again wasn't going to be good for business.

"Tristan?" Aria asked.

I responded way too quickly. "Yes?"

She pointed up to the top shelf of the closet. "Can you get that stuff down for me?"

I looked up to where there were some boxes stacked in the top of the closet. "Yeah, of course."

Stepping forward, I reached up towards the top shelf, pinning Aria between me and the back of the closet. She elbowed me, trying to maneuver in the little amount of space. "Wait. Let me back out then you can do it."

"I've almost got it. Just hang on." The boxes were pushed further back, so even with my height, they were difficult to reach. I leaned forward on my tiptoes and reached as hard as I could, in spite of the fact that Aria was pushing me away from her. "Aria, stop. I can't reach it with you doing that."

"Then move and let me out and you'll have more room."

I growled in frustration. "Fine. Hang on."

"Shutting this for a second," a voice called from outside the closet.

"Huh?" The door of the closet hit my back and pushed, forcing me against Aria and shoving us both deeper into the closet. I looked over my shoulder and clicked my teeth. "Idiot. Why would he shut it with me in here?"

"He probably didn't see you in here," Aria hissed. "Can you move over?"

"It's not like there's a ton of room in here. I'm not trying to make you uncomfortable."

She scoffed. "Then don't stick around and sign up to clean the same area I agreed to clean."

I sighed. It was a low blow, but I deserved it. "I'm sorry. I just want to talk to you but you won't even look at me."

"I told you, we have nothing to talk about." She reached around me for the door handle, but struggled to reach it. "Can you please open the door so we can get out?"

As much as I wanted to trap Aria inside so she had no choice but to hear me out, forcing her to deal with me wasn't going to be productive. I fished a hand behind me and grabbed the handle to the door, but when I pushed, though the door moved, it didn't move far.

"Shit," I hissed.

Aria let out an exasperated sigh. "Very funny."

"I'm not kidding," I said. "I can't get the door open."

"What?" Aria wrapped around me, sliding a little too

close to me and encircling me with the smell of her delightful perfume. She squeezed between me and the door, setting her full backside right at my waist and tried to force the door open, unintentionally rutting herself back against me. "Dammit. I think those idiots stacked the desks in front of the door."

"Can you turn around?" I asked, begging my lower half to behave itself.

"No. I don't wanna talk to you," Aria said.

"Fine. I won't talk, just turn around." I moved as far back as I could, but the closet wasn't very large.

This was bad.

Aria pounded on the door. "Hello? Can you move the desks? We're stu—"

And at that moment, the fire alarm went off. The blaring was much louder than Aria's screams to try and get us out of the closet, and we could hear the shuffling of feet as those left rushed out of the room and then eventually silence.

"Did she not notice that we aren't with them?" I asked.

"Everyone's running in and out while cleaning. She may not have even been in there when it went off." She set her forehead against the door, once again accidentally sticking her butt further back and rubbing it against me. In terms of punishments for my past misdeeds, it was by far the worst. "We're just going to have to wait until she takes roll outside and notices we're missing."

"Whatever," I squawked out in desperation. "For now, please for the love of god, just turn around."

17

ARIA

*H*earing the strain in Tristan's voice, I turned around so that I was facing him, and he let out a sigh of relief. There were beads of sweat licking at the edges of his hair and he was releasing clenched fists.

"Are you claustrophobic or something?" I asked at his obvious discomfort.

"Sure," he said. "Let's go with that."

"Okay? I've turned around. We're stuck in here, so what did you want to talk about?" I asked.

His eyes went wide. "Really?"

I shrugged. "What else are we going to do?"

We were nearly face to face, in fact, if it wasn't for the height difference, our faces would probably be touching. Making everything worse was the fact that Tristan looked incredible in an understated outfit of gray sweatpants and a black t-shirt. He normally dressed way up, wearing multiple layers and bright colors, but the simple look was good on him too.

I stood there, waiting for him to say something, but he

just stared down at me with an intense gaze that made my skin burn. "If you keep looking at me like that, I'm turning back around."

Tristan shook his head. "That is *not* a good idea."

"Why?" I said. "So you can keep staring at me until my resistance has waned?"

He raised an eyebrow. "Would that work? Because I'll do it."

Scoffing at him, I started to twist my body around again, in spite of Tristan begging me not to. It was stupid for me to even consider giving him a chance to speak up anyway, so if he was just going to play games, I wasn't going to play them with him. I turned until I was facing the door again and pressed myself as far forward as I could, but it didn't create any space between us. We were still touching.

"Aria, please, I'm begging you to turn back around," Tristan huffed into my ear.

"No. I'm not falling for that." I forced as much severity into my voice as I could, knowing full well that I was at a disadvantage. *I* was the one that had feelings for Tristan unimpeded by any friends or need to maintain some dumb status quo. If he continued to look at me like that, or even if he continued to talk to me in that husky, attractive voice, I was likely to give in. "Just sit still and be quiet until Mrs. Hammerskill comes back."

Though I could hear him straining behind me, he listened to the directive and stopped talking. I tried to imagine in my mind how long it would take Mrs. Hammerskill to notice that Tristan and I weren't outside with the rest of the class. We were on the top floor in one of the back classrooms, and with everyone flooding out of the school at the same time, they probably weren't even outside yet. Then once they were out there, before jumping to any conclusions, Mrs. Hammerskill would likely look around to see if she saw Tristan and me first before coming up to investigate.

Minimum we were stuck in there for at least fifteen minutes, but it was probably going to be closer to twenty or thirty.

The real question was, would my resolve last that long?

We stood in silence for about five minutes and I was committing myself to just remaining motionless and speechless until we were discovered, when all of a sudden, I felt a poke behind me, right at my ass. My heart started to beat a little faster as my mind jumped to conclusions, but I tried to shove that idea out of my mind.

"Did you move?" I asked.

"No," Tristan replied, sounding defeated, almost as if he knew where my mind had already gone.

"Then…"

Almost like he wanted to prove it, Tristan shifted slightly to the side and the bulge poking at my back moved with him.

It *was* what I thought it was.

I glanced back over my shoulder and he was straining just like he had been before. Goosebumps covered my skin and images of my dream from a few weeks prior and when we'd made out came flying to my mind. "Are you serious?"

"I *told* you to turn around. What do you want from me?" he huffed back.

I rolled my eyes. "I'm surprised you can get it up for a fat girl."

Tristan's hands came up and settled on either side of

me. "I shouldn't have said that, Aria. Nothing could be further from the truth, I…" He let out a breath and it was hot against my neck, elevating my own feelings. "I think you're sexy."

The word hissed across his lips like a commandment and it started to turn me on. It was the same way he sounded in my dream and there was nothing I wanted more than to be able to indulge in him. I tried to remind myself this was *his* fault, but in that moment, all I could think about was how close we were and the fact that I couldn't second-guess his words with his arousal stabbing me.

Unable to take the feeling of it, I turned around and looked up at him. "Really?"

Tristan looked down at me with the most serious gaze I'd ever seen. His arms were still situated on either of me, and though I was trying not to look down, I could still see that his boner was tenting his sweatpants.

"Aria, I like you," he said in a moment of total honesty. "Is that a crime?"

The pain in his voice as he said it made me equal parts sad and angry. I felt the same way. The issue wasn't me, it was him.

"I don't understand," I said. "If that's the way you feel and that's the way that I feel, then what the… fuck?" I barked, trying to keep my emotions at bay. "We made out at your party, it wasn't like there was any big secret that I had feelings for you. We were going to meet up and pick up from where we left off. If you liked me and I liked you then why wouldn't you say *that* instead of all that horrible shit you said about me?"

"Because I'm a terrible person. I was trying to impress

people who, in the long run, don't really matter to me and it cost me someone I care a lot about. I'm sorry, Aria. I shouldn't have said that stuff to them and I swear to you, I will never say it again," Tristan said.

Whether I could trust him or not, I wasn't sure, and it left me painfully conflicted. I wanted more than anything to believe that Tristan could move on from whatever weird attachment he had to his awful friends so that we could be in a relationship for good. When I thought about being with him, it made me feel like it could be the last relationship I was ever in. After all the years we'd been apart, we found our way back to one another and that had to count for something.

But was I being stupid and just walking face first into my own heartbreak? I'd already been hurt by Tristan once. Could I really believe him when he said he wasn't going to do it again?

"I want to trust you so much, I really do. I… I like you too. After that first day when I saw you again, I thought we were on the road to somewhere and you proved me wrong."

Tristan's hands drifted down from the wall and wrapped around me. My skin prickled where his hands were resting on me, and I looked up into his eyes, wondering if I could safely choose hope.

"This is what matters to me. *You* are what matters to me. If you can just give me one more chance, I promise, I won't waste it." He whispered.

It took active effort to force out all the voices in my mind telling me it was a bad idea. Arden, Lucky, Zameera, my mom. Everyone who had listened to me lament and believe that Tristan was a bad guy. I knew better. I knew he wasn't that man, it was just whether or not he was strong enough not to pretend to be that man.

"This is the last chance I can give you," I said. "If you hurt me again—"

"I swear, I won't."

Tristan leaned in and I found myself craning up to meet him. Our lips found one another in the dull light of that closet and my mind started to go foggy. There was something about kissing Tristan that just felt *right*, like it was something I always should have been doing. I bent against him, letting my arms slide up around his neck and hold him close. He pressed himself even more firmly against me and eventually left my lips behind to move to a spot on my neck. He kissed me there for a moment, but when I leaned my head back, giving him better access, he stopped and snickered.

"What?" I said.

"This is definitely not helping my boner, but I do *not* want to stop," he said.

"So don't," I said. "There's more than one way to get rid of one."

He looked down at me with a surprised expression. "Well then…" He squeezed, his hands moving down on my body. "Tell me more."

His lips found a spot on my neck again, and I unlaced my hands from his neck and started to move them further and further down his torso. "We probably can't do *everything*, but I can help at least."

My fingers tucked under the waistband of his sweatpants and my heart was racing at top speed as I got closer to grabbing him.

Then we heard the screech of desks outside the closet.

Tristan snapped back from me and jumped to the side, landing on a pile of boxes, which caused the bottom of the stack to crumple and for him to still smack his head. His leg flew up and if I hadn't swung my body backwards, he would have kicked me right in the face.

"Tris!"

He groaned, rubbing his head, and the door behind me opened, revealing Mrs. Hammerskill with a panicked look on her face, which quickly turned to relief when she saw us standing inside. "Jesus, I'm so sorry you two. I saw them block the door, but I didn't realize you were inside. My god. Get out here."

I stepped out of the closet and Tristan grunted as he got to his feet and squeezed out of the closet. He seemed freaked out and was keeping a distance from me, but I figured that was just because he was still half-hard. I respected the space he needed to try and calm himself down as Mrs. Hammerskill shooed us out of the classroom.

"You two get started heading down. I need to call the principal and let him know I found you."

I nodded and led the way out of the classroom with Tristan not far behind me. My heart was still pounding, but more than anything I was annoyed we'd been interrupted. I looked back over my shoulder to see how Tristan was managing, but not only was he really far behind me, he was on the other side of the hallway from me.

"What are you doing?" I asked.

Tristan shook his head. "N-nothing."

No.

Studying him as we walked, I tried to step a little closer to him when I was certain there was no longer an arousal issue, but he damn near crashed into the lockers to keep the space the same between us. I waited a little bit and then tried to get closer again, but once again, he moved as close to the wall as he could to keep the space between us. There was no one else in the hallway, but we were headed towards the front of the school where the entire student population would be waiting and likely see the only two stragglers left behind and the reason why the drill had lasted so much longer than it was supposed to.

He wasn't embarrassed about his boner, he was making sure he wasn't seen with me.

Every part of me wanted to say something. To cuss him out or throw something at him or tell him to fuck all the way off until he couldn't anymore, but I was fighting just to hold back tears.

We got to the front doors and he pulled back, and I pushed through one, dragging all of the attention to me. Out of the corner of my eye, I could see him slink out of one of the doors and immediately cut to the left and out of sight, managing to avoid most people's gazes.

The only record faster than how quickly he'd let me down was how quickly I'd let myself down.

How big of an idiot could I be?

18

TRISTAN

hank god for fast reflexes, because when I placed my hand inside Aria's locker in an attempt to stop her from walking away from me, she didn't hesitate at all to slam the door shut. The metal grazed my fingers as I yanked them back, and the locker slammed with a resounding clang.

"Aria!" I called out as she turned to walk away, but she turned around and threw me a harsh glare that melted me where I stood. I made no attempt to step any closer or follow her as she left.

I'd really screwed things up for good this time.

"Tris." I looked over my shoulder and saw Ceradi, Josh, and Hannah coming down the hallway towards me. "There you are," Ceradi said. "Why weren't you at lunch *or* at the fire drill?"

"Um, I looked for you guys during the drill, but I couldn't find you," I lied, feeling like an actual piece of shit. "And Coach bought lunch for anyone who agreed to stay behind and clean."

Josh's jaw dropped. "What? She didn't say she was going to do that. I would have stuck around and helped."

"That's why she didn't say anything, most likely," Hannah said. "She didn't want a bunch of people doing it for the free food, so it was more a happy surprise for the good people who actually chose to do it."

Ceradi crossed her arms and raised an eyebrow at me. "I thought you said you were going to the gym to play games? How did you end up cleaning the classroom?"

"Uhhh." My gaze shifted towards Hannah and she rolled her eyes immediately, having figured it out, but didn't say anything. "I saw how few people were staying back and felt bad."

Ceradi shook her head. "Your chivalry is borderline irritating."

"Yeah, come on dude. What are you doing cleaning the class? Aren't there people who work here and get paid to do that?" Josh asked. "You make the school famous from the field, not sweep the floors."

"Yeah," I said, rubbing the back of my head. "I guess it was pretty stupid."

"It wasn't," Hannah said. "If you stayed back because you wanted to be helpful, I think that's a good thing."

I looked over at her, as did Ceradi and Josh. Ever since the altercation with Aria and Arden, Hannah had been standing up for me more. Fortunately, she hadn't had to hang her neck out on anything truly insane, but in little moments like that, she defended who I was, which I appreciated.

Even if I was totally lying.

"Well, whatever," Ceradi said. "Mop floors if you want

to, you totally missed my impromptu photoshoot. It's blowing up on the socials."

"Oh no," I said flatly and Hannah quietly laughed, shaking her head.

"Don't worry. I'll fill you in at dinner," she said.

I side-eyed Hannah, exhaustion likely prevalent all over my face. "Dinner?"

Hannah shrugged. "We decided we're all gonna get dinner together tonight since you guys don't have football practice."

I couldn't think of a single thing I'd rather do less than that, but no one seemed to be picking up on that apart from maybe Hannah, but she wasn't about to stop it from happening. So instead of taking issue with it and making my day worse than it already was, I just went with the flow. Hannah came with me to collect my things from my locker, but seemed to be able to read my mood and didn't ask about what was going on.

There was a high-end restaurant a little outside of the city where Ceradi liked to go because everyone fawned over her and it made her feel fancy. It was just Ceradi, Josh, Milton, Capito, Hannah and I, but that was more than enough people to make me wish that I was just at home.

When I could, I sent Aria a text, hiding it from any onlookers, but the message bounced back immediately.

I'd been blocked—no shock there.

"Oh, Tristan," Ceradi said, bringing my attention to her. "Did you see that Aria was so late coming out of the fire drill?"

Hannah watched my face, reading my expression, but hopefully I was hiding it well when I said, "No, I was too busy looking for you guys. I didn't notice."

"Well, obviously she was last," Josh said. "It's not like she can move all that fast."

Ceradi's shrill laughter filled the restaurant and it brought rage bubbling up to the surface of my skin. I slammed my hand down on the table rattling all of the silverware and plates. "Stop it!"

"What?" Josh said.

"Don't talk about her like that. You don't even know her. She didn't do anything wrong to any of you and doesn't deserve to be treated that way!"

Hannah, Milton, Josh, Capito, and Ceradi were all staring at me in utter shock, along with several people at the surrounding tables. My nostrils flared out with anger, and I glared at Ceradi so hard I thought my eyes may fall right out of their sockets.

"Are you joking right now?" Josh asked.

Ceradi was leaning forward in her seat, almost like a beast preparing to jump all over its prey. The people whose attention I'd attracted from nearby tables were murmuring and pointing at me, and were more than enough of a hungry audience for Ceradi's torment if she threw into a fit. Under the table, I could feel a stabbing into my leg, and I noticed that Hannah's hand was under the table and her fork was missing.

This was what Aria was talking about, right? Standing up for her? Not letting her down?

Then again, I'd pretty much already done that in a way I was quickly learning was irreversible.

So then what was the point?

"Yeah," I said, relaxing in my chair and throwing on a fake laugh. "I'm kidding."

Josh, Milton, and Ceradi all erupted into laughter, but

Hannah, and for some reason, Capito were both watching me with concerned gazes. I forced a smile on to pretend as if I was okay, but I had a feeling that they both knew I wasn't. The conversation carried on, trashing Aria even more, but Capito and Hannah stayed out of it. The rest of the meal was arduous, but I made it through by the skin of my teeth, and was so exhausted when we were leaving that I considered getting a ride home and coming back for my car.

"Close call," Hannah whispered to me as we were walking out. "Don't you dare drive away until we get the chance to talk about it."

We said goodbye to the others, with hugs and waves, then all climbed into our cars and waited for everyone to pull off. Hannah was parked next to me and I assumed she was going to come over to my car, but she continued to sit there until I finally got a text that simply said:

Capito's still here.

I looked over, and sure enough, Capito's car was still parked in the parking lot and he was staring back in my direction as if he was waiting for something. I opened the door of the car and climbed out, and as soon as I did, both Hannah and Capito did the same. Hannah lingered back, but Capito crossed the parking lot, tucking his hands into the pockets of his letterman jacket. He was a tall, thickly-built Hispanic guy, with a closely shaven head and a budding goatee. He carried toughness like most people wore glasses, so seeing him staring at me like I was a puppy cowering in the middle of a busy highway was disconcerting to say the least.

"You, uh, wanna talk about what happened back there?" he asked.

My heart thudded once, and I looked back at Hannah for guidance, but she seemed just as confused. Turning my gaze back to Capito, I read his face for signs of deceit or trying to trick me for Ceradi, but he seemed genuine.

"I'm… in love with Aria," I chose to say.

He puffed up a bit and then let out a long breath. "Fuck, man. Why didn't you say something sooner?"

"Tris," Hannah warned, but I just shook my head at her.

For some reason I trusted that everything was okay. "You see how Ceradi is about it."

He scratched his head. "Yeah. That's a tough one. I'm sorry for anything shitty I've said about her. Just trying to fit in and all that."

I laughed. "Yeah. Trust me when I say I know how that goes."

Hannah made her way over to us and stood next to me. "Did something happen?"

It felt a little weird having Capito there, but it also felt like I was gaining an ally, which in a really strange way, gave me some of the confidence I'd always lacked. "Yeah. We got locked in the closet and I told her how I felt. She feels the same way and things got… hot. But when Coach showed up to let us out, I jumped back and then wouldn't go within ten feet of her. I just panicked. Old habits die hard. I wish I could redo it and just walk out of that school holding her hand."

As shocking as it was that Capito was there, it was even

more shocking when Hannah reached up and whacked me across the back of the head. "Ow! Why?!"

"You are such a chicken shit!" she screeched.

"What?" I said. "You're the one who's been telling me to let it go."

"Yeah, let it go, not continue to keep her hanging on and then shame her afterwards. I'm beginning to think you really *are* just as bad as Ceradi." There was fury in her face that I'd never seen before. "I think it's a bad idea, but if you're going to do it, then you need to do it. If you're not going to get over yourself then you need to leave her alone." She looked me up and down then hissed, "Dick," and stormed off towards her car, getting in and starting it up and screeching off right away.

"That was unexpected," I said.

Capito nodded. "Yeah. She's right though."

"Yeah…" I looked up at Capito, knowing that he had very little of the story and wondering if that would make his advice more or less helpful. "What would you do if you were me? I wanna be with her, but Ceradi isn't going to let that happen without a fight."

"You just gotta decide what means more to you, man," Capito said. "I don't know, I think if I had a girl that really cared about me, I wouldn't give a shit what Ceradi thought." He made an awkward, twisted expression with his face before continuing. "I know this sounds weird, but back in there when you defended Aria, I really felt that, ya know? I hate being one of these people. That's the first time I really felt like maybe we're not all bad. I kinda thought you were as bad as Ceradi too. My parents can't stand you."

"Hey," I said.

He shrugged. "You're one hell of an actor."

I swallowed hard. It did *not* sound like a compliment. "Why does it have to be one or the other? Why can't I be with someone I care about so much and keep you guys as friends?"

"That's how shit shakes out I guess," Capito said. "Anyway, if you run off and start dating some chick you're in love with, regardless of what Ceradi does, that's not gonna create any problems between you and me, and it seems like Hannah's got your back too."

"Thanks," I replied. "Why do we choose to put up with this shit?"

"I don't know man, maybe we're stupid."

I laughed. "I keep fucking things up with Aria, so I am for sure."

19

ARIA

"Fuck," I barked as I dropped yet another bowl, shattering it on the ground.

I was at work, in the middle of serving chili for the afternoon lunch, but every time I thought about Tristan I got angry all over again, and my hands shook so much that I was dropping things left and right. Kneeling down, I started collecting the shards of the bowl, trying extra hard not to cut my hands even more, which I'd done already twice that day.

"Aria, can you please be more careful?" my coworker Henri said softly. "Any more glass on the floor and we're going to have to close down the cafeteria."

"I'm not doing it on purpose," I snapped, and he recoiled.

"Whoa," Travis, another one of my coworkers, said. "He's just reminding you, Aria. Relax. We know you're not doing any of this on purpose, you're just usually more careful."

"I'm not allowed *one* bad day?" I screeched. "You two certainly fuck around enough."

"Hey!" Zameera barked, having stepped out into the line. Even some of the homeless men and women who'd shown up for the meal were steering clear of me. Zameera stood to the side and pointed towards the back. "Off the line, now." I opened my mouth to argue, but she held her hand up. "I don't want to hear it. Get in the back now."

My nose was already burning as I fought to hold my frustration back, but my eyes were blurring as I passed Zameera and fell under her direct scrutiny. I kept my head low and listened as she walked out to the line to apologize to those people who had heard me snap. She told Henri and Travis to give her some time, and I'd be back with an apology.

"Don't bother," Travis said. "If she's gonna be like that, we're better off without her out here."

"Agreed," Henri said.

I supposed I deserved that for the way I was acting, and I sunk down into one of the break room chairs and dropped my head to the table. It probably wouldn't be too difficult to call out sick at this point, no one wanted me there anyway. I just wanted to go home and crawl in bed.

"Aria, look at me," Zameera said in a stern tone. I lifted my head and looked up at her, tears already plucking at the corners of my eyes. "You need to explain yourself right now. That kind of behavior is *not* okay."

"I'm sorry," I whimpered. "I'm having a bad day."

"You've had bad days before, I've seen it. You tried to come to work the day your grandmother died, and put a smile when you showed up the day after. You simply aren't that person," she said. "As your boss, I need to inform you that it will not be tolerated here. Everyone is working just as hard as you, and a bad day does not give you the right to speak to your coworkers like that. You will apologize to them, and if I hear it again, you'll be written up."

I nodded. "Yes, ma'am."

"As a friend," Zameera said, sitting down across from me and reaching across to rest her hand on top of mine. "I know that you wouldn't do that unless you were extremely pressed. What's going on?" All at once, all of the emotions I'd been holding back came clamoring over the edge and I started to sob. It immediately concerned Zameera, who stood up and walked around the table to lean over me and rub my back. "Oh, honey, what's going on?"

"Tristan told me that he had feelings for me yesterday, but even after he promised he wouldn't do the same things that he'd been doing, he turned right around and acted like he was ashamed of me. I forgave him and it was like no time at all before I learned why that was a mistake." I dragged my palms across my eyes, trying to take the tears away, but each time I did it, new ones came along to replace them. "It just broke me. I pretend like I'm this confident person, but I know that I'm fat, and I know that I'm ugly, and I know that I'm a dork. Telling myself that those things are fine only gets me so far. When stuff like this happens, it just reminds me that I'm grasping at straws."

"Aria," Zameera sounded blown away. "You are one of the most beautiful women I've ever known. Inside and out. So what you've got some curves, there are supermodels who weigh more than you. You're the kind of desirable that people realize they want when they get out of this petty, must be barbie-doll-perfect phase of their lives. All the men around me, they want women who are shaped like you, and it's evident in the way people interact with you. Half the reason people come through those doors is to look at you. Don't you dare let some stupid boy make you second guess your own beauty. He sounds like a fucking idiot to me."

I nodded, whimpering, "He is a fucking idiot, but…" The words I wanted to say just wouldn't come out of my mouth.

But I love him.

"No buts," Zameera said. "You deserve someone way better than that."

"I can see that he's telling the truth when he says he cares about me. When he promises to do the right thing, I know that, in his gut, that's what he wants, but for whatever reason the pull of being known as a popular kid is more important. I'm not worthy of the life he's established," I explained. "I just want to be with someone who loves me for me and isn't ashamed of me."

Once the words left my lips, Lucky stepped around the corner from the back and looked at me with a face of determination. "Aria." Zameera and I looked at him, shocked, and it made my face burn with embarrassment to know that he'd heard all of that. "I'm in love with you."

"Oh my," Zameera said. "Why don't I give you two some privacy?"

She stood up and walked through the door out to where the others were serving food, and shut it behind her, leaving Lucky and I alone. His eyes were wide with passion as he stormed over to the table. "I want to be with you. I've wanted that since we first met." He reached down and grabbed my hand and held it close to him. "I wouldn't hide you away. I would never be ashamed of who saw you. I want to post it all over my social media that I'm fortunate enough to be with someone like you."

"Lucky…" I wiped my nose and eyes. "You've never… I had no idea you felt this way."

"I was afraid of ruining what we have, but now that this guy is in the mix, I know that I have to say something. I can't just stand by and let him take you. He's not even worthy of you," he explained. "Go out with me, Aria. I love you."

It seemed like strange reasoning. If he had feelings for me all this time, what did the sudden appearance of Tristan have to do with it? What was more than that, Lucky was holding my hand, and staring at me, and as frustrating as it was, I felt absolutely nothing. Maybe, if I'd known years ago, but I saw him more like a brother now.

He didn't do half to me what Tristan could do with a single glance.

"I don't know what to say." Mostly I was angry. Why couldn't Tristan have Lucky's fearlessness when it came to me? Or why couldn't Lucky be as appealing to me as Tristan was? Why was I helplessly snagged between these two people?

Didn't I deserve happiness?

Thinking about it more sent my tears running again and I started to cry again. Lucky got afraid and took a step back. Instead of being understanding, though, he looked angry. "Is the thought of being with me that bad? I just want to love you, does that make me a villain or something? At least I won't mock you in front of other people. I'm sorry you'd rather be with someone who treats you like he does."

"N-no," I said, feeling slighted by how defensive he got,

and no longer feeling like I could share my real feelings. "I just can't think straight right now."

"Oh." The anger left Lucky's gaze and he dwarfed inside himself a little. "I'm sorry. I didn't mean anything by it. I'm…"

"I just can't do this right now, Lucky," I said. "I'm sorry, but I don't have an answer right now. Can you give me a little time to compose myself and sort out my feelings?"

A small smile came across Lucky's face that crushed me. "Of course! Take all the time you need." It was clear he was hanging onto a hope that I was going to say yes at the end of the day.

Things were just going from bad to worse.

TRISTAN

*S*omewhere in the distance, I heard my bedroom door open and close, and when I looked back, the dishes that had been stacked on my desk were gone. It was likely Andrea that had come up to collect what I'd neglected to bring down in two days' time, and even though she wasn't my favorite person in the world, she had at least had enough sense to just leave me the hell alone. Friday night and all day Saturday, she'd brought my meals up to my room, slipped in long enough to set them on my desk and left without saying a word. Then, some time after each meal, she'd return to collect the dishes, equally as quiet.

I'd have to muster up the kindness to thank her at some point, because it meant that I literally didn't have to leave my bedroom all weekend. I'd come up to my bedroom straight away after my game Friday night and neither my dad nor Andrea had seen the whites of my eyes since. I hadn't even moved from my bed a whole lot, occasionally moving to the armchair to play video games for a bit, before crawling back under the covers, starting a show on some streaming service, and turning into a potato. It was already leaning into Sunday afternoon, and if I didn't have to leave for another two weeks, I wouldn't.

Hannah was right, I *was* wearing things with Aria like a breakup, but that was honestly how it felt. We got so close to moving to the next step, and thanks to the fact that I was, as Hannah so lovingly put it, a chicken shit, she wanted nothing to do with me and I couldn't blame her.

I wouldn't want anything to do with me either.

A knock on my door had me looking over my shoulder in confusion. "Tris?"

I sat up a little, shocked by whose voice I heard. "Taylor?"

"Can I come in?" he asked.

He sounded more reasonable than he had the last few times we'd spoken, which was nice. Though we stayed in close communication after my birthday party, Taylor had been treating me very differently. It was like he said, he struggled to be friends with me after he'd seen the way I acted at the party. For the last two months, Taylor was just my brother and nothing more. He loved me, that was obvious, but a lot of the friendly stuff we'd done had come to an end. Between him being angry at me for the past two months and Hannah not having contacted me since we left dinner Friday night, there was no one to guide me through the weekend.

So… I was a potato.

"Yeah," I called back.

Taylor took one step into my room and then slapped his hand over his nose and backed out. "Holy shit, it's *rank* in there. Have you not bathed, like… at all?"

I looked down at the sweats and t-shirt I was still

wearing from when I'd gotten dressed for school Friday morning. "Um… no."

"Okay, well I can't talk in there with it smelling like that. Open a fucking window, leave your door open, go take a shower, and meet me downstairs."

I turned my back to him and pressed the spacebar on my laptop to resume my show. "I don't want to."

"I swear to god, Tristan, if I have to wade through this sulfur pit to drag you out, I am not going to be happy about it," Taylor said.

"So don't," I snapped back. "Just leave me alone."

"Jesus," he huffed. "What the hell is wrong with you. You *never* act like this. Dad was right to call me."

That made sense. My dad had made a few attempts throughout the weekend to discern what was wrong with me, even going as far to offer to play video games with me to try and coax it out of me, but not only did I not want to revisit the pain that it was causing me anymore than I had to, I didn't want to deal with the fact that I was my own problem.

And I'd rather talk to my dad about it ten times over before talking to Taylor. He already told me how frustrated he was with me. The most recent fuck-up was only bound to make him angrier.

"I don't want to talk about it." Aria's smile skidded across my brain and made me sick to my stomach. At the end of the day, what happened was in her best interest. She deserved a *way* better guy than me. "Sorry to have wasted your time."

Taylor let out a long, loud groan. "I am going to have to shove your funky ass in the shower. I am not happy."

"No you don—" but before I could say anything else,

Taylor's hands were on my back, ripping me backwards out of my bed. "Fuck off! Let me go!"

I tumbled onto the floor, grabbing Taylor around the shoulders and taking him down with me. Like a child, when we were face to face, I breathed right into his nose and he gagged. "Disgusting!" We continued to wrestle, the noises of which brought Andrea and my dad rushing up the stairs.

"Stop it!" Andrea screeched.

"It's fine," my dad said. "At least he's out of bed."

"Taylor, let me go!" I growled.

"Dad, can you go start his shower?" Taylor grunted out.

"Yep." My dad stepped into the room, groaning and stopping briefly to say, "Ugh, Drea, go grab a spray." Andrea walked away, and my dad continued into my bathroom, moments later starting the shower.

"Okay, up we go," Taylor said.

He flipped around until he was at my back, then he wrapped an arm around my chest and jabbed his knee into my back, holding our weight with his other leg, which forced me up onto my feet unless I wanted his knee to split my vertebrae. He was hissing out a flurry of swear words in my ear as he shoved me forward into the bathroom and towards the running shower.

"I'm still dressed!" I barked.

Taylor stopped pushing me. "I'll let you go if you promise to get in."

"Fine!" I said. "Just let me go." Taylor unwrapped me and took a huge step back. My dad walked past us, tapping Taylor on the shoulder as he passed and left the room. "That was unnecessary."

"Seemed pretty necessary to me," Taylor said, then he sniffed his shirt. "Great. I smell like your funk." He speared a finger in my direction. "Go fucking bathe and meet me downstairs."

I tossed him a glare, but listened, lifting my t-shirt up over my head, and pleased that I was going to do as told, Taylor left the bathroom, shutting the door behind him.

As much as I hated to admit it, but once I was in the shower, I already felt much better. I turned the water as hot as I could stand it and tried to ignore the sludge color the water was turning as it washed off my body. In no time, I was offended by how gross I'd let myself get, and settled into a deep cleanse including washing my hair twice. By the time I'd gotten out, my entire room had been sprayed down with something that smelled nice and fresh, and a candle had even been lit and set on my desk to change the aroma in my room.

I was grateful.

I changed into a pair of jeans and a t-shirt with a sleeveless vest over it, then slipped on one of my favorite pairs of tan boots and walked downstairs. Andrea, Taylor, and my dad were sitting in the living room and all looked as if I'd just walked into the room wearing a ball gown when they laid eyes on me.

"Okay," I said. "Maybe I let it get a little bad."

"Your bedroom smelled like it was the cabin of a man who'd been stranded in the jungle for two years," my dad said. "We don't pay half a million dollars for this house so you can turn your bedroom into a cesspool."

Shockingly, Andrea reached over and whacked my dad's arm. "What are you talking about? That's *exactly* why we pay that much for it. If he's going through something, then I'll just clean his room. It's fine."

"Thanks," I said to Andrea.

She smiled back at me. "Of course."

"I won't let it get like that again. I'm sorry."

She shook her head. "I'm serious. It's just a bedroom. I was more concerned about you."

Andrea was Aria 1.0. All she'd been doing ever since she married my dad was try and be the best mom to me that she could be, and I let the asshole tendencies I'd developed under the guise of survival make me unreceptive to it. "I'm okay, mama. I promise."

Andrea's eyes widened and then started to blur, and even my dad and Taylor seemed to get a little emotional. Andrea nodded, stood up and gave me a kiss on the cheek, then fluttered away. My dad stood up to go after her, hooking my head over to him for a kiss on top of the head as he passed, then he walked off after her.

Taylor leaned forward, setting his elbows on his knees. "See? That wasn't so difficult, was it."

I thought of the big deal I'd made of being popular or fitting in and the fact that it'd officially cost me Aria. "No. It wasn't."

Standing up and walking over to me, Taylor slapped the side of my face gently and it felt closer to the friendly relationship we normally had. "Come on. Lunch on me. I gotta hear about what turned you inside out."

We left and went to one of our favorite restaurants that sat right on the edge of a cliff in the mountains and overlooked the valley below. They served typical American food. We got a table near the windows and placed our order, including an appetizer of a blooming onion, my favorite, then Taylor chucked his straw wrapper at me.

"Alright. Out with it," he said.

"Well, if you were looking forward to thinking I'm a

better person, this conversation is going to let you down," I said.

Taylor shrugged. "I don't know. You sure made Andrea's whole life back there, and you seem pretty aware of it. I think you're in the self-loathing phase of changing who you are for the better."

"I apologized to Aria for the things I'd said about her. I even told her that I liked her, though my feelings are much stronger than that honestly," I explained. "She said she liked me too and we made out." I chose not to mention the almost-handjob part of the story. "Everything was going so well, but then as soon as I thought someone was about to see us…" I made an explosion sound with my mouth and motion with my hands. "I suck."

"If you know that, then why do you do it?" Taylor asked.

"I don't know. It's an impulse. I don't want these people to judge me."

Taylor shook his head. "If you love Aria," he made the leap from *like* on his own, "then why does anything else matter?"

"I'm afraid!" I yelped and Taylor recoiled. "These are the only friends I've ever had! Are they great people? No, some of them are really fucking shitty, but what the hell am I supposed to do? They're the only ones I got. I don't have a supply of friends on standby. Even Hannah tells me not to go for it with Aria because she's afraid I'll fall out of our friend group. Doesn't that mean if that happens, she'll leave me? She's my best friend. Though she's not even talking to me right now, because I keep pushing and pulling with Aria and hurting her instead of just letting it go." I hadn't put my straw into my drink yet and I was bending it in my hands, probably breaking it beyond repair. "What if they put shit on social media? What if they get me kicked off the team? They have so much more power than you think. I worked hard getting to this place. It sucks, but it's safe. What do you want from me?"

Taylor stared back at me in shock for a second, then he softened entirely. "Oh. Tris, I'm so sorry. I get it now."

I lowered my gaze at him, unsure of if he was being sarcastic or not, but he sounded genuine. "Really?"

"Yeah. You've weighed what you have now against what you could have with Aria, and have decided this is more important," Taylor said. "That's totally understandable." I didn't like the way it sounded even though Taylor did appear to be significantly less frustrated with me. "Hannah's right, though, you have to just let Aria go then. You can't just keep her dangling on. If your friends are what are important to you, then you have to let her go. That's the best option." He reached across and set a hand on my head. "I'm sorry. I didn't understand. I shouldn't have gotten so mad. It'd be scary thinking you're going to lose all your friends."

It actually made me a little emotional. It *was* scary. The thought of starting over from scratch kept me up at night. I wanted Aria, I really did, but I simply didn't think I was strong enough for that. "Yeah."

"I won't bring it up again, I promise. You have to let Aria go though. It'll hurt for a while, maybe a long while, until you leave for college and never see her again. First loves suck, but you'll move on eventually. Trust me," Taylor said.

Like a lightning bolt striking from the top of my head down to my feet, something hit me. "I don't like that."

"No one does, baby bro. Heartbreak is a bitch," Taylor said.

"No," I said. "The thought of never seeing Aria again."

Taylor tilted his head. "Well, you'll go your separate ways after you graduate, I imagine."

He was right. Right now, I could still see her and talk to her, even if it was laced with all the nastiness between us, but we were seniors and would graduate at the end of the year. I wouldn't have the summer to learn and grow and see if we could make it work next school year.

I wasn't just risking losing Aria right now, I was risking losing her forever.

TRISTAN

There were audible groans coming out of me as I walked down the hallways now drenched in decorations for the Sadie Hawkins dance. Thanksgiving break was in two weeks, which meant the dance would be next Friday. Along with the posters advertising the dance and reminding students to purchase tickets through their school app, the fronts of several lockers were decorated, a tradition around the school when anyone wanted to ask someone else to the dance.

All of the couples in school were being super lovey dovey. I'd even seen some of the teachers who were dating outside of school getting flirtatious with one another.

"Ugh, fuck happiness," I groaned.

"Well, that's not very nice." I jumped so far to my side that I crashed into a set of lockers and fell under a hail of points and laughs. Hannah grabbed my arm and pulled me back over, before brushing me off. "What the hell? It's just me."

I wrapped my arms around her and pulled her into a big hug. "You're not mad at me?"

She squeezed me back, circling her arms around my back and holding me tight. "I needed a break from you, but I could never stay mad at you. Especially not when you're going through all this shit."

I stepped back from her and frowned like a little boy that had just fallen down. "I'm sad."

It broke Hannah in an instant, who gave me a pitying expression. "Oh, honey, I know." She reached a hand up and scratched the side of my face. "Have you spoken to Aria?"

"No. Even if I wanted to be that much of a sadist and keep in contact with her, she's blocked me on damn near everything. Not that I don't deserve it."

"Well, you do," Hannah said.

"I know," I said.

Hannah looped her arm through mine and we started for the stairs that would take us up to where our lockers were. "Look, at least you can put all of this behind you now."

"That's the thing though, Hannah," I said. "I don't want to put it behind me. I don't want Aria behind me. I'm… I'm in love with her."

Hannah looked at me with sympathy. "I know. Unfortunately, I think that ship has sailed."

Knowing she was right severed me in two pieces. All I could think about after talking to Taylor on Sunday was the thought that Aria and I would graduate and I would never see her again. I'd already been through that pain once, when we were pulled away from each other in elementary school. I was too young then to know just how painful it was, but I never got over it. It was the main reason why I was so over the moon when I saw her again the first day of school. It was what allowed me to fall so hard for her so fast. After finding our way back to one another after all this time, I didn't want to just walk away and never see her again. I didn't want her to be a what-if in my past that I constantly thought about until reuniting at a high school reunion ten years from now.

I wanted to be with Aria, and I knew now that I'd give up anything for that chance, I'd just figured it out too fucking late.

I carried myself forward through sheer force of will. When we got to my locker it was as bare as it was any other day, and I threw Hannah a frustrated gaze. "Couldn't even decorate my locker? It would have made me feel better."

Hannah raised an eyebrow. "What are you talking about?"

"Well, I know we're not going together romantically, but you did it last year when we just went as friends and it made my day," I said.

"I didn't decorate your locker because I'm not asking you to Sadie Hawkins," Hannah said.

I and several girls nearby looked at her with shock. "Wait… what?" I asked.

"I already told you, I'm asking a guy I grew up with. I've already asked him and he said yes," Hannah explained.

"Who is this guy? You've never mentioned him before that one time," I said.

She shrugged. "We just recently reconnected. He found me on social media. We've been talking for a few weeks, and then I invited him to the dance. I figured it'd be safe since he doesn't go here, and when I told him, he was really excited about it. I am too actually. I think I like him."

"What's his name?" I asked.

Hannah eyes the people standing around us and intently listening to our conversation. "You'll meet him at the dance."

"So I'm going stag?" I moaned.

Hannah nodded in the direction of all the onlookers. "Uh, it looks like you'll have plenty of options to me."

My locker would probably be decorated before lunch, but that didn't matter to me. If it wasn't Aria or Hannah, it wasn't worth my time.

We walked to our first class with several people pointing and whispering, and the news that I wasn't going to the dance with Hannah was spreading fast. As if I needed anything to upset my world, I'd be turning people down for the next week and a half.

Great.

It took Hannah swatting me every ten seconds in our first class to keep me from just staring at Aria. If I stood up and made a public declaration in front of Ceradi and the others, would that be enough to convince her to forgive me? One last chance and I wouldn't mess it up?

Aria…

Getting through one class was hard enough on its own, but it was the second class that was the nail in the coffin. Aria was much later getting there than normal, but the reason became clear when, seconds before the bell rang, Aria came waltzing into the classroom with a large bouquet of yellow roses and a huge box of chocolates. She was wearing a really cheesy straw hat, but it looked perfect on her.

"Arden!" Aria exclaimed, then extended the flowers and box of chocolates out towards her. "Will you make me the luckiest woman in the world and…" She fake cried. "Attend the Sadie Hawkins dance with me?"

Arden jumped up, clasping her hands around her face. She fanned her eyes as if she was crying and trying to stop her nonexistent makeup from running. "Yes, a million times yes!" She took the flowers and chocolates and gave Aria a big hug before stealing the hat and putting it on her own head. "Let's be honest, this was made for me."

"That's why I bought it," Aria replied with a laugh.

A few of the students around the classroom started whispering to themselves, but it appeared to be rolling off Arden and Aria's skin. "Whisper all you want," Arden said. "The hottest girl in the whole school is bringing *me* to the Sadie Hawkins dance." She stuck out her tongue.

I looked at Hannah and frowned. "She *is* the hottest," I whimpered.

Hannah rubbed my back. "Yeah, she is gorgeous."

I lifted my head and my jaw dropped. "What are you doing? Why have you never told me you felt that way before?"

Hannah looked at me as if I asked her the strangest question she'd ever heard. "You never asked."

It was such a simple answer and it made me feel like an absolute moron. "Can you please just write down *all* the ways I'm an idiot?"

She scoffed. "Oh honey, I don't have that much paper." She glanced over my shoulder, and a look of honest sadness registered in her gaze for a moment.

My stomach twisted and I reached across and put my hand on *her* back instead. "You okay?"

Hannah shook, washing the look from her face and went back to her ground zero, aloof look. "I'm fine."

As expected, several different people asked me to the dance throughout the rest of the week after learning I wasn't going with Hannah, but I turned them all down as nicely as I could. After the seventh or eighth girl, I finally started telling them that I didn't think I was even going to the dance, which bothered Hannah more than I expected it to.

"You can't just *not* go. It's your senior year. You will never get these moments back. You're supposed to enjoy them."

"I'm just not in a very Sadie Hawkins mood," I said. "I'd rather stay home or go over to Taylor's for dinner and movies."

"Come on, Tris. Just because I'm not going *with* you doesn't mean I don't want you there. What if things go south with this guy?" she said.

"Ceradi, Josh, Milton, Capito, and all the rest of our friends will be there, you'll be fine."

"Just like that you're not going?" Hannah said.

I nodded. "Yeah. Just like that."

"I'll cancel with my guy then, and go with you," Hannah said. "I really want you there."

"No," I said. "You're not canceling and I'm not going. You're going to have a great time with this guy, and if you don't, just tell Ceradi and she'll mock him until he wishes he wasn't born. You want me to get over Aria, right?"

Hannah sighed. "Yeah."

"Then I need to not go to a dance where she's probably going to look unbelievable and spend the whole night dancing and laughing with someone else," I said.

"It's not like things are romantic between them," Hannah said. "Arden's gay, but Aria isn't."

"No, I know that, but it doesn't change the fact that I would spend the whole dance watching her and wishing that was me." I put my hands on her shoulder. "Trust me, you don't want me there. If something really goes wrong with that guy, you can call me and I'll come get you. We'll make Taylor buy us beer and watch B movies in his basement all night."

Hannah nodded. "Fine, but I'm going to miss you."

"I'll miss you too," I replied, "but I'm certain that this is for the best."

2 2

ARIA

I pulled up in front of work and parked my car and then slammed my head on the steering wheel. I'd been considering calling out sick all week, but Arden talked me out of it, saying that avoiding the inevitable was only going to make everything worse. She was right, I knew she was, but that didn't change the urge I had to flee as I sat there. Lucky's car was already parked out front as well, and if the look of hope that he had on his face when I saw him last was any indicator, he was probably waiting right inside to hear what I'd decided.

I fished my phone out of my bag and quickly navigated to Arden's number and pressed the button to video call her. It rang a couple of times before a very close up and unkempt image of Arden appeared on the screen.

"For what reason do you call me so early, my liege?" she said. "The serfs also need their sleep."

"I'm sorry, I'm so sorry, but I'm sitting in front of work and I'm seriously freaking out. I can't do this. He flipped out so much last time," I said. "He's my best friend. I don't want to lose him."

"Aria." Arden sat up in bed and ran her hand through her hair. "I know that you guys were close, but if he gets 'nice guy' syndrome about this, then he was never your friend to begin with. It's important that you're up front with him, and if he *really* cares about you, he'll understand."

"What if he doesn't?" I said, welling up at the thought of never talking to Lucky again after everything we'd been through together.

Arden frowned. "Sweetie, I know this is hard, but if he doesn't then this might be the end of the road for you two. Do you want someone sticking around you like that? Look, I'm not even kidding, if I thought you were even marginally gay, I'd be going for it, but you told me you weren't and I let it go. That's what friendship is, understanding that, even in spite of pesky feelings, you can get around it and still be friends. I just want you to be happy, and if he's your friend, that's what he'll want for you too."

"Yeah. I know you're right," I said. "But maybe I could tell him that next week."

Arden laughed. "Or, you could woman up and go tell him right now, and I'm not just saying that because I want to go back to sleep." I giggled. "I'm saying that because the longer you draw this out, the worse it's going to be for both of you. He needs to know, and you need to not have this cloud of doubt looming over you. You are never going to be able to take over the world if you're too busy wondering if your best friend has an ulterior motive."

"Yeah," I said. "Yeah! I need to not let this hinder me anymore. Just like I straight up let Tristan know we were done, I can tell Lucky that too."

"That's my girl!" Arden said. "Now please, my lord, may I return to my cot."

"Go, go. I'm sorry for waking you up," I said.

She winked at me. "Don't worry about it. You know I'm here for you day or night."

"I do know that. Thanks."

"Love ya, kid," Arden said.

"Love you too," I replied. "Bye."

Hanging up the phone and sliding it back into my bag, I took a huge breath in, held it until I started to feel light-headed and then I let it out. My heart was pounding and my hands were clammy, but I knew it was time to do this. Arden was right, Lucky deserved the truth, and so did I.

Rehearsing the lines I'd said to myself a million times in my bed until I fell asleep the night before, I got out of my car and headed into work. I offered Billy a tepid greeting and then stepped nervously into the break room. I'd be lying if I said I wasn't hoping that Lucky had already been called out into the shelter to handle some task or another, but he was sitting at the break table and looked up the second I walked in.

He shot up and took a deep breath. "Aria."

"Hey," I said weakly. I hadn't spoken to him all week, avoiding him while I tried to figure out the best way to tell him that I didn't reciprocate his feelings. Once again, I was realizing that Arden was right. At least if we had made small talk throughout the week, it would feel slightly less monumental, but having the first thing I'd said to him in seven days be a rejection, it felt a little harsh. "Um… can we sit? I wanna talk to you."

That seemed to give Lucky hope, even though that wasn't my intention. "Yeah. Of course."

"You two." Zameera poked her head into the break room, looking as frantic as ever. "Sorry, the cold rush has started already. I know neither of you are supposed to be clocked in for another fifteen minutes, but can you please come out right away. Lucky, I'm hoping you can help with breakfast, and Aria, can you go help with intake. You're a calming presence."

"Sure!" I said, a little too eagerly.

Lucky frowned. "But…"

"We'll talk later," I said, quickly rushing and putting my things in my staff locker and then running off to help out. I knew Arden was right and we had to discuss things, but I was glad for the disruption. I'd get around to it eventually, but maybe the busy day would buy me a little more time.

The morning was a whirlwind of an influx of people coming in off the streets who actually needed to stay long-term. The shelter handled a lot of short term stays throughout the year, on top of a soup kitchen for anyone who just needed to eat, but once the cold started to set in around mid-November, more and more people showed up hoping to stay for the entire winter. Anyone staying at the shelter for more than a week at a time had to be reported to the state, which made the intake process a little more intense.

Dedicating my mind to the task of aiding the social workers in getting everyone's paperwork filled out actually made me feel the best I'd felt in weeks. When I was just doing the work I loved and didn't have to think about feelings my best friend suddenly has for me, or the guy I have feelings for being ashamed of who I was, I felt much more like my normal self. It was needed, even more so than I realized.

"It seems like you're feeling better," Dani, one of the social workers, said. "I heard that you got a little nasty last weekend. I could barely believe it."

"Yeah." I still felt bad even though I'd apologized to those I was terrible to over and over. "I'm going through a bunch of stuff. I let my emotions get the best of me and took it out on a few people who didn't deserve it. I hate that I tarnished my good name of being someone you all could rely on *not* to do stuff like that."

"In all honesty, Aria, it made me feel a little better about you. You wear this atmosphere of perfection, and don't get me wrong, there's nothing bad about striving for the best, but I was kind of becoming afraid you weren't human. Hearing that something had gotten you in such a foul mood that you were spitting nails at people actually humanized you a bit, which is good."

I grinned at her. "Wow. Thanks. That actually makes me feel a little better about it."

"I just think you bear so much yourself. Don't be afraid to rely on the people around you," Dani said. "Zameera says you have a friend now that you can lean on a little bit."

Arden's bright pink hair and sly smile cracked across my brain. "Yeah, Arden. She's awesome, and has certainly been bearing the weight of holding me up lately."

"That's good. You hold so many other people up all the time. Let someone hold you up for once," she said. "I know you love Lucky, but I can tell he relies on you a lot. It probably has never bothered you, because you have a hero complex, but if someone can finally take care of *you* a little bit, you deserve it." Then she leaned in a little bit with a sly smile on her face. "Wanna talk about what happened? Free therapy."

I snickered. Most of our social workers had other talents. It was necessary for our line of work. "Well, it was kind of two-fold. There's a guy that I'm kind of crazy about, and he has feelings for me too, but he's really popular and kind of embarrassed of me. Then there's another guy, who would scream from the rooftops that we're together, but I don't feel that way about him."

"Oof, that's a shitty feeling," Dani said.

"The thing is, the guy who suddenly revealed his feelings for me, they sort of came out of nowhere."

Dani raised an eyebrow. "After you mentioned the guy that you like?" I gave her a gaze and she nodded, knowingly. "So this other guy, as sweet as he may seem, was almost worse. He had feelings, but assumed you'd always be available and didn't think to act on them until there was a risk of losing you. At least the other guy was up front about his feelings."

That was the first time that the circumstances held Tristan as the better guy instead of Lucky. I didn't want to think that Lucky was just sitting around assuming I would never be picked up by another guy, but hearing Dani lay it out like that, it made it seem like that was really what it was.

"That sucks feeling like our whole friendship was just a means to an end," I said.

"Yeah. The one way to know for sure," she started.

"Is to tell him I don't feel that way and see how he reacts?" I replied. "That's Arden's advice."

"Sounds like a smart cookie, that one," Dani said. "She's totally right. If this guy actually cares about you as a friend, he'll respect that you don't feel that way about him."

"And the other guy?" I asked. "The one I like? Well… I think I may more than like him."

"If he's really embarrassed of you, then screw him, but I wouldn't just write it totally off. I was one of the popular kids back in high school, and the pressure to perform in a certain way is immense. If this has been this whole guy's world before you came along, he could just be feeling terrified of turning his life upside down." I snickered at first, then let out a full laugh. "What?" Dani asked.

"Nothing. I just wish I'd talked to you sooner," I said.

"Well, I'm always here. If you ever need more advice, I'm only an office away." She slapped her hand on top of the stack of files we finished and smiled. "Okay. I think we're good for a little bit if you'd like to go and take your lunch break, Aria."

I nodded with a smile. "Okay. I can come back early if you need me. Just text me."

"Will do, but I think I just heard them release Lucky too. You guys enjoy your lunch together. Don't worry, there will be plenty of work waiting for you when you get back."

And just like that, reality had come back to smack me in the face. "O-okay. Thanks."

I couldn't really blame my coworkers. As far as any of them knew, Lucky and I were best friends who enjoyed going on our breaks together. I hadn't made it clear to Dani that *he* was the friend who liked me that I didn't reciprocate the feelings.

But Dani had helped me enough, and as long as Lucky and I both still worked there, I didn't want there to be gossip or drama, so I didn't mention it. It was time to get it over with anyway, and with Dani's advice under me, my confidence to do so had certainly been bolstered. It was going to be hard for Lucky to hear, but if he actually cared about me as a friend, not just as a potential romance, then we could get through it.

I just hoped I wasn't about to lose my best friend.

"Hi," he greeted me as soon as I walked into the break room. "Are you on break?"

"Yeah," I said, trying to seem as serious as possible.

"Can we have that talk now, then?" he asked.

I nodded. "I think that's a good idea."

Rather than going for my lunch, I sat down at the break table across from where Lucky was sitting. There was still hope coloring his gaze, but I didn't let myself get sucked in. I just kept telling myself it would be better once he knew the truth. Lucky was my friend and he would understand. Those things were true, I had to believe it.

"Lucky, listen…" I started. "I was flattered by what you said last week, obviously, but um… I don't feel that way about you. We've been so close for so long, and I think of you more like family. I think you're incredible and are going to make some woman really happy one day, but I am not that person."

Lucky stared back at me in total silence. I studied his expression, trying to see which way he was going, but for a while it was just ghostly and plain. He watched me and I waited, unsure of if I should say something or not to break the silence, until finally, Lucky shook his head.

"No," he said. "I don't accept that."

My heart started to pound. "What?"

"I don't accept that answer," Lucky said. "I've been there for you through all of this shit. We've been together forever. Is it because of Tristan? Even though he treats you like that? I've been nothing but wonderful to you. How can that be your answer?"

I gulped, hearing Dani's words in my mind. "It's not like you've shown any romantic interest in me before. For me, this flew in out of left field."

"I just assumed that one day we'd get there," Lucky said. "We were halfway there already. I'm a guy and you're a girl. People joke that we'd be great together all of the time. What has all this been for if it wasn't headed anywhere?"

That question broke my heart. "So… that's all our friendship has been for you? A trajectory towards romance or nothing at all? I thought I meant more than that to you." Tears filled my eyes and I tried to blink them back, though it wasn't going all that well. "I thought you actually cared about me."

"N-no. Of course I care about you. You mean the world to me." He blinked a few times, then frowned and looked away from me. "I do just want you to be happy, even if that's not with me. It's just hard for me to hear is all."

That would make more sense to me if it hadn't been for the outburst. "I really hope that's true, because you're my best friend and I don't want to lose you."

"It's true," Lucky said. "I just need some time to recover from this, but I'm not going anywhere."

Whether he was telling the truth or not, I wasn't sure, but a person was only so strong. I let the conversation die there, because just like Dani had said about Tristan, I was afraid. Everything in my life was changing so fast, and I didn't want to keep going and lose my best friend forever, too.

23

TRISTAN

The week of the dance, the entire school was buzzing. Teachers were smart enough to know that students were more excited about the dance and the following partial week for Thanksgiving break, so a lot of classes were working on big end of the semester projects that would be due not long after the break was over, and studying for major tests. For seniors specifically, a lot of teachers opened their doors and allowed students to go deal with other tasks if that was what they needed, like speaking to counselors, or studying in subjects where they needed more help.

Or if you were friends with Ceradi, it meant moving into the cafeteria at the beginning of the day, and not leaving until the end. Hannah and I did better in our courses than the rest of our friends, so I actually felt bad for them. They should have been using the time to their benefit, rather than sitting around listening to Ceradi talk about nothing and take pics for her social media.

The only good thing it did for me, was keep me out of

classes where I'd have to stare at Aria all day and wallow in my own heartbreak. If I felt like it would do any good, I'd tell Ceradi to fuck off, but Aria wouldn't talk to me even if I did, so what was the point?

"You okay?" Hannah asked, noticing the slump I was in.

"I will be." I looked at her and frowned. "It's just hard, and I haven't gotten a lot of sleep. I'm tired."

"Tris!" Ceradi slid up next to me and held out her phone for a selfie. I smiled and let her snap the pick, and then my face immediately went neutral again as Ceradi reviewed the picture. "Oh, you look exhausted in this. You need to start doing my face cream regimen."

"I'll think about it," I replied flatly.

"Who did you end up deciding to go to Sadie Hawkins with?" she asked. "I know a bunch of people asked you. My dad is going to get us a limo to go, and I need to know if it's someone I'm okay with having ride with us, or if we'll need to meet them there."

I bit the inside of my lip to keep from lashing out. "I decided not to go."

"What?" everyone at the table said at the exact same time.

"What do you mean?" Ceradi said. "This is our last Sadie Hawkins together. You have to go."

"Did I miss something?" Josh asked. "I thought you were going with Hannah?"

Hannah let out a loud scoff. She'd mentioned the fact that she'd asked someone else a dozen times or more, but given that no one paid much attention to anything they weren't legitimately interested in, people kept reiterating the concept.

"No," Hannah replied through gritted teeth. "I invited someone from a different school. I said that already."

"Seriously, Tris, don't be a baby about the fact that you can't go with Hannah. You've got a million invites, just pick one."

"I don't want to do that," I snapped at Ceradi. "I don't just want to go with someone for the sake of it. I'm sick of doing vapid shit just to make it look like we're happy when we're not. I want to go with someone because it means something to me, and because I can't do that, I'm not going."

Everyone looked back at me in shock, and for the first time, Hannah didn't try to back me down. I'd finally had a moment of real honesty, and she was allowing it to happen without interference, which I appreciated.

"Is that a joke?" Ceradi said with a knowing smile.

It was code for 'Take it back, or prepare to get reamed.' A week or two ago, it might have scared me, but I was in a different place now. "No, it's not. I'm serious. If I can't go with the girl I like, then I don't want to go."

"Wait, you *like* Hannah?" Milton asked. "I thought you two were just friends."

"Whatever, when you turned down Colleen, she asked me instead, and she's smoking hot," Josh said. "So whatever the reason, I'm thankful."

"That's my point exactly," I said. "And no. Not Hannah."

Ceradi leaned forward, perching her head on her hand. "Ooh, you have a crush on someone else? Who is it?"

At the exact same time, both Capito and Hannah tipped their drinks over. It was like there had been a glitch in the matrix. Ceradi stood up, yelping, and Josh and

Milton toppled over to get away from the spill as the rest of our friends at the table sprung into action spreading their napkins over the liquids. Ceradi took off far from the table, screeching about not being able to sit there because she was going to stain her expensive clothes, and eventually everyone gravitated off in her direction, leaving Capito, Hannah and I sitting there alone to clean up.

"What the hell was that?" I asked.

Hannah laughed. "Nice teamwork there, Cap."

He nodded. "I saw you going for it and jumped in."

"What's going on?"

Capito reached across the table and knocked me on the top of the head. "Has *nothing* we've talked about sunk in?"

"Seriously," Hannah said. "How dumb can you be?"

"What? I'm not being ashamed of Aria anymore," I said. "I don't care if people know how I feel."

"That's fine, but think of how that's going to reflect on Aria," Hannah said. "If Ceradi finds out you're into her, she's never going to let her live it down, and maybe if you two were together it'd be worth it, because you could actually help her through it, but you're not."

"We've been through this, Tris. You have to let her go, and certainly don't go running around starting fires where you don't need to," Capito finished.

"I don't want to let her go."

Hannah put her hand on my head. "I know you don't, honey, but remember what we said before? She's not likely to forgive you at this point. I'm not saying this for the same reasons as I was saying it before. This time it's totally about her. Even if you're willing to give everything up, don't make her life even harder than you've already made it."

I slammed my head on the cafeteria table. "This sucks."

If only I could get Aria to trust me one last time, I could show up the way she was expecting. The idea of starting over from the bottom didn't scare me as much as losing her forever. I wished I could tell her that, but Hannah and Capito were right. If I wasn't going to be able to be with her the way I knew we both wanted, then dragging her into Ceradi's bullshit was only going to hurt her more, and I'd done enough damage.

"Are you really not going to Sadie Hawkins?" Capito asked, swiping the drenched napkins off the table and tossing them with skill into one of the garbage cans nearby. "That's what sucks. I feel like you and I are actually becoming *real* friends, and I was looking forward to having you there."

"I told him the same thing," Hannah said.

I dragged my head up and looked at Capito and he seemed truly sad. It made me feel bad, but also much better. "That's sweet."

Hannah glared down at me. "But me begging you to come for the past week isn't?"

"Of course it is, it's just that I kind of expected it from you. I wasn't expecting it from Capito," I said. "You really want me to come?"

Capito laughed. "Yeah man. Let's go to the dance. No one who asked me really excited me either, so I'm going stag. We'll just be two bros at the dance wondering why we can't have deep, meaningful relationships."

"Wow. Are you smart or something?" Hannah asked.

Capito leaned in a little bit. "I wanna be a psychologist, but don't tell Ceradi."

Hannah and I both smiled, and I chuckled. "How have we missed this whole time that you're one of us?" It felt like a true relief to know that we weren't just anomalies."

"I don't know, but I'm glad we all figured it out. I hated being in this group before, but now I feel much better."

Hannah continued to rub my back as she said, "Same."

"Okay," I said. "I'll go to the dance."

"Yeah?" Capito said. "Alright! I won't be the only loser!"

"Glad that our years of friendship hold such a persuasive control over you," Hannah said sarcastically.

I sat up suddenly, and wrapped my arms around her, pulling her in for a hug. "You know I love you. Let's enjoy the dance together."

She hugged me back, just shaking her head. "I really can't stay mad at you."

"Is this what *real* friendship feels like?" I asked, smiling at Capito and Hannah. "Because I like it."

24

ARIA

When Arden and I did our big reveal to one another in the living room, we both gasped and then immediately started laughing. Arden had braided her hair and was letting it hang down the side of her head. She had on a fuschia button-up shirt with dark purple suspenders that connected to a pair of black slacks. On her feet, she wore shimmery purple boots and she'd done a light coat of makeup, just enough to give her eyes a matching purple shadow and her lips a dark color similar to the suspenders.

"You look awesome!" I said. "I love it!"

"You said purple so…" She fanned her arms out on either side of herself. "I'm purple."

"It's perfect. I couldn't have put something better together for you if I tried."

"Well, not compared to you," Arden said. "I mean, you look drop-dead gorgeous!"

I spun around, letting my purple sleeveless flare dress

spin around me. "Thanks!" I had a pair of black platform pumps on and was carrying my items for the night in a black sequined clutch. I pinned one side of my hair back while the other hung down the side of my face. "We are *easily* going to be the best looking couple there."

"Oh," Arden waved her hand in front of her face. "I knew that when you asked me to go with you."

"Oh wow!" My mom walked into the living room and put her hands up to her mouth. "You two look amazing!"

She had her phone up and was already snapping tons of pics. I skipped most dances in the past because the torment of my bullies was not worth spending a few hours in a hot gym, sweating until I couldn't breathe, just to listen to music and dance with Lucky, who was my only friend at the time. This time around, though, I was drawn in by the fact that I was a senior in a new school who wanted to make the most of my final high school experiences. And now I had Arden and a whole bunch of other friends that I could enjoy my time with. I was actually feeling like it'd be worth it to go.

For this reason, my mom hadn't got to enjoy the experience of having her only kid get all dressed up to head out to a dance. She'd been denied the fun of taking pictures and cooing over the date, so she was leaning far in now.

"I'm happy to finally meet you, Arden," she said, walking up to Arden and pulling her into a big hug, then she looked over at me and raised her eyebrows. "So... is this...?"

"No, mom. It's not romantic," I said. "Arden and I are just friends. She's way out of my league."

"Ha!" Arden said. "That's funny."

A frown crossed my mom's face. "But she's so beautiful and she seems like a lot of fun."

Arden wrapped an arm around my mom's shoulders. "I like her."

"Everything you've just said is very true. Arden is incredible. I'm very lucky to have her, and believe me if it was something that could work, it'd already be happening," I said.

"Alas," Arden exclaimed. "The gods of fate save all of the best women for…" She sighed. "Straight men."

"Well, even if, I'm glad my Aria found you. You've been taking such good care of her. She talks about you nonstop. I'm happy that she could find such a wonderful friend."

"Believe me," Arden said, looking over at me and smiling. "I'm the lucky one."

I grinned. "You really do make me wish I was gay."

She shrugged. "Nah. You'd be *way* too overpowered. If you were this beautiful, this smart, *and* gay, it would just be unfair. Had to nurf you somewhere, kid. Sorry."

"Okay!" My mom said, clapping her hands and motioning us together. "Come on. Let me be the annoying mom and take some pictures."

Arden and I squeezed together for a bunch of photos and then loaded into my car and headed out for the dance. It actually made me laugh as we pulled into the parking lot. I had never seen a school at night. The closest I got to visiting school for any reason that wasn't related to academics, was debate tournaments that took place on the weekends. Seeing my school all lit up for the night with music thundering from inside was a sight to behold indeed.

It wasn't quite prom, so people weren't dressed to the nines, but everyone had put on their best semi-formal attire and was filtering through the front door with energy buzzing all around. Sadie Hawkins was traditionally a country-themed dance, but instead of going kitschy with hay bales and blow-up animals, they'd gone for a country chic motif, decorating the inside of the auditorium like the inside of a barn, but one that had been decorated for a wedding or other formal event.

Twinkling lights hung from fake beams, and barn doors stood against the walls in different places for people to take pictures in front of. The typical vault of the auditorium had been mechanically lowered to create a flat surface, and all the seats were gone, folded into the floor. Instead there were tables with school colored tablecloths and floral arrangements on top. There was a band performing on the stage, and the people playing looked familiar to me—I was pretty sure they actually attended the school. For about fifty feet between the stage and the tables, there was a rustic barn dance floor, and to the left and right of the dance floor, decorative barrels and crates were topped with food and drinks.

"Wow," I said as I walked in. "This is much nicer than anything my old school ever did."

"When you live in the rich district, this is what your tax dollars pay for," Arden said with a smile. "Come on. I want one of those lame couple-y pictures in front of the barn doors. I'm feeling nostalgic."

Arden and I drifted over to one of the photo stations and took a few pictures just the two of us, and then when we noticed more of our friends standing nearby, we invited them for some as well. In another feat of technological marvel, the pictures were automatically sent to our school apps when we scanned a podium near the camera so that we could print them or upload them to social media.

"Oh, I'm having this one framed," Arden said, holding out one of us with the rest of our core crew from debate. "I'm setting it right on my desk."

I was flipping between a couple of me and Arden together and my stomach tightened. We looked so happy, and I couldn't remember any time that I'd looked *that* happy with Lucky. All of Arden's jokes aside, she was just a really good friend. Had I just been that blind to Lucky's phony friendship all along?

"Uh, Aria?" Arden said.

"Sorry," I said, not looking up. "I was just missing Lucky."

"Well, you don't have to miss him for much longer," she replied.

I looked up at her. "What?" She nodded in the direction of the door, and Lucky was wandering into the auditorium in a black button-up shirt and black slacks. "What?!" He was scanning the growing sea of students, and terrified he was looking for me, I grabbed Arden's arm and snatched her behind one of the barn door setups. "What is he doing here?"

"Creepy," Arden said. "Do you think he's like stalking you now or something?"

A shiver ran down my spine. Had *that* much insanity been hiding just beneath the surface the entire time. "How did he even get in? You need a school app with tickets!"

"Your guess is as good as mine," Arden said. "Wait…" Her eyes zeroed in, and it looked as if someone had smacked her across the face with a frying pan. "No… I'm not seeing what I think I'm seeing, right?"

Following her gaze over to where Lucky was standing, I watched in shock as Hannah walked into the dance and locked her arm in his. He smiled at her and pointed further into the dance, and Hannah nodded and then they set off in the direction of the dance floor.

"He's here with Hannah?" I said, then I looked back at Arden, who was still staring after them like she was in physical pain. "Arden?"

Arden retreated totally behind the barn doors and slapped herself up against the wall. "Are they dating, do you think?"

Oh...

"I mean, last week notwithstanding, Lucky and I had been talking constantly. I imagine if he was dating someone who went to *my* new school, he would have mentioned it. Especially someone like Hannah." Then it hit me. "Yeah. He just confessed to me! I would certainly like to hope that he wouldn't do that if he was seeing someone."

Arden nodded. "Yeah, that's true, but then I'm back to thinking he pulled all of this to come here and keep an eye on you. Either way, I'm quickly learning I do *not* like that guy. He's screwing with you *and* Hannah."

"You stay here," I said.

"What?"

I stormed around the barn doors and threaded my way into the crowd. Hannah had stopped at one of the tables where I noticed some of the Pops were already standing, including Tristan. He looked unbelievable in a dark blue blazer with matching pants, pointed light gray shoes, and a matching undershirt. His hair was simply styled, and he had a silver watch on his wrist. He was smiling and laughing with his friends, but his eyes caught mine as I was passing. My stomach clenched and a swell of emotions burned up inside of me.

He gave me a gentle, warm smile, and so much passion poured from the look in his eyes that it almost froze me in place. He lifted his hand and waved, which I was surprised to see on its own because all of his friends could clearly see him do it. When they noticed it and followed his gaze over to me, he didn't stop, keeping his hand up, and I didn't know what to make of it.

Had something changed?

I broke his gaze and continued towards the dance floor. Lucky was standing near one of the food setups, and figuring out what was up with him was my goal for the time being. I couldn't afford to be distracted by Tristan. Lucky's presence there was problematic for more than one reason, and I had to get to the bottom of it.

When I finally reached him, I tapped him on the shoulder and he turned around, lighting up when he saw me. "Aria! I've been looking all over for you!"

"What are you doing here?" I asked.

"I came with my friend Hannah," Lucky said. "We lived in the same neighborhood growing up. We weren't incredibly tight or anything, and we never went to the same school, but we reconnected a handful of months ago."

"You mean around September when I started going here?" I asked.

Lucky's eyes widened and then softened. "I... was worried about you."

"Does she think you're here because you like her?" I asked. "You confessed to me just two weeks ago. What if I had said yes?"

"Then I would have stopped talking to Hannah immediately," Lucky said.

My jaw dropped. "Don't you hear how fucked up that is? How can you say it so simply?" Then I recoiled. "Oh my god. It's because she's friends with Tristan. It was the same thing with her. You were just dealing with her so long as you could use her, just like me?"

"No!" Lucky yelped. "You mean way more than that to me."

"I can't believe it. How long have you been this horrible of a person?" I asked.

Lucky reached out. "Aria…"

I smacked his hand away. "Don't. Don't touch me. You need to tell Hannah what you're up to and leave."

"Why should I?" Lucky said. "I'll stay here if I want to." His demeanor shifted in an instant, and my heart broke.

What happened to my best friend?

"I feel like I don't even know who you are anymore."

All I could do was turn around and walk away from him. Emotions were welling up in my eyes, and I knew I needed to step outside and get some fresh air for a moment. It was upsetting to me that I'd been tricked into such an empty and meaningless friendship. This man that I thought actually cared about me was willing to go to such nasty lengths to stake some unearned claim on me like that.

There were still a lot of students arriving at the dance, so once I was out the front door, I cut to the left and walked over to one of the outdoor work pods and sat down. Was I just *that* terrible at reading people? How many other people in my life was I completely misjudging?

"Aria?" I looked over and Tristan was standing there,

watching me with concern. "Are you okay? You bolted out of there kind of fast."

"I'm fine," I said. "You can go."

"Okay…" he said, turning to walk away, but then he stopped and turned back. "Actually, no. I'm sorry. Whatever your answer is after this, I'll drop it, but I just have a few things I have to say."

25

TRISTAN

I looked down at Aria, knowing that I shouldn't say anything. Hannah and Capito were right about the things they said, but they were assuming that all chance of me being with Aria was totally gone. It was clear in the way she looked back at me and the magnetic energy bouncing between us even then that it wasn't the case. If there was even a small part of Aria that would be willing to take one more risk with me, then there was a world in which I could be with her and just give up the worst of my friends and still be just fine.

Happiness wasn't totally out of my reach yet.

"I'm in love with you," I started. It was maybe too heavy of a way to go in, but I had to get the most important words out first. "I know that sounds kind of crazy because we haven't really dated or anything, but everyday I see you it gets worse. You're the only person I want. I haven't been sleeping well. Haven't been eating well. I just think about you and how much I fucked up. I'm not even going to beg you to forgive me for that stuff, because honestly, I don't deserve forgiveness for that."

"Okay…" Aria said.

She looked so beautiful in the glow of the moonlight, and I decided to take a risk and step a little closer to where she was sitting. She didn't stop me or back away, so I kept going until I was able to sit down next to her on the bench. My whole body throbbed with a desire to reach out and touch her, even just to hold her hand and pray that my feelings would bleed through me to her, but I kept myself at bay. Unless she invited it, I wouldn't do anything other than sit next to her.

"After my dad took me away from you, I was terrified. It wasn't just that I couldn't stand up for myself, even though I couldn't, it was that a really big piece of me still hung back with you. The part of me that wanted to boldly do the things I loved, the part of me that was willing to stand up in the face of adversity. Aria, you *were* my strength, so when we were taken from each other, it was like I didn't really have any anymore. Yeah, I worked out in the gym until I got physically strong, but that didn't change the fact that I never knew how to be strong from my core, like you were."

"That's obvious," Aria grumbled and I smiled. "It's not that hard, you know?"

"You know, if you'd said that a few weeks ago, I might have argued with you about it, but you're right, it's not. Not everyone is as strong as you, but it's easy to stand up for the things you care about. I'd spent so long doing the exact opposite of that, that when you needed me to show up and prove that I could do it for you, I didn't know how. I didn't have any of my own strength to use, but I found it. Wanna know how?"

"How?" Aria asked.

I sighed, looking up at the few stars I could see dotting the sky. "I was talking to Taylor at lunch a couple of weeks ago, and he said that I would maybe get over you when we graduated and I never saw you again. And I realized, nothing in my life scared me more than the thought of losing you again." I looked over at her. "I can't do it. I won't survive going back to a life without you in it. I don't want to do that."

Aria nodded lightly. "I understand what you mean."

"Really?" I asked.

She looked at me through an annoyed, although pained, gaze. "Yeah. How do you think I felt? We bumped into each other again and I couldn't believe it. After being snatched away from you, I thought we were just going to pick up where we left off. I thought we were headed… somewhere, but then you were all ashamed of me and—"

"I'm not ashamed of you, Aria," I said. "I never was."

"That's not true. You trashed me in front of your friends. You ran away from me so that they wouldn't see us together in public," she said.

"That wasn't about you," I said. "What about you would I be ashamed of? I wasn't embarrassed of you, I was embarrassed of me."

Aria sat up a little straighter, furrowing her brow. "What?"

"Those times when I was pulling back from you, it was because I was embarrassed that I was just this joke. I wasn't the guy that my friends thought I was, I wasn't the guy that you thought I was. Hell, I wasn't even the person I thought I was. I was an embarrassment to myself."

"Well, knowing that now, have you learned anything else about who you are?"

I nodded. "Yeah. I've learned I'm a guy with very strong feelings for a pretty astounding woman. She won't talk to me, but I can't blame her." That brought a small smile to Aria's face. "I'm a guy that actually does have some true friends. People who wouldn't mock me or leave me just because I want to be in a relationship with that woman. In fact, Hannah even admitted that she thinks she's beautiful."

Aria raised her eyebrow. "She didn't say that."

I held up my hand. "Hand to god." I took a deep breath. It felt like it was going well. Just taking the honest road. Not being afraid of the consequences. Being with Aria was worth any cost. "I'm a guy who knows how badly he fucked up and knows that he doesn't deserve forgiveness, but if you were willing to give it. I promise I won't let you down this time. We can walk back into that dance right now hand-in-hand, I wouldn't give a fuck."

"Really?" Aria said, her smile growing.

"Really."

She looked at me for a minute and I could see her mind calculating. I waited, not about to pressure her into doing anything, when all of a sudden, she threw herself forward and her lips landed on mine.

And I melted so hard we almost fell off the bench. I threw my arms up and wrapped around her and held her close and her arms encircled my neck and held on just as tight. Like all the other times we'd touched, having our hands on one another didn't stay kosher for too long. Aria's fingers caressed the back of my neck, sending chills down my spine, and my hands eventually found their way down to her exposed thighs. I pushed, pressing her to the back of the bench and leaning against her instead, and Aria's breath quickened, but she didn't stop me.

"Shit," I grumbled. "We can't do this out here." Aria pulled back and I clenched onto her. "Not because I'm embarrassed, just because the things I want to do would definitely get us arrested if we were caught out here doing them." I kissed her again and flicked her hair out of her face. "Wanna get out of here?"

She looked conflicted, which didn't make me happy. We'd been stopped twice before, this time, I wanted things to unfold as we clearly both wanted them to.

"I shouldn't leave," she said. "I'm here with Arden and…"

I sighed. "Right. No. You're right. That'd be a shitty thing to do. I mostly just came out here to make sure you were okay. You looked pretty disturbed."

"Yeah. It's a whole situation…" She frowned. "In fact, I should probably get back in there. Arden needs me, and as happy as I am to hear you say we could go in together…"

"No, no, I get it. You're here with someone, I understand." I was disappointed, but it felt like we were headed in a better direction. "Okay, well… Can we see each other tomorrow maybe? We could get dinner?"

Aria nodded. "Okay. Yeah. I'd like that."

Relief didn't describe my feelings. I'd done it. I'd actually convinced Aria to give me another chance.

I wasn't going to fuck this one up.

"Okay. I'd say I'll call you, but you're gonna have to unblock me first."

Aria blushed a little, but chuckled. "Yeah. I'll do that right away."

"Okay." I stood up, taking her by the hand and pulling her up with me. She fell a little off balance, which was fine by me, because I caught her and used the momentum to kiss her one last time for the night. "I'll see you tomorrow then?"

"See you tomorrow."

We peeled ourselves apart, as difficult as it was, and Aria walked back towards the door. Just before she walked in, she turned and looked over at me and waved. I waved back and she played coy and bolted inside.

I sunk back down onto the bench in the work pod and sighed. Victory had never felt so sweet before. Starting tomorrow, everything changed, and for the better at that. I no longer had any fear that the friends I was closest with would judge me for my relationship, and the woman of my dreams was finally going to be mine.

Whatever deed I'd done to earn that night's fortune, I was glad I'd done it.

Eventually, I made my own way back inside and returned to the table where I'd left my friends. Hannah seemed poised to start asking questions right away, but something much more important caught my attention.

The guy that Aria had spoken to right before running outside was sitting next to Hannah at our table. "Who are you?" I asked.

Hannah held out her hand. "Oh, Tris. This is Lucky, my date."

"Wait… *this* is the guy from the other school?" I asked. I'd just assumed he was a kid lower on the totem pole that I didn't recognize. "If you don't go here, then how do you know Aria?"

The question seemed to make Lucky immediately

nervous and Hannah shifted her gaze slowly in his direction. "You know Aria?"

"No. Who's that?" Lucky responded.

"What?" I said. "I watched her walk up to you and then you two got into what appeared to be a very heated argument. You even tried to grab her arm a few times. I was about to come over there when she suddenly ran outside and I went after her instead."

Hannah watched him with fury in her gaze and it was clear she had no idea that Aria and Lucky had any connection to one another. "How do you know her?"

"W-we… uh…" Lucky flipped his eyes between me, Hannah, and the others sitting at the table, then finally he jumped up. "I gotta use the bathroom," he blurted and bolted out of the auditorium.

Nijah, who was also sitting there, took a sip of her drink. "Uh, looks to me like that guy was playing you. Is he an ex of Aria's or something?"

Hannah pulled out her phone and navigated to a few different social media sites until she was able to find one for Lucky. She flipped a bit down the page, until we started to run into selfies of Aria and Lucky together. It was obvious from the way the pictures were notated, that the two were just friends, but then what would Lucky go to such lengths to come to the dance for?

"I didn't even think to check," Hannah said. "He told me he didn't do much on socials because he wasn't a computer guy." She slammed her phone down. "I'm so fucking dumb."

"No," I said, putting an arm around her. "That guy was clearly up to something. I just wish I had any idea what it was."

26

ARIA

After what had happened with Tristan and Lucky showing up out of the blue with Hannah, it became clear very quickly that it was better for Arden and I to just leave the dance. We hung around for another forty-five minutes tops, then we said goodbye to our friends and just left.

Arden was clearly out of sorts after seeing Hannah with Lucky, even more so after I told her what he'd said. At first, I believed that the situation between Arden and Hannah was just friends gone wrong, but after seeing the shattered look on her face when she thought Hannah may be dating the guy, I realized that my understanding was totally false. I felt like a shitty friend. She'd been doing so much holding me up while I was dealing with all the drama with Tristan, that I didn't even notice the way she was feeling about Hannah.

And I was keeping her and Hannah in close quarters while I went back and forth with Tristan. I was being horrible.

So it was time for me to take care of her. We stopped by a convenience store on the way home, loaded up on ice cream, chips, and just about any other junk food we could find, then we went back to my house and buried ourselves beneath mountains of covers. I gave Arden some cozy pajamas to sleep in and let her borrow my bed and Hazelnut for the night, while I cozied up in a recliner I had in the corner of my room.

"Okay, out with it," I said. "Tell me about Hannah." Arden took a big scoop of her ice cream and put it all in her mouth all at once, then looked at me as if she couldn't speak. I shook my head. "That's fine. I'll wait."

Arden sighed, but worked her way through the rest of her bite and then frowned at me. "I don't really like talking about it."

"Well if you don't want to, that's fine, but you've been there for me for all this Tristan stuff and I want to be there for you too. Even before I give you the update."

She tilted her head. "There's an update."

"Yep, but I don't want to bother you with anymore Tristan stuff until you're feeling better. I saw the look on your face when you saw Hannah with Lucky. Do you wanna talk about it?" I said. "If I've learned anything from our friendship, it's that people like us who allow our friends to rely on us, tend not to rely on others. It wasn't until I met you that I allowed someone to bear some of my weight, and let me tell you, it makes a world of difference. Use me that way too. Let me bear some of your weight. I promise, you'll feel better."

"But, ugh, feelings," Arden whined.

"I know. They're awful. Do it anyway," I said.

"Fine." Arden set her bowl off to the side. "Well, I guess you could say she was my *awakening*."

"She's how you knew you were gay?" I asked.

Arden nodded. "Yeah. I mean when I was younger, I didn't really get it. You know, I was always just really excited she was coming over to hang out, and I figured when we were playing family and she was the mom and I was the dad that it was normal because we were the only two there and we each had to play a role. Then at one point in middle school, I mentioned that I would like it if I could marry her one day, and they told me that I had to marry a man. I didn't understand that and it seriously fucked me up."

"Well yeah," I said. "How could it not."

"But you know, I thought maybe I'd just gotten it wrong. So then when all my friends were developing crushes, I tried to force it a few times, but it didn't matter what I did. The one I liked and wanted to be with was Hannah. That never changed. I thought I was messed up in the head or something. My grades started slipping, I started using drugs, it was bad." Then Arden smiled. "But Hannah pulled me back. She told me she loved me, in a friendly way, and that she didn't want to see me hurt myself. All our freshman year she was like this annoying gnat. Are you eating? Did you bathe? Did you go outside today? You didn't do any drugs did you? Let's go shopping. Let's go to the park." She laughed. "She wouldn't leave me the hell alone for more than a few minutes."

"And you fell in love?"

"Hard," Arden said. "And fast. I came to terms with my sexuality after that. I learned about what it meant to be a woman who liked other women, but really even that didn't matter to me. It wasn't like I wanted just *any* woman, I wanted Hannah."

"Then you guys fell apart sophomore year?" I asked.

Arden nodded. "She grew boobs, which, by the way, was another confirmation that I was, in fact, gay."

I laughed. "Well, sure, that'll do it."

"She got her dorky braces removed, which I actually thought were really cute. She used to keep her hair cut in a bob, but she let it grow out and fall all over her shoulders and started wearing clothes that showed more of her skin. It was like a scene out of a movie when we walked into school the first day of 10th grade. Everyone stopped and stared. To me, she'd always been beautiful and was even more so with confidence. It was just like they were all seeing what I'd seen all that time. Then Tristan asked her out, and she was *so* excited to be one of the popular kids. She didn't even really like him, I don't think. Just accepted."

"Maybe that was why their relationship didn't last long?"

Arden shrugged. "Maybe, but I think Hannah would have forced it. It was Tristan that ended things with her. Though in hindsight, looking at you and looking at her, he probably just didn't realize he had a type and she didn't fill it." She scoffed. "Hell, it may have even been Ceradi that coaxed him into doing it."

I took a handful of chips and crushed them over what was left of my ice cream and took a huge bite, letting the salty-sweet combo melt in my mouth. "I could see that. She's nuts."

"That's an understatement," Arden said. "Well, you

pretty much know the rest of the story. She cut me off, and that was it."

"I'm sorry," I said.

"I tried my fucking damndest to get over her, but fuck, love hangs on," Arden said.

I nodded. "So I'm learning."

"Okay." She held up her hands. "I'm tapping out. Your turn."

"Now I feel bad," I said.

"Why?" Arden said. "If one of us is having some luck, it should be celebrated."

"Tristan… I think he finally gets it. He said all the right things, even said that those times when he was retreating from me, it wasn't because he was ashamed of me, it was because he was ashamed of himself."

Arden started to clap. "Yes, Tristan."

"We kissed… well, we did a little more than that," I smiled, my skin burning as it remembered his hands sliding up my thigh.

"Aria," Arden said in a fake shocked voice. "Exhibitionism."

"Amost," I said. "He wanted to leave, but I had a date I couldn't ditch."

Arden's face turned into a touched expression. "You turned down sex with the guy you like for me?"

"I did." She jumped out of the bed and leapt over to where I was, wrapping her arms around me and squeezing me, nearly toppling over the armchair. "We're gonna fall!"

"I'm the luckiest girl in the world," Arden said. "Never leave me."

I hugged her back. "I don't plan to."

With all of our emotions out in the open, we both felt much better and spent the rest of the night laughing at stupid movies until we eventually passed out from a sugar-crash. My dreams were filled with blissful images of me being in a happy, loving relationship with Tristan and having Arden at my side as my best friend. It was the life I'd been after so long, and I couldn't believe I was right on the precipice of it.

At least I thought I was.

"Aria," Arden whispered as she shook me awake. "Wake up." I rubbed my eyes and looked up to where Arden was hovering over me with a look on her face like she'd just seen a ghost. "I'm sorry to wake you up for this shit, but I wanted you to see it as soon as possible to try and do damage control."

"Damage control?" I said. "For what?"

Arden handed her phone to me and my heart jumped into my throat when I realized I was looking at a picture of Tristan and I making out from the night before. At first it didn't seem so bad, but then I noticed where the picture was posted. It wasn't on Tristan's personal page as a decla-ration for our new romance.

It was on a page called "Plow the Cow."

I looked down at the picture's caption and read it aloud. "Today's entry comes from Tristan Castrone from North-west End High School, who earns a whopping one hundred points for his photo. Fifty for the plow and fifty for the cow."

Arden sank down onto the edge of the bed. "That's fucking cold."

"It's got over a thousand likes and comments already

and it's only from an hour ago," I said. My stomach was completely sick and I felt like I was going to pass out. After everything he'd said. After how close we'd gotten. How could Tristan do that to me?

It was all just an elaborate joke?

27

TRISTAN

"I'm gonna fucking kill him!" were the first words I heard in the morning, followed quickly by the feeling of being snatched out of my bed. I hit the floor with a painful thud, half a second later feeling a fist across my face.

"Ow!" I clamored my eyes open to see through the haze and pain and Taylor was hovering over me, already pulling his fist back to bring it down and punch me again. "What the f—" He slammed it down and I just barely managed to duck out of the way. "Taylor? What the hell are you doing?"

"Shut the fuck up!" Taylor lifted his fist again, but my dad bolted into the room and hooked his arm around Taylor's and dragged him backwards off of me. Taylor fought against his hold. "Let me go! He thinks he's a big man who can just do whatever he wants to people, I'll fucking kick his ass like a man!"

My dad slammed him up against a wall. "Calm down and watch your mouth in my goddamn house."

Andrea slipped around them and into the room, where she must have noticed me bleeding because she clawed a shirt up from my floor and held it up to my nose. "Tilt your head back." She walked around me to go into my bathroom, but the second she was out of the way, Taylor charged me again, slamming me backwards onto my bed, causing it to splinter and snap beneath our weight. "Taylor!" she screeched.

Taylor grabbed the edges of the shirt I was sleeping in and lifted me a little before slamming me down. "How could you do something like that?"

"What are you…?" I finally got a good look at his face and saw that there were tears in his eyes. He was furious, yes, but more than that he seemed heartbroken. I thought we were in a better place after we hashed things out about Aria at lunch a couple of weeks ago. In fact, I couldn't wait to make things official with Aria so that I could surprise him by posting to my socials about it. "What are you talking about?"

"Don't play stupid with me. I'll punch you again," Taylor said. "Explain yourself!"

"What'd you do?" My dad asked behind Taylor.

I held up my hands. "I swear to god, I have no clue what he's talking about."

"Taylor," Andrea snapped. "Get up."

Taylor's nostrils were flaring, but after staring down at me for a few more minutes, he got up. Andrea helped me carefully navigate the wood of my broken bed frame and guided me over to sit in my desk chair. My back stung and Andrea lifted my shirt and whimpered. "Oh no. Okay. Take this off. You're bleeding."

My dad facepalmed Taylor and shoved him to the side

so hard he fell over. "Don't just fucking storm in here and start fighting! You seriously hurt your brother!"

"Stop it!" Andrea yelped. "No one else touches anyone unless it's me tending to injuries!"

Taylor stood up off the floor and sat down in my gaming chair, and glared at me. "You still haven't explained yourself."

"I already told you I don't know what you're talking about," I hissed back, letting out a yowl when Andrea touched my back with a towel that I assumed she'd maybe put some sort of peroxide or other cleaning agent on. "Don't come in here and fucking punch me for nothing."

"If you both don't stop swearing in my goddamn house —" my dad started, but then Andrea glared at him and he recoiled. "What? I'll take it outside."

"No more violence," she said. "Honestly. You're peas from the same pod."

My dad looked at Taylor. "Even if he knows, we don't, so tell me what the hell you're talking about."

"Tristan thought it would be real funny to play a big, elaborate joke on a girl whose only crime was liking him," Taylor said.

"What?" my dad said. "What kind of joke?" Taylor pulled his phone out and I watched in confusion as he handed it over to my dad. He took the phone and looked down at it, scrolled a little bit and then looked over at me. I'd never seen my dad look at me in such a way, and more than it was scary, it was upsetting. "How could you do this? I've raised you better than this."

"Do. What?" I growled.

My dad walked over and handed me Taylor's phone and I looked down at it, with Andrea looking over my shoulder. On the screen was a picture of Aria and I kissing from the night before on a hate social page called "Plow the Cow." I'd heard of it before from Ceradi, but I knew for a fact she hated the page because someone submitted a picture of her to it once, sending her into a tizzy, not to mention an insanely unhealthy diet.

Under the picture was a caption that said I was the one who'd submitted the photo and was the day's victor with a hundred points, fifty for the cow, and fifty for the plow.

"How could..." Andrea started and I opened my mouth to respond, but then she shot a look in my dad and Taylor's direction. "How could you honestly believe that he did this? You're his two biggest role models and you respect women more than yourselves. Watching you, how could you think that he'd do something so horrible. Honestly. I'm disappointed in the two of you."

"It says his name and handle," Taylor said.

"So? It's the internet, people can say whatever they want. It could have been anyone who knew his name and handle that submitted the page under his name. He clearly wasn't aware this photo was being taken."

I looked up at Andrea. "Thank you."

I walked over to my busted bed and pulled my phone from the wreckage and saw that my phone was blazing with notifications. Despite the fact that Ceradi hated the page, my group message was alive with them telling me how funny it was. They were being particularly cruel, but I knew they weren't the ones who submitted the picture.

I had a feeling I knew who did it, though.

Instead of explaining myself to Taylor, because I was still hurt that he honestly believed I'd do that, I just took a shirt from my dresser and limped out of the room.

"Where are you going?" my dad asked.

"To figure this out," I said. "I think I know who did it."

"Tris!" Taylor bolted out from my bedroom and I stopped in the hallway and looked back at him. "I'm… I'm sorry."

"It's my fault. Because of the way I acted at my party, it made you believe I was capable of this." I swallowed to hold back emotions. "Can you see if you can get the picture taken down?"

Taylor nodded. "Something like that has to be illegal. I'll have the whole page down within an hour."

"Thanks," I said. "See if you can find out who sent it in. An email address or handle maybe."

"Yeah. I'll call you when I know more," Taylor said.

It was still pretty early in the morning, but I didn't care. I got in my car and started off for Hannah's house. I needed to be with a friend and I needed to get to the bottom of the post. I was so close to Aria and now this?

To confirm what I already feared, I tried to call her, but the call never went through. I was blocked.

Not shocking.

It was the same thing with Aria. Because of the way I'd already behaved, it made this not that far of a stretch.

Failing with Aria, I called Hannah, getting an answer immediately after the first ring. "Tristan."

"Hannah, I swear to god—"

"Who do you think I am?" she snapped. "I know you didn't do this. Not with the way you feel about Aria. You know who I *do* think did it though?"

My hands strangled the steering wheel. "Lucky."

"That must have been what he was up to last night," Hannah said. "He told me that he had to use the bathroom not long after you went outside. He must have followed you, heard you guys talking and decided to take matters into his own hands. Can you come over? I've been looking into him all morning."

"I'm already halfway there," I replied.

When I got to Hannah's house, she came out instead of inviting me in. She hopped into the passenger's side of my car and looked at me sadly, then her eyes popped out. "My god! What happened to your face?"

"Taylor thought I did this," I replied.

Hannah's sad expression came back. "My parents have seen the post and are pretty livid too. Until we have definitive proof that it wasn't you, I should probably keep you out of there."

"Great," I said, irritated. "At least Taylor knows it wasn't me now. He's working on finding out directly from the page who sent the picture and then is going to get, at least the picture taken down, but he's hoping for the whole page."

With nowhere to go in particular, and not feeling confident that any place we went would be safe, I just started driving around the city while Hannah gave me the rundown of what she'd found.

"Apparently, Lucky and Aria are best friends. They went to high school together before she transferred, and even work together. But then a couple of weeks ago, he started sharing really creepy, 'nice guy' posts and stuff about being friendzoned. I think he confessed to her and she turned him down. He even talks about guys being able to be horrible and still get the girl while guys like him can't get a leg up. She must have mentioned you at some point."

"When did you two start talking?" I asked.

She let out a little growl. "Yeah, that's the worst part. Lucky added me as a friend a long time ago, back when it was exciting to just have as many friends as possible, but only reached out to me *after* you and Aria reconnected. I'm not quiet about our friendship. If she mentioned to him that you two had run into each other and he realized you were my friend, it's highly likely that that's the *only* reason he reached out to me. To keep an eye on you, or try and ruin your reputation or what, I don't know. When I brought up Sadie Hawkins, he jumped all over it. I'm certain his plan was to do this to you to get Aria to leave you alone and go with him."

"If he cared about her at all, how could he ever let a picture of her be on a page like that?" Rage boiled up in my body and I wanted to get my hands around that guy's neck more than I could say. My car phone rang, and I slammed the button to answer so hard, my finger stung. "Hello?"

"The page is gone," Taylor said. "Once I mentioned a class action lawsuit of all the people whose pictures they uploaded, they were quick to oblige."

"Did you get any info about who *actually* sent the picture?" I asked.

"Yeah," he replied. "The handle was LuckyLuck121090."

Hannah held up the social media page she was looking at, and the handle was the same. "There's our proof."

"Thanks Taylor," I said.

"Yeah. I'm sorry again," he responded, then just hung up without waiting for a response.

"He's not having a good day," Hannah said.

"No, but I'll deal with that later. For now, I need to show this to Aria. Will you come with me?" I asked.

"Of course," she said. "Do you have her address?"

I sighed. "No, and I'm blocked so I can't call her."

"That's okay. I have it," Hannah said.

I looked over at her. "How do you have it?"

She gave me a nervous glance, but then took a deep breath. "Back when Arden and I were still talking, we joined a location group so we could see each other. I still have hers, and I can see she's not a home. With all this shit, I'm guessing she's at Aria's."

"Why do you still keep up with her location if you aren't friends anymore?" I asked.

But Hannah ignored me entirely, plugging her phone into my stereo system and starting the navigation to Arden's location. She clearly didn't want to talk about it, and in the state I was in, I was in no place to help her. We had to take our problems one step at a time, and the current problem was letting Aria know that her best friend was a total fake before he could hurt her any further.

TRISTAN

When I pulled my car up in front of the house that Hannah's directions took us to, I recognized Aria's car in the driveway outside. There was another one parked on the road, but I could tell by the look on Hannah's face that it was Arden's.

"When was the last time you talked to her?" I asked. "Like not indirectly."

Hannah took a deep breath. "Two years ago."

"Are you sure you can do this? I don't want to drag you into anything that's going to hurt you. I've done enough hurting the people around me," I said.

She nodded, though still with her glossy, far-off gaze. "Yeah. I can do it."

"Okay. Thank you." I reached over and rubbed the top of her head. "You're an amazing friend."

She forced a smile, but it was ingenuine. "We're about to be face to face with someone who would argue that point to their grave."

"Maybe we deal with that problem next?" I asked. "It's probably high time that you guys hashed it out."

"Believe me when I say this," she said, taking a deep breath. "It is a much bigger problem than it seems like on the surface." She shook her head, closing her eyes for a minute, then when she opened them again, she locked them into mine. "Let's go deal with Aria. Now's not the time for all of this mess."

"Okay," I said. We climbed out of the car and walked up the path, and to my surprise, Hannah rushed a little ahead so that she was leading the way. "Hannah—"

"Trust me. Arden's opening up this door, and if she sees your face, she's swinging. You've been punched enough for the day."

"Really dedicated friend, huh?" I said.

She shook her head. "You have no idea."

Taking her advice, I kept myself back a little as Hannah walked up to the door and knocked. There was silence for a minute and I was beginning to wonder if they'd seen us approaching and were choosing to ignore us, but then the door opened and, as Hannah expected, Arden appeared on the other side.

There was pain and anger in her face as she looked down at Hannah. "What are you doing here?" Then her eyes drifted up to me. She threw out a finger in my direction and her eyes went wild with fury. "No!"

"Arden, listen to me," Hannah said. "He didn't do this."

Arden scoffed. "It has his fucking name on it. I'm not dumb. All his friends have been commenting on the picture congratulating him for the past hour."

Hannah nodded. "I know. I know how bad it looks, but

we have proof." Arden was still glaring at me, so Hannah reached up, put her hands on either side of Arden's face and forced her to look at her. I could see in both their reactions as they touched that there was a lot more between them than I knew. "Listen to me. Would I be here if I wasn't serious? Trust me. We have proof that this wasn't him, and Aria deserves to know who is really trying to hurt her."

Arden went quiet, watching Hannah with conflict deeply seeded in her gaze. "If he hurts her—"

"He's not going to hurt your precious Aria," Hannah snapped, pulling her hands back. "Please? Can we come in and explain?"

I made a note to myself to unpack things with Hannah a little more thoroughly when all of this was over. Clearly, I'd missed a lot.

Finally, though, Arden stepped aside and let us into the house. It didn't seem like Aria's mom was home, which was good. Arden hissed, "Wait here," and walked up the stairs, leaving Hannah and me standing alone in the front hall.

"Are you okay?" I asked. Hannah shook her head and turned towards me, tears in her eyes. She buried her head into my chest and I wrapped my arms around her. "Hey, it's okay. I'm sorry for bringing you here. I didn't know."

"It's okay," she whimpered. "I don't want you and Aria to end up like us. I'll be okay."

"End up like you?" I asked. "Hannah, what haven't you told me?" She looked up at me, her eyes glistening, and it broke me. I just pulled her head back against me. "Don't worry. We'll talk about it later."

"Thank you," she said.

After about five minutes, the time I imagined it took Arden to convince Aria to come down at all, they came down the stairs. Arden led, keeping a defensive position in front of Aria, and I could see Aria's red eyes and puffy cheeks behind her. It killed me. If I ever got my hands on that Lucky guy, he'd be sorry.

"Aria," I said.

"Arden said you have proof this wasn't you," she said, cutting straight to the chase. "Show me."

We walked into the dining room and sat down around the table. Hannah sat in the seat between Aria and I so that she could show her the different things she'd found on her phone, including the posts on Lucky's social media about being a nice guy and friendzoned. She explained the suspicious timing with which Lucky reached out to her to begin with and then looked at me to finish things off.

"Taylor's a lawyer, I don't know if I ever told you that or not. Anyway, I asked him to look into the page, and he confirmed the handle of the person that sent the picture into the page was LuckyLuck121090," I explained.

Hannah slid her phone over to Aria and pointed at the handle. "It's the same."

Arden had been scrolling through the page on her own. "Aria, do you have this social media page? He's like… obsessed with you."

"No. I didn't even know he was on social media. He would tell me all the time that he didn't like social media," Aria said.

Hannah nodded. "Yeah. He told me the same thing."

I saw the wind knocked out of Aria's sails, and I felt bad. "How long were you two friends?"

"Since the sixth grade," she said. Tears rose to her eyes, and while Arden put her hand on Aria's back to rub,

Hannah put hers on Aria's hand. "I can't believe it was all nothing."

"I'm sorry," I said.

"For what? This isn't your fault," Aria replied.

"I mean, maybe not, but you never would have believed it if I'd treated you better. We probably wouldn't have even been in that situation at all if I wasn't such an idiot. I'm sorry that anything I did has caused you pain."

Aria looked up at me and forced a smile. "It's okay. I'm glad this wasn't you." Then she turned and looked at Arden. "I have to go talk to Lucky."

"I'm coming with you," Arden, Hannah, and I all said at the exact same time.

Aria let out a little chuckle which made us all smile, but she shook her head. "I know you all have your own reasons for wanting to come, but I need to do this on my own."

"I'm not letting you go there alone when he's unhinged," Arden said.

"I feel the same way," I said. "He's already hurt you enough."

Aria looked between Arden and I. "If either of you come, there's gonna be a fight, am I wrong?" I looked at Arden and she looked at me and we both knew that she was totally right. "And Hannah, I don't know you very well, but your issues with Lucky and mine are totally different. I think you should kick his ass, but that's not really what I'm going there for."

Hannah nodded. "Yeah, you're right."

"I'll meet him in a public place and be totally safe," Aria said. "I'll be okay. I'm no weakling."

"That's for sure," I said.

"Thank you guys for coming and explaining everything. I feel better," Aria said, then she smiled at me. "Thanks."

"Of course," I said. "I'd do anything for you." Arden and Aria walked us over to the door so we could leave, but before I got too far, I grabbed Aria's hands and looked her in the eyes. "Can we meet up later? Talk?"

"Um…" She was still just barely holding her emotions back. "I think I need to take things just one step at a time right now."

It was frustrating, but I was understanding. I wanted to give her as much space as she needed to sort things out. I didn't want to risk the little bit of trust I'd built back. "Yeah, of course. Take your time." She pulled her hands from mine and it left me with a sense of foreboding, but I did the best I could to ignore it. "Just so you know, Taylor got that entire page pulled down. So our picture isn't up anymore."

Aria nodded. "Thank him for me."

"I will. You be careful?" I said.

Aria took a deep breath. "Don't worry. I will."

29

ARIA

I had no qualms about lying to Lucky to get him to come and meet me. I wanted his guard down so that when I confronted him I could catch him off guard and make sure that I got the full truth. Hannah and Tristan had enough to prove that Lucky had been the one who sent the photo into the hate page, but the rest of the details were only what they surmised. I wanted the full story, not just about how the picture ended up on the page, but about our entire relationship and how things went so wrong.

So I told him that I wanted to talk to him in the wake of Tristan posting the picture and asked him to meet me at a cafe nearby. He was all too eager to come, probably feeling like he could be the knight in shining armor while I was upset about Tristan.

Boy was he in for a surprise.

The cafe was nice and busy for a Saturday morning, and because neither Lucky nor I had work for the day after the dance, we had plenty of time to talk. He owed me an explanation for everything that had happened and I wasn't leaving the cafe until I found out the truth.

"Aria!"

I looked over and Lucky was walking into the cafe, as I expected, full of light and hope. He held out his arms for a hug, and though it was ill-advised, I gave him one. He was my best friend after all, or he used to be, and I figured I could muster up that much. He gave me a tight squeeze, almost refusing to let go when I started to pull back, but he eventually released me, and I settled down into one side of the booth, Lucky into the other.

"So," I said. "I assume you've seen the post?"

"Yeah," he frowned, and it seemed so genuine that if I didn't know for a fact it was him, I could have almost been swayed that it wasn't. "I'm so sorry that he did that to you."

"It's crazy. He'd just told me that he was in love with me before that. I believed him, too. I nearly said it back," I said.

Lucky's expression went ghostly. "You're in love with him?"

"I think I might be," I said. "Although I might be in a bad situation. What do you think?"

"What do I think? Isn't it obvious? You need to stay away from him. Look what he did to you."

"Yeah, I mean, anyone who would send a picture like that of me to a page like that, must actually hate me, don't you think?"

Lucky stopped for a minute and then soldiered on. "Obviously."

"Because it's vile. I mean, not only is it a total invasion of my privacy, but to shame me and my body in that way. There would be absolutely no reason why I should forgive someone who has done that to me. There's no excuse for it."

"N-none," Lucky said. "None at all."

"So what should I do to the person who shared that picture of me?"

"You should never speak to them again, obviously," he said. "Cut them off for good."

I nodded. "Oh, good, thanks for that advice," I responded. "So before I walk away from you and never talk to you again… You need to tell me what I've done to you that is so horrible that you could send a picture of me to a page like that."

Lucky froze. "What?"

"I know that you're the one who sent the picture. Tristan's brother is a lawyer. They confirmed your handle, on the social media page that you told me that you don't have. You told Hannah that same thing, right? So neither of us would see the obsessive behavior on your page."

I could see the panic rising in Lucky's face, which was exactly what I wanted. I didn't want to give him a heads up that I was onto him, because I didn't want him to have a chance to weasel out of it or explain anything away. In the moment, he was freaking out, and couldn't find answers to my questions fast enough.

Even though it was clear in his gaze that he was trying.

"Don't," I said. "Don't look for an answer. Don't try and come up with an excuse. Be honest with me. If you ever want to breathe the same air as me ever again for the rest of your life, you need to tell me everything. The truth. From the beginning."

Lucky took a deep breath and then nodded. "Okay."

"Has our friendship ever been just a friendship, or has it

been this crazy, obsessive, entitlement from the beginning?"
I asked. "Be fucking real about it. Don't lie to me
anymore."

"No," Lucky said. "I mean, not in the sense that you're
saying. I've always had feelings for you since we first met.
You're beautiful and strong and smart. You stood up for me
when I couldn't stand up for myself, and in the years that
we were friends, I always wanted more with you. I really did
just think it would happen naturally. I was afraid of rejection, so I just kind of hoped we'd just wake up one day in a
different place and head in that direction. You kind of
became my whole world, so when you transferred schools, I
panicked. I had a feeling you'd meet someone, but then you
mentioned Tristan, and all that history that you guys had. It
wasn't just that I was jealous, but I saw the way you lit up
when you talked about him. I realized that you had never
looked at me like that. I think it let me know definitively
that we would never be that."

"So then you just threw away our friendship after that?
All I meant to you was a possible girlfriend in the future and
when it couldn't be that anymore, you figured that was it?"
I said.

"I made some bad decisions. I thought that maybe there
could still be a chance if you could see that Tristan didn't
care for you and how much I did, that you'd choose me.
The picture... it was a knee-jerk reaction when I heard him
say all that stuff to you and saw that you were giving into it.
I regretted it immediately, but it was already done, so I
guess I figured I may as well benefit from it if I could."

"You know, I'd mostly managed to fly under the radar
of the bullies at my school," I said. "They're probably
putting ammo in their guns for me right now."

Lucky's expression twisted in anguish. "I'm sorry."

"I don't want to hear it," I said. "I love you so much as my best friend, and if you had just come to me respectfully and said that you had feelings for me, but if I didn't reciprocate, then we couldn't be friends, it would have broken my heart, but I would have done that because I would never have wanted to hurt you. You didn't feel the same way I guess."

"I should have handled things differently," Lucky said.

"You shouldn't have handled things at all," I snapped back. "This wasn't a decision for you to make. You don't get to decide how my relationships go with everyone around me if they don't benefit you. That's not how friendships or romantic relationships work, and you're going to need to figure that out if you want to have any hope of having a meaningful relationship with someone again. As far as you and me goes, we're done." I stood up to walk past Lucky's seat and he reached out and grabbed my wrist. "Let me go."

"You said if I told you the truth, that there was a chance," he said.

My eyes widened and my jaw dropped. "I said no such thing. I said if you ever wanted to breathe the same air as me, you'd be honest. Think of what you just told me. Do you honestly expect me to stay friends with you after that? How delusional do you have to be."

He yanked on my arm so hard it hurt. "You don't get to just walk away from me after I bared myself like that."

"Watch me," I said, trying to pull my hand away, but he kept a firm grip. "Lucky. Let me go."

"No," he said, yanking again, and that time it attracted the attention of some college-age guys at a table near ours who immediately started to stand up. "You owe me."

"I don't owe you anything. Let me go."

"Hey," one of the guys said. "You heard her. Let her go."

"Mind your own fucking bus—" He didn't get the rest of the sentence out as my fist collided with his face. Everyone else in the cafe yelped or gasped, apart from the college guys, who cheered.

"Stay the fuck away from me, Tristan, and Hannah. If I catch you within 500 yards of any of us ever again, not only will I call the police, but I'll let the guy you tried to frame fuck you up the way he wants to."

Lucky glared up at me, but I had no sympathy for him. I stormed out of the cafe, thanking the college guys for their offers of help as I passed them, and drove myself back home. Though I wanted to just go in and take a bath and melt away for a bit, my mom's car was in the driveway, which wasn't a good sign considering she was supposed to be working all day.

"Mom?" I called out as I walked in.

"Aria!" she yelped. "Where have you been? I tried to call you."

"Sorry. I was taking care of some business," I responded. "What are you doing home? I thought you had to work this weekend."

"I heard some craziness about a page and a picture of you and Tristan? What's going on?"

"Lucky tried to sabotage things with Tristan and me by sending a picture of us kissing to a nasty body-shaming page and saying it was Tristan. Taylor, Tristan's older brother, already got the page shut down, and with the help of another girl Lucky tricked, we found out it was him and that he did it for crazy, obsessive reasons. I just got back from telling him to fuck off."

"Oh, honey. I'm so sorry. I know how close you two were," she said.

I shook my head. "Turns out most of it was just fake anyway. He was phoning it in trying to get a relationship out of me, and then when he realized I didn't feel the same, he tried to trick me into it."

"And what about Tristan?" she asked.

I sunk down onto the couch and my mom sat next to me, wrapping her arms around me. "Ya know, mama. I think I love him. I really think I do, but I'm so scared. Every time we get close to being together, something else happens to stop it. I kind of feel like it might be the universe telling me we're not supposed to be together."

"Hmm," she hummed. "I've been in that situation before."

"You have?" I asked.

She nodded. "I was never going to tell you this story, but I think it could help you, so forgive me, okay?"

"Okay?"

"There was a man in college that I was absolutely crazy about. We flirted all the time, and I knew he had feelings for me and he knew I had feelings for him, but it was kind of the same thing. We could make out at parties or whatever—"

"Gross, continue," I said.

"But when it came to dating, we just struggled. It wasn't that he didn't want it or that I didn't, I think we just both realized it wasn't movie love. It was the kind of love that takes hard work. Constant attention. Regular tweaks and checkups, and we were still both in that romanticized place where we felt like, because things didn't come along smooth sailing, that it meant we weren't meant to be together. We decided not to date, and then we graduated and moved on. I actually looked him up on social media not too terribly long ago, and he's married with kids."

"Why wouldn't you tell me that story? Just because you looked him up? I mean, it's not like dad is still around, or that you were even together when he was."

"No. I wasn't going to tell you because, to this day, I believe from the bottom of my heart that he was my soulmate." It covered me with goosebumps and gave me a rare insight into my parents' relationship that I wasn't expecting. "I loved your father, don't get me wrong, and it broke me up when we couldn't make it work, but I think that's why we didn't work out and why I've never had any serious relationships since." She pet her hand along my hair. "Sometimes love isn't like you see in the movies or read in books. In fact, I daresay it's rarely that. You and Tristan were both very fractured people who suffered a lot of trauma in your own ways. If you decide to forgive him and see past everything that's happened—and I'm not saying you should one way or the other—I need you to know that your love can be just as beautiful even if it isn't all sparkles and rainbows. Learn how to see things from one another's point of view and don't be afraid of the work it may take. Hard and hard work are different."

"Thanks mama." I set my head on her shoulder. "He wanted to meet up tonight, but I think I'm just going to sleep on it."

"I think that's a great idea," she said.

"You give really good advice," I said.

She gave me a light swat. "Yeah. When you turn down the angst, you'll find I'm actually quite useful."

"I love you," I said.

She set her head on top of mine. "I love you too, sweet girl."

30

TRISTAN

*A*ria hadn't called me for the rest of the weekend, so to say I was discouraged by the time Monday came around would be an understatement. There was something about the way she responded to me at her house after Hannah and I told her the truth about Lucky that left me with a feeling of unease. If I were to guess, I would say she was still second-guessing me based on how easy it was for her to believe I'd actually sent that photo.

The news about Aria being sent into the slam page wasn't being talked about as much as I figured it would be, but it didn't stop pretty much everyone except for my friends for giving me nasty looks as I walked the hallways. How ironic that after months of trying to keep myself from being bullied, I was still being treated like shit, and it wasn't even for something I actually did.

Is that what they call cruel irony? Or just karma?

Capito sat down at the lunch table and pushed my lunch tray closer to me. "You need to eat. The playoffs are coming up and we're going to be working extra hard. If you fuck it up, I'm gonna slug you."

"Aw, I missed you too," I said flatly, though it was enough of a motivator for me to lift the bland cafeteria food to my mouth and start eating. I didn't want to run myself into the ground or risk football on top of everything else.

"People are dragging you for that post," Capito said. "When are you planning on telling people it wasn't you?"

"What's the point?" I said. "Aria's going to suffer for it regardless. At least this way, I can bear some of the weight."

Capito was mid-bite, but stopped in response to my statement. "Oh wow. That's actually really sweet."

I twirled my finger through the air. "Yay. I've finally figured it out."

Hannah sat down next to me. "Warning. Ceradi incoming, and she's realized that a better stance to take on the Plow the Cow thing is that you're a horrible person."

"Of course," I said, thinking of all of her messages of praise in our group chat. "Whatever. Let her do her worst."

"Tristan, Tristan, Tristan," Ceradi started as if on cue. She set her tray down on the table and sat down before looking across at me and shaking her head. "How could you do something like this? I mean it's harsh even for you. We're the popular kids, sure, but we're not cruel. That was just sadistic."

I felt Hannah rear up in her seat next to me, and for the first time, it was me sticking my arm out to stop her from unnecessarily getting on Ceradi's bad side. I was a sinking ship. There was no reason to take the whole crew down with me. On top of that, if Ceradi was planning on just bullying me and leaving Aria out of it, that was a much better response than the alternative and I would take it without issue.

"What can I say?" I said. "I'm a terrible person. I learned from the best."

Ceradi's feathers were immediately ruffled and she puffed up a little bit before giving me an evil gaze. "Well, you'll understand if we don't necessarily want to be associated with someone who's capable of that sort of vile behavior. I mean, honestly, how could you just blindly torture someone like that?"

"The same way you commented under it mocking her too, Ceradi," Capito said suddenly, snapping everyone's attention to him. "Do you honestly think people didn't see it?"

Ceradi started to stutter and stammer. "People know I'd never—"

"Face it. Everyone in this school thinks we're all pieces of shit. They want to be one of us, but that's mostly because you project a very friend-or-foe type attitude, and people would rather be on your side rather than in your crosshairs."

"So what are you saying?" she hissed at Capito.

"I'm saying, maybe we don't judge Tristan for something that could have easily been any one of us." Then he side-eyed her. "Especially you."

Their gazes were locked for a moment, then Ceradi just rolled her eyes. "Whatever. Tristan, you had better not do it again. I won't be so forgiving next time."

I looked across at Capito and mouthed 'Thank you,' and he nodded before returning to his lunch without a care in the world. The rest of us set into our food then, eating mostly in silence, until someone stood near our table and cleared their throat. I looked over, as did everyone else, and saw Aria standing there with Arden at her side.

"Aria…" I whispered.

"I just wanted to come clean and say that this was all my fault. I tricked Tristan into kissing me and then I had a friend take and upload the pictures," Aria explained. "It wasn't Tristan's fault."

"Why?" I said.

She looked down at me. "I'm sorry for the trouble I caused you."

Ceradi let out a loud, dramatic scoff. "Honestly Aria, what kind of person does something like that? Because you're jealous? Because he turned you down? How sad!"

"No!" I stood up. "That's not true. That's not what happened."

"Don't," Aria said. "I'm trying to help you."

"I don't want this help!" I reached out, wrapped my arm around Aria's waist and pulled her towards me, setting my lips on hers. The cafeteria went totally quiet except for a few scattered gasps. I released Aria, but held her gaze as I announced, "It wasn't Aria nor I that sent the picture. A jealous friend of hers saw me confessing my love for her and did it to try and sabotage us."

"Love?" Ceradi said. "With this girl?"

"Yes," I glared at Ceradi. "With this incredible, intelligent, beautiful person whom you could *never* hope to measure up to. I have the messages of you congratulating me for the post."

She immediately became nervous. "Uh, I did no such thing."

"You didn't?" Josh said. "Then who were these messages from?"

Milton smacked him across the back of the head. "Shut the fuck up, you idiot."

"Aria," I said, turning my back to Ceradi and the others. "Thank you for trying to save my friendship with them, but I don't want to be friends with them if it means I can't be with you. Will you please go out with me. Just one date to prove that I'm serious."

Everyone in the cafeteria was watching us, including the few teachers who were usually tasked with keeping things on the up and up. It was probably against the rules to allow two students to kiss and shout in the middle of the room, but given the tension and the fact that everyone was watching, they probably figured it was just best to let it play out.

"I know that I hurt you," I said. "I know that you don't trust me."

"I'm struggling," Aria admitted.

"But whatever attachment I had to these vapid relationships, is gone. I have real friends." I looked down at Hannah and Capito. "Who aren't going to leave me just because I choose happiness. It's going to be scary, but…" I grabbed her hand. "Please give me one last chance."

Everyone was waiting with bated breath like they were watching a television show. If I'd gotten my way, I might have liked to have a more intimate conversation with Aria, but this was a good opportunity to prove that I wasn't going to let her down again. I'd very clearly and boldly stated my feelings in front of everyone.

All that was left now, was for her to trust me.

"I can't handle another blow, Tris," Aria said.

"I know. I won't give you one," I replied.

"Okay then," she said, blinking away tears. "Yes. I'll go out with you."

ARIA

*A*rden and I decided to play hooky on debate practice after school because after agreeing to go out with Tristan, I'd melted down into a mess that she was struggling to pick up. I honestly wasn't expecting to take it as bizarrely as I did, but after months of getting close only to have something step in the way, the fact that we actually had a scheduled date and so far nothing had clawed its way out of the grave to interfere, I was so nervous it made me sick to my stomach.

"Okay. One black coffee, because you're an eighty-year-old woman apparently," Arden said, setting a cup of coffee down in front of me on the table. "And one strawberry cream-cheese danish."

"Thank you," I said, giggling at her. "The black coffee is to help calm my stomach. If I put a whole bunch of cream and sugar in it, on top of the danish, I'll be sick all night."

Arden hunched over suddenly like she was an eldery woman. "Oh, you kids," she said in a crotchety voice.

"That sugar will keep you awake. That and your damn cell phones."

"Ha ha," I said.

She laughed and sat down in the chair across from me. "If it's all the same to you, I'm going to have my hyper-sugary frappuccino with added espresso, and then I'll just stare into the darkness fearing adulthood until three in the morning like a normal person."

"How strange. I already do that without the aid of sugary beverages," I said.

Arden snickered. "Oh, Aria. Our banter is next to none. Never change."

"If we could just keep it up until Saturday, that'd be good." I took a large gulp of my coffee. "Thank god we only have two days of school this week, because if I had to look at him all week knowing what was coming, I'd never survive."

"I don't get it. You two have come close to fucking, what, three times? You certainly weren't nervous through all of that," Arden said.

"No, because all of that just happened. I was on a speeding bullet train and I didn't have control over what was happening regardless. I was letting my impulses operate the controls. Now it's like I'm sitting at a stoplight waiting for it to turn green," I explained. "Besides, this is more than just coming close to hooking up. This is an *actual* date. Spending the whole day together. Having to find stuff to talk about that whole time. Not living in constant dread that after all the shit we've been through to get to this point something is going to fire up and ruin it."

"You can't think like that," Arden said. "You're going to sabotage it."

"Don't say that!" I yelped. "Now I'm afraid I'm going to sabotage it!"

"Oh my god, you are painful to be around like this. I hope this date goes well, because this is disillusioning." Arden took a bite of the pastry she'd gotten for herself, then noticed my serious expression and flicked my nose. "Oh relax. You know I'm obsessed with you."

The tip of my nose stung, but it was oddly grounding. "I really am afraid though. This just feels like another setup. What if we see someone while we're out and about and he gets all weird again?"

"Someone other than the people he made a *very* public display of love for you in front of?" Arden said. "Aria. You're freaking out over nothing. In my honest and expert opinion, Tristan has finally proved that he's ready to take this seriously. All you have to do is show up and start off on your road of romance and true love. It's very exciting."

"Don't sound so cynical when you say that please. I know I'm projecting onto you, but it terrifies me," I said. "Are you sure you're okay talking about all of this? I don't want it to be like I'm rubbing it in your face or anything."

"Aria, I'm *fine*. Hannah and I have nothing to do with this. Hell, there isn't even a Hannah and I. That's ancient history. Right now, we're focusing on you and you not being self-destructive in what I truly believe, could be a serious thing for you. This *is* what you want, isn't it?"

"Of course it is," I said. "But isn't it okay to be a little skeptical after how things have transpired up 'til now?"

"Sure, be a little skeptical, but not so much so that you aren't seeing the good when it's right there in front of you. Just promise me you aren't going to go in there flinging shit all over the place just to find a reason to not like it. Be vulnerable."

I winced. "Ooh, vulnerable? I don't think I can do that."

"I'm gonna smack you," Arden said.

I laughed. "I'm just scared."

"I know, babe, but everything is going to be fine. Trust Arden, you know her. She loves you. She's your very best friend. She is both incredibly intelligent and unimaginably beautiful. She wouldn't steer you wrong."

"That's true," I said. "Not to mention an amazingly talented inventor."

"Oh, Aria," Arden waved her hand at me. "Flattery will get you everywhere."

"You really think Saturday is going to be okay?" I asked.

"Honey, I'm certain of it. This is what all of this has been culminating to. Don't put too much pressure on it, don't expect too much or too little, just let it happen naturally. You and Tristan have chemistry that comes from the soil. It'll do its job. I promise." She took another sip of her coffee. "But of course—"

"If it goes badly you're available for a drunken hookup?" I cut in.

She gasped overdramatically. "I am hurt that you would even think I'd say such a thing." Then she glanced up over her cup at me. "But if that's what you need, I want you to know I am always there for you."

"I love you," I said, glad that I had her. She always knew the perfect thing to say.

She smiled at me. "Aw. I love you too."

TRISTAN

I took a deep breath before grabbing the bouquet of purple tulips I'd bought for Aria and climbing out of my car. The sun was shining and it was still late morning, exactly the time I'd planned to give Aria the date of her life. I'd be lying if I said I wasn't nervous, but I believed the worst of it was behind us. There was no longer a jealous best friend, or evil popular kids, or my stupid insecurities standing between us. All we had to do at this point was nail the date.

This should be the easy part.

I pressed my hand against the doorbell and rang it, and then took another deep breath while I waited for someone to answer the door. I could hear some hushed tones coming from inside, then, to my surprise, Arden opened the door.

"Hello young man," she said in a very low, bassy voice. "How are you today?"

"Um, confused mostly."

"Well that's not the kind of thing we're looking for.

Goodbye." She started to seriously shut the door, so I shoved my hand out.

"No, wait. I'm sorry. I'm here to pick up… your daughter? I was going to take her out on a date."

Arden folded her hands in front of her and reared forward on the balls of her feet and then back onto her heels. "Ah, yes. You must be this *Tristan* she's been talking non-stop about. Come in."

"This is weird," I murmured to myself as I passed through the doorway.

"What was that?" Arden huffed.

"Nothing… sir? Ma'am?" I replied. "You."

"He's right," I heard Aria's voice from someplace I couldn't see. "This is weird."

"Aria," Arden whined, stomping her foot like a little kid. "I'm playing a role. Don't interfere with my process."

"Fine," Aria said flatly. "Continue, but do it quickly."

Arden cleared her throat, then turned to face me and started to shout, "Just what are your inten—"

"Whoa!" Aria yelped, hopping out from the kitchen doorway. "Why are you yelling all of a sudden?"

"That was my dad voice," Arden said.

"What happened to the regular volumed one?"

"Wow," I said breathlessly, taking in the sight of Aria. "You look beautiful."

She turned and looked at me, then smiled, blushing a little. "Thanks."

She was wearing a sleeveless sundress that started a deep pink at the top and faded down to a dark purple at the bottom. She appeared to be wearing roman sandals around her well-pedicured toes. Her hair was pinned back on both sides, giving me a perfect view of her magnificent eyes. It was so simple, but she wore it like she could walk it down a runway.

It was perfect.

I was glad I went simple, with black jeans, a white t-shirt, and a blue jacket over it. Whatever I wore was going to pale in comparison to how incredible she looked.

"You said dress comfy, but I still wanted to look good, so…"

I snickered at that. "You were going to look good regardless, but… Yeah. This is a good look."

"Thanks," she said.

I held out the flowers. "These are for you."

She grabbed them and took a big whiff of them. "Thank you. They're lovely." Then she turned and extended them out to Arden. "Uh, dad, do you think you could put these in water for me? There are vases under the sink in the kitchen."

"I suppose I could do that," Arden said, then looked at Tristan. "I guess I'll ask you about my intentions later."

"You already know my intentions. You were there when I said them," I replied.

Arden guffawed at me, but walked away nonetheless, taking the flowers with her. Aria stepped closer to me, and I leaned in. It wasn't until halfway through the action that I realized she was probably just coming closer so we could walk back out the front door, but she didn't pull back and my lips set gently on top of hers.

She grinned as I pulled back. "Getting the awkward kiss out of the way, I guess."

"Yeah. Is that okay?"

She nodded. "More than." She looked back over her

shoulder and muttered, "Wait for it," then as soon as she heard water running, called out, "Dad! We're leaving!"

"Not fair!" Arden called back. "You wait for me!"

"Go," Aria said, pushing me towards the door.

I opened the front door and stepped aside so that Aria could walk out first, then we left, closing the door behind us. I held the passenger's side door open so Aria could climb in, then got into the driver's seat myself.

"What was that?" I asked. "The whole dad thing?"

"She's actually been at my house since Thursday. She has trouble with her extended family because they're hyper-religious and she's gay, so she spent Thanksgiving with us. My mom had to work today and couldn't be here to send me off, and I had disclosed to her that I was sad my dad couldn't be here to meet you, so… Arden became my dad."

"Oddly that makes sense," I said. "That sucks about her family though."

"It really does. I don't think my mom would care if I dated a garden gnome so long as they treated me right. I can't imagine being outcast like that." As we pulled away from the curb, I took a risk and lifted Aria's hand to my lips and kissed the back of it, then kept it gripped firmly in mine. An adorable blush rose to her cheeks and she looked away to keep me from seeing. "So. Where to today?"

"I've got a few things planned that I think you'll like," I replied. "It's a surprise."

The silence that fell over the car then was perfectly comfortable. We didn't feel the need to fill it, and I just enjoyed seeing Aria out of the corner of my eye and feeling her hand in mine. We were really here. It was really happening.

Finally, we pulled up outside of our first destination and

I walked over to her side of the car and opened her door. She stepped out and snuck a kiss in, which surprised me at first, but then sent me shooting to cloud nine. I laced her hand into mine and walked her into the building we'd parked at and when we got inside, her jaw dropped.

"Oh my god." Dogs were running around in different rooms, and several families were walking around, petting and playing with the supply of animals. "A shelter!"

"Once a month they bring all the dogs out like this to try and get more of them adopted and raise money." I pulled out the check for five hundred bucks that I'd coaxed out of my dad and dropped it into the donation bucket on the way in, and then Aria and I started our rounds.

We had a blast walking in and out of the different rooms and getting our fill of all of the dogs. One of the rooms in particular was just puppies, and Aria just sat on the floor and let them pile on her like a swarm of bugs, albeit the cutest, fluffiest ones around. I couldn't help myself and took a series of pictures of her with the adorable animals. As cute as they were, they had nothing on the look of pure bliss on her face as she was overtaken.

Closer to the back of the shelter was where all the birds were stored, where I learned that Aria had a way with all animals, and where she learned that I had a slight fear of birds. She had a little too much fun letting the animals perch on her and watching me squirm as they perched on me. Then we snuggled some kittens on our way out, which nearly resulted in me adopting one because I'd found a little, fluffy white one that wouldn't leave me alone.

"I might be back," I told the shelter worker.

After playing with animals until we were covered in fur, I drove us not far to a boardwalk that overlooked a man-made lake, and we got froyo and walked and talked while the sun set. For the fact that I was actually afraid Aria and I may have trouble filling the void, there was no shortage of things for us to talk about. We spent a good amount of time catching one another up on what had happened in the time we were apart, then shifted to the many things we had in common. When my phone went off, the alarm reminder I'd set for thirty minutes before our dinner reservation, I couldn't believe so much time had passed.

On the other side of the lake we were walking around was a really nice dinner place simply called "Y." Because of its closeness to the boardwalk and the beach, it didn't have a dress code, but still had a romantic atmosphere. I'd made sure to reserve a table near the windows where we could continue to watch the sunset.

Aria's phone buzzed in the middle of dinner, and she apologized, recognizing the specific ringtone as belonging to her mother and brought it up to her head. "Hey mama." I set my head on my hands and enjoyed the perfect vision of her against the setting sun behind her. It was the kind of beauty one should have to pay to see. I still couldn't believe I was actually out with her. "Okay, no problem. I'm out with Tristan now, but I'll be home after that." She rolled her eyes. "Yes, Arden is still there. She wants to gab about the date, so I'll send her home after that. Okay. Don't work too hard. Love ya. Bye."

"Mom's working late?" I said.

"Yeah," Aria said, "but I lied. Arden already went home."

Her eyes locked into mine and my heart slammed so hard in my chest I was shocked it didn't cave in. "Oh. That is wonderful news. Can't wait to see what we'll do with this fortune." Aria laughed at first, but then her eyes glossed over and her smile faded a little. "What's wrong?" Was she not attempting to be spicy, so my spice applied unwanted pressure? "Uh, we don't… If you don't…"

"Oh, no," Aria said. "Sorry, my mind was on something else."

"Oh, good," I replied, though I was still a little nervous. What was that all about?

After dinner, I drove Aria back to her house and promised myself I'd play by vampire rules. She'd alluded to me coming in at dinner, but she had to explicitly invite me or I wouldn't go. I didn't want her to think I was expecting anything. I was just happy for the date.

"This…" Aria started softly as we approached the door. "Was incredible."

"It really was, wasn't it?" I said. "I'm… glad you agreed to give me another chance." We got to the door and stopped. Aria faced me and I reached out and took her hand in mine, looking down because I was suddenly super nervous. "Not to be *that* guy, but… does this mean that we can be together?"

Aria was quiet after that. I looked up, but rather than the joy I expected to be on her face, there was only anguish. "No," she said. "I'm sorry, but we can't be together."

ARIA

"What?" Tristan said, looking at me, truly shocked. "Why not? I thought today went so well. It… Why?"

Emotions were burning in my nose and sending tears to my eyes. "I'm so scared."

"Scared? Of what?" Tristan said.

"I'd spent all this time trying to believe that all these insecurities I had about myself weren't true, then things got heated, and…"

"Oh…" Tristan said. "Aria. I swear to god, that stuff had nothing to do with you or your body, or anything. I was being an idiot. You are so perfect."

I shook my head. "I'm so afraid that it's all just gonna turn on its end again. This was so good, it felt so good. Like how I always imagined it would be. When I think of you, I think of the future. That's what I want, but what if you change again? I can't just live in fear of that."

"I love you, Aria," Tristan said.

"I know, I love you too. I really thought you were going to be my forever," I said. "I don't think I can handle the fear."

"Aria, our forever starts tonight. Right now," Tristan said, bringing my hand to his lips and kissing it. "I know I've lost your trust, but please give me some time to earn it back. I promise, you'll never feel that pain again. I won't stop until you trust from your gut that I would never hurt you ever again."

I thought of my mom's story and the guy she felt was her soulmate, but she was afraid of how much work she thought their relationship might take. I didn't want to be like that. I didn't want to be looking back in twenty years wondering what if about a guy I loved.

But could I trust Tristan?

"You can't hurt me," I said. "I can't take it anymore."

"I won't," Tristan said, even some tears coming to his eyes. "I hate how much I've hurt you already. I want to spend the rest of my life making it up to you. Please, give me that chance."

"Okay," I said. "Yeah. I wanna take the risk."

Tristan looked at me with passion deep in his eyes. "Open the door."

I did as he said, opening the front door and letting us inside. We barely made it past the front doorway before Tristan's hands were on either side of my face pulling me to him. I closed my eyes just as his lips pressed to mine and a few tears ran loose. Tristan pulled away from my lips and kissed my cheeks where the tears had fallen. He pressed me back against the wall and his fingers combed up into my hair as he moved down the side of my neck, dragging his lips down the curve of it. He wrapped around under my chin, then stuck out his tongue and licked his way back up and slipped it back into my mouth. I gripped his sides, that alone keeping me on my feet.

"Let's go upstairs," I said.

He nodded. "Okay."

We tripped and fell our way down the hallway, stopping every ten or fifteen feet to make out some more. We could barely keep our hands off of each other, to the point that I was shoving Tristan's jacket and peeling his shirt off when we were still in the hallway.

Thank god my mom was working late.

We got to my room and I opened the door, sending us falling inside. We just barely made it to my bed, with me landing on my back and Tristan hovering over me. Based on our previous circumstances, that was exactly where we would have been interrupted, but not that time. There were no party guests arriving, no dream to wake up from, no teacher coming to the rescue. It was just me and just him, and his breath was hot on my skin as he held the same anticipation I did.

At the same time, one of his hands worked my dress up my legs, while the other folded the top down to reveal my strapless black satin bra. He kissed across my chest and down my breasts, until he got to where he could peel the cups down and spring my breasts free.

I wasn't a virgin, but as coy as I felt laying under Tristan, I may as well have been. His hand under my dress squeezed my ass, while his mouth moved over my waiting breast. My body pulsated with heat, and I leaned my head back and huffed out a quiet moan as he began to lick. He took handfuls of me below until finally working his hand around and between my legs to rub me over the fabric of my panties.

A muted moan came out of me again, and I covered my mouth to hide it. Tristan took my hand and moved it away. "No. I want to hear you."

He kept his head above me and looked down as he started to rub a little faster below. His eyes were dark and lust-filled now, and it gave me goosebumps. My legs twitched as his ministrations brought me closer and closer to climax. Mewls of pleasure came out of me in a continuous stream, and when Tristan slipped his hand under my underwear to rub directly against me, it finally sent me over. I threw my head back and let the vibrations wash over my body. Tristan tucked his head against my neck and started to suck as he rubbed me through.

It was ecstacy.

As the haze of my orgasm faded, I managed to get my hands between us to start unfastening the button of his jeans. He took over, leaning back, and shoved his hand into his pocket to pull out a condom. He looked down at me, briefly freaked out.

"I don't want you think that I brought this because—"

"Tristan, shut up," I cut him off.

"Right," he said with a smile. "Sorry."

He ran his hand through his hair and the moonlight coming in through the window cast across his chiseled abs. He perched the condom between his teeth so that he could pull his pants and boxers off and…

Holy shit did he look sexy.

Keeping the condom held in his teeth, he rolled my dress down and off, followed by removing my bra and panties. My whole body felt like it was going to melt from the feeling of his hands on me. He kept a hold of the condom in his mouth and peeled against it to open it, then he brought the condom down to his…

"Are you serious with that?!" I yelped.

He froze. "What? I thought we were."

I stuck my hand out and ran it along the length. I'd been so focused on him and his beautiful face that I hadn't looked down that whole time.

He was massive.

"No way you're this good-looking, smart, talented, and working with *that*?"

He had his eyes focused on me stroking him gently. "What can I say?"

"It's all mine?" I asked, then, then I rigidified, looking up at him. "Oh my god. I can't believe I Just fucking said that out loud."

Tristan only seemed more aroused. He rolled the condom on and brought his face down to mine, pushing me back on my back. He lifted my leg up over his shoulder and smiled. "Yeah, Aria. It's all yours." He poked himself at my entrance and slowly started to push in. I seized up almost immediately, and he got nervous. "Are you okay?"

"Yeah, just go slow," I said. "Don't break me."

"You got it," he said.

He listened, working himself into me in slow, enticing centimeters. Though I stung at the outset, the fullness threatened to make me pass out from pleasure. I couldn't move in any way and not feel him inside of me, and it had me at a fever pitch.

"Oh god," I hummed. "Yes."

After loosening me up enough, Tristan picked up the

pace, moving in and out of me at faster intervals until he was slamming in and out of me. Any pain associated with his size was diminished by the fact that every spot he struck seemed to send a stream of pleasure flowing from my head down to curl my toes.

Oh, so it could be *that* good.

"Aria," Tristan huffed. "I'm close."

I couldn't return the sentiment, because in truth, I'd had several orgasms already. For not being used to it, I was close to exhausted and actually a little relieved. Though every time he targeted me deeply, I wished it could last forever.

Unexpectedly, I came again, shuddering as I did so, and Tristan growled and pushed himself all the way into me. His fingers dug into my leg and I temporarily lost sound.

"I hate," Tristan said just as it was coming back to me. "That we were stopped from doing that sooner."

"Same here," I said, nodding. I turned my head to the side and closed my eyes. "I can't believe you're…"

And I fell asleep.

Months of worrying. Months of fears. Months of doubt all culminated in that moment, and I simply couldn't keep myself conscious anymore. I only barely heard Tristan whisper, "I love you," as I drifted off, wanting to say the same back, but not having the energy to do so.

The sun was bright and painful against my face the next morning. I looked around, but expectedly, Tristan wasn't there. He'd been smart enough to get the hell out of Dodge before my mom got home, but then my eyes landed on the vase of flowers he'd gotten me sitting on my bedside table. They hadn't been there the night before, so he must have brought them up as a way of silently telling me that all was well.

I was buried in the blankets of my bed, and a shirt I didn't recognize had been pulled over me, but when I sat up Tristan's cologne wafted off of me and I smiled.

Good call.

Hazelnut was curled up at my feet, just like always, so rather than disturb her, I lifted my phone from the table where I'd set it and unlocked it. Immediately, I was hit with a rush of notifications, specifically those that said people were liking and commenting on a post I'd been tagged in on social media. My stomach knotted and I was sure I was about to walk into the same situation that happened the night after Sadie Hawkins.

I unlocked my phone and nervously clicked on the notifications to take me to the picture, but when I saw it my heart soared.

It was a picture of me, covered in puppies from the shelter the day before. It was posted directly to Tristan's page, and had the caption, "I am one hell of a lucky guy."

There were dozens of comments beneath it, and apart from an isolated few from his former friends dogging us both, most of them were comments about how cute we were as a pair, ribbing Tristan and asking him how he landed someone so hot, and someone even commented "#Prom2021" which had garnered a lot of likes. As I was looking at it, comments from Taylor started pouring in, in all caps, cheering on the relationship. I liked a few of them, which only seemed to spur him on.

I could have kept looking at it all day, except my phone rang in my hand. I answered it and Arden's face popped up on the screen. "Hey."

"Hi," I said with a smile.

"Didn't I tell you, it'd all work out?" she said.

"Oh, so *now* you can say I told you so?" I asked.

She nodded. "Hell yeah. This one feels much more vindicating."

TRISTAN

*R*iding to school with Aria sitting next to me was like a dream I couldn't have imagined would ever come true. I had one hand on the steering wheel, one hand sitting on her leg, and it should have been a sin to be as blissful as I was.

We pulled into the parking lot, and even though I'd been excited for the date, and certainly for what came after the date, I was excited for this part too. This is what I'd been waiting to show Aria most, and even though I gave her a preview of it when she tried to take the fall for the post that Lucky had done, I wanted her to see it in action.

How unashamed I was to be with her.

I parked in my typical spot and then climbed out of the car and walked over to her side to open her door. Several people standing around stopped and looked, a few even cheered, which made Aria a little coy, but I was happy for it. She deserved all the attention, and I wanted her to see me boldly loving her regardless of who was watching. I pulled both her and my backpack out of the backseat of my car and threw them over my shoulder, then I laced my fingers into hers, kissed the back of her hand, and we started off for the front of school.

My post had been up for a couple of days, so it wasn't like it was news that we were together, but there still seemed to be a handful of people who were shocked to see it. Every chance I got, I kissed her hand, or better yet, her lips, and kept her close to me. I wanted everyone to know that she was mine.

Did I throw petty gazes at guys like Devario and Yunmir as we passed them, maybe? I didn't feel bad about it.

"Well if it isn't the happy couple!" Arden greeted once we got through the door, then she faked like she was emotional. "My baby's all grown up."

"So where are we on the Arden as Aria's filler parent thing?" I asked. "Because I gotta be honest… freaks me out."

"That's fair," Arden said. "I can't promise it will stop. I can't even promise I will try." Arden's voice went up at the end of the statement, so I waited patiently for the end of it, but then she just said, "Oh, no. That's the end."

"Great," I said, and Aria laughed.

I felt a hand on my back and turned around to see Hannah standing behind me. She had a huge smile on her face and I released Aria only to give her a hug. "Congrats," she whispered in my ear.

"Thanks," I said. "Couldn't have done it without your help."

She shook her head. "Well, I don't know that that's true,

but I appreciate you for saying it." She ducked around me and walked up to Aria. "Hey…"

Aria smiled. "Hi."

"We're friends-in-law now, so you have to deal with me," Hannah said.

It pulled a chuckle out of Aria. "I'm okay with that." Then she opened her arms and Hannah walked into her embrace and they hugged. It made me happy to see the two women I cared about most getting along. I was actually a little nervous, but it was clear I had no reason to be.

But then Hannah turned around and came face to face with Arden, and things got awkward fast. "Hi," she said.

Arden's gaze was shifting side-to-side uncomfortably. "Hi."

Hannah looked as if she wanted to say more, an array of emotions flashing across her face, but she opted not to say anything at all. She took a step backwards and I met her, wrapping my arm around her shoulder and holding her so that she knew I had her back. With Aria and I dating now, things were bound to dredge up between Hannah and Arden, whether she was ready for it or not, and I wanted her to know that we were going to get through it together. She smiled up at me and I could read thanks in her eyes, so I left it at that.

"Aria, right?"

We turned and Capito was behind us. Aria looked up his full height and gasped. "Y-yes."

"I'm Capito," he said. "One of the aforementioned *real* friends."

"Ah," Aria said. "Nice to meet you."

"You take good care of my boy, you hear?" He tapped the top of my head. "And you take good care of her."

"Yeah," we said in unison.

"I'll see you guys at lunch then," Capito said, walking around us waving as he went. He was such a tell-it-like-it-is kind of guy, and having him as a friend had certainly changed the dynamic in my life. That one outburst at dinner gave Capito the insight he needed to open up to me, and I was glad for that. Painful though it had been, if Aria and I hadn't been estranged at that moment, it may have never happened.

Just another thing I could thank her for.

"Oh, so now that giant guy is going to sit with us at lunch," Arden said. "Cool. I like giants."

The bell rang and everyone dispersed for their first classes, leaving Aria and I standing alone once again. I caught Ceradi up ahead watching us through a narrowed gaze, so I curled Aria towards me and gave her a huge kiss, which Aria then punctuated by flipping Ceradi off. She stormed off down the hallway, and though we both knew it wasn't the last we'd hear from her, neither of us were too worried.

We watched as Arden introduced Capito to some of their debate friends, while Hannah stood awkwardly behind them, and Aria laughed.

"That is quite the sight," I said, noticing some of the people standing around looking in awe as one of the largest football players in the entire school exchanged comic book notes with the debate team. "I don't think anyone here has ever seen anything like that before."

"I certainly haven't," Aria said. "The drama may have ended, but it looks like the fun is just beginning."

I nodded. "Yeah." Then I pulled her close and kissed her on the forehead. "But I knew that when I looked up the first day of school, and realized that you had found your way back to me."

"I love you," she whispered up to me.

I looked back at her, thanking whatever god of fate brought her to me. "And I love you."

EPILOGUE

ARDEN

*B*eing extra careful not to splinter the old wood as I climbed, I lifted one foot over the other to bring myself up into the treehouse that I hadn't been in for ten or more years. For a while there, it was just about the fact that I was a big kid, and the treehouse had been built for a much younger version of myself, but then once Hannah and I fell apart, I could barely bring myself to look at it.

For some reason, I woke up that morning compelled to climb up into it and smoke a little weed. I wasn't sure if I was expecting it to make me feel better, but when I crouched and twisted to shove myself inside, the position I had to contort into in order to fit seemed to fit the circumstances perfectly.

Just like my relationship with Hannah.

"Arden?"

I didn't move, mostly because I was afraid if I did, I'd break something. "Up here, gorg."

Dragging the papers and weed out of my pocket to start

rolling a blunt, I waited until Aria's head popped up through the opening in the base of the treehouse that allowed entry. "Wow," she said. "A true blue treehouse. I honestly didn't think these things existed outside of old movies."

"You wanna come in?" she asked. "I'm sure we can both fit if we're willing to get a little cozy."

Aria raised an eyebrow. "Are you just trying to feel me up?

I snapped my fingers. "Foiled again."

She tapped my leg. "Yeah, move over. I'm not going to see an actual treehouse and not sit in it."

Repositioning myself, and sticking my leg clear out of one of the makeshift windows, I made enough space for Aria to squeeze into, which she did by pushing her legs into the corner parallel to my head and laying her head in my lap. "Hey. Careful of the weed," I hissed.

"Sorry," she giggled.

I finished filling the paper and lifted it to my lips to perch between, then I fished my lighter out of my pocket and lit the end, letting the dusky taste and smell of the weed fill my head and help relax me a bit.

"So. Did you get the treehouse in as cliche circumstances as most treehouses came to people?" Aria asked.

"Yup. My dad built it for Hannah and me when we were like six. It was our big clubhouse. We called it Mount Ardannah."

"Cute," Aria said with a chuckle.

"Well, sure, if you don't count the fact that he built it while reciting several passages from the Noah's Ark area of the Bible and then made me pick and carve my favorite verse into the wood."

"Obviously, Arden. What is childhood playtime without some intense Christianity?" Aria replied.

"That's what they say."

"Do you come up here often?" she asked.

"No. This is the first time I've been up here in a long time. Just got a lot on my mind and I figured at the most it would help, and at the worst, I could smoke without my parents smelling it and lecturing me for the next two and a half hours."

"Did it help?" Aria asked.

"Smoking without lectures? So far so good. Clearing my mind? Not so much," I said. "It's just making me think of Hannah, but I don't really know what to make of her right now, so it's really just making my mind more muddled if anything."

The longer I sat there, the more I was reminded of the games we used to play as kids. From pirate adventures, to the domestic bliss of playing house, there wasn't a story Hannah and I couldn't tell when we played together. We'd so carefully built a foundation, and though I believed it was as well-constructed as the treehouse that could hold two, fully-grown, eighteen-year-old women without cracking, it was crafted much more like my first invention, a makeshift zipline which snapped and sent me crashing to the ground the second I put my weight on it.

The feeling of having the wind knocked out of me was the same, but the pain of losing Hannah was much worse.

"How was your date with Tris last night?" I asked.

"It was wonderful. He took me to that flea market downtown and we had a battle for who could find the silliest thing to buy as a gift for the other. I really thought I was going to win with this rank, old doll I found that had a hanger through the head for hanging displays I guess, but he found a bedazzled throw pillow that, when the sequins were pushed one way was Mahatma Gandhi, and when pushed the other way was Snoop Dogg."

I coughed on the current puff of my blunt. "What, why?"

"I don't know that I want to know," Aria replied. "The mystery of it is kind of what makes it so incredible. Tristan thinks it has something to do with achieving higher enlightenment. I think someone just had bizarre tastes in men."

"Those two things are not mutually exclusive," I said, and Aria laughed.

"You are not wrong." She let her laugh die down, then she turned and looked at me with a sad expression in her eyes. "I feel like I owe you an apology."

"For what?" I said with my brow furrowed. "We've been over this, Aria. I don't *actually* have a crush on you. Unless it's something you're receptive to, is it?"

"Not that," Aria said. "For… bringing Hannah into our lives through Tristan. Don't get me wrong, I'm so happy that her and Capito and some of his other friends chose to stay by his side after Ceradi dumped him, but I can't imagine how hard it must be for you."

I took a long drag of my blunt before responding. "It's a tough one, but I'm upset with her, not you."

"Do you think you could ever forgive her?" I asked.

"For the first offense? Maybe. For the more recent one? That's the toughie."

Aria tilted her head. "What do you mean?"

"Well, yeah, she completely cut me off when she became a Pop, which was painful, but I suppose that could be forgiven. I mean, Tristan has told me about how she said she did it for me, because she knew she wasn't strong enough to stand up for me and *blah blah blah*. Maybe we could work our way through that because high school politics are shitty, but you know, that's not the thing that bothers me the most lately."

"It's not?"

"Nope," Arden said. "It's the fact that when Tristan fell under scrutiny, she stuck by him. She even stood up for him. When it was me and our fifteen years of friendship, she threw it down the drain in two weeks because she wasn't up to the task, but two years with Tristan and suddenly she's a powerhouse who can stick by her friends? I don't know. That shit is fucking with me right now. I know it makes me sound like a bad person. I'm not saying I wished she'd done the same thing to him…"

"But if she had then it would just be a facet of her personality, and not like he means more to her than you did?" Aria finished.

I poked her in the forehead. "Bingo."

"So what does that mean?" Aria asked. "Even with all of these feelings you have, you're just going to let it all go. You're nothing like Lucky. You could put your feelings aside and just be a good friend if that was what you wanted to do."

"You're not wrong. I just don't know that that's what I wanna do," I replied. "I mean, why should I? What has she done to earn that from me at this point? I lost all respect for her, and whether I love her or not, it doesn't change the fact that she made a very clear decision about me two years ago, and continues to rub it in my face to this day. I don't know. I'm not gonna make trouble or anything, I just don't think I can forgive her for that."

"I understand," Aria said. "It's just a bummer."

"Yeah, well, this world is bummer's house. We're just the lucky assholes who get to live here," Arden said.

"So no more Hannah?" Aria asked.

I nodded. "I think that's it. No more Hannah."

Aria closed her eyes and took a deep inhale of the weed smoke. She didn't smoke herself, in fact she was staunchly against influences of any kind, but she'd come to enjoy a nice contact high since establishing our friendship. "Well, there's gotta be someone incredible out there for you. You're too awesome not to have a crazy love affair."

I smiled. "I don't know. I kind of like the idea of being your future kids' crazy, spinster aunt."

Aria laughed. "You're going to be that regardless."

I nodded. "Right you are."

"You ready to go get lunch?" Aria asked.

I took a deep pull of my blunt and blew out the smoke, focusing my attention on Hannah and my names carved inside of a heart in the space between the windows. "Nah. Let's stay here just a little bit longer."

Meet Tristan and Aria again in book 2, I LOVE YOU MORE THAN I'M AFRAID, featuring Arden and Hannah's story.

WANT MORE STORIES LIKE THIS ONE?

Go to www.RebelHart.net/Stories for a full list of my books.

WANT TO BE A REBEL?

Join my FB Group of Rebels to chat with me and other fans. I'd love to have you there!

Thank you for reading this series!
If you loved it, consider leaving a review on Amazon. Just 1 or 2 lines would be amazing!

Get an alert when I release a new book:
SMS: Text REBEL to 77948 (US only)
EMAILs: join at www.RebelHart.net

Rebel Hart is an author of Contemporary and Dark Romance novels. All her books are FREE in Kindle Unlimited. Check them out at author.to/RebelHart.

NEVER MISS A NEW RELEASE:
Follow Rebel on Amazon
Follow Rebel on Bookbub
Text REBEL to 77948 (US only)
Sign up at www.RebelHart.net to get an email alert when her next book is out.

authorrebelhart@gmail.com

CONNECT WITH REBEL HART:
www.facebook.com/groups/RebelHart

ALSO BY REBEL HART

For a full list of my books go to:

author.to/RebelHart